I0762530

HOW TO CHEAT YOUR OWN DEATH

ALSO BY KRISTEN PERRIN

How to Solve Your Own Murder
How to Seal Your Own Fate

HOW TO CHEAT YOUR OWN DEATH

A NOVEL

Kristen Perrin

DUTTON

DUTTON

An imprint of Penguin Random House LLC
1745 Broadway, New York, NY 10019
penguinrandomhouse.com

Book design by Ashley Tucker

LIBRARY OF CONGRESS CATALOGING-IN-PUBLICATION DATA
Names: Perrin, Kristen author
Title: How to cheat your own death : a novel / Kristen Perrin.
Description: New York, NY : Dutton, [2026] | Series: Castle Knoll mysteries; 3
Identifiers: LCCN 2025048849 | ISBN 9798217047505 hardcover |
ISBN 9798217047529 ebook | 9798217181469 export
Subjects: LCGFT: Cozy mysteries | Novels | Fiction
Classification: LCC PS3616.E785 H65 2026
LC record available at https://lccn.loc.gov/2025048849

Printed in the United States of America
1st Printing

The authorized representative in the EU for product safety and compliance is Penguin Random House Ireland, Morrison Chambers, 32 Nassau Street, Dublin D02 YH68, Ireland, https://eu-contact.penguin.ie.

CAST LIST

Annie Adams: a twenty-five-year-old aspiring writer

Laura Adams: Annie's mother, who was a famous modern artist in the 1990s, but whose career has flagged

Sam Arlington: Annie's estranged father, whom she hasn't seen since she was a baby

Detective Rowan Crane: Castle Knoll's lead detective, who grew up in the village

Reggie Crane: Rowan's father, also best friends with Laura Adams and drives a taxi in Castle Knoll

Felicity "Fliss" Rowe: Rowan's ex-girlfriend and Laura's new apprentice

Peony Lane, aka Ellen Jones: a fortune-teller local to Castle Knoll, who told Frances she'd be murdered one day

Jenny Chen: Annie's best friend, an artist who designs elaborate window displays for Harrods

Lord Rutherford "Ford" Gravesdown: Frances's late husband, who inherited the Gravesdown estate when his family was killed

Frances Adams: Annie's wealthy great aunt, who inherited the Chelsea townhouse Annie and Laura live in, as well as the Gravesdown estate and fortune, when her husband died

Vera Huntington: a wealthy socialite who befriends Frances while she's at university in London

Dr. Alasdair Huntington: Vera's husband, a renowned heart surgeon several decades her senior

Max Torrence: Vera's brother, who is at university with Frances

Elaine Cook (later Torrence): Max's girlfriend, and also a student at university with Frances

Professor Dane: professor of psychology at UCL

Marie Cavanaugh: a volunteer at an art gallery in Knightsbridge

Brian Folkestone: a police officer in Soho who knew Frances, who later works as a private investigator

Archie Foyle: Frances's gardener, who lives on the farm adjacent to the Gravesdown estate

Beth Takaga-Foyle: Archie's granddaughter, who runs a deli in the village but also did some cooking for Frances

Miyuki Takaga-Foyle: Beth's wife, who runs a large-animal veterinary clinic on Foyle Farm

Dr. Kabir Banerjee: a pathologist at University College Hospital who helps Annie and Crane in their investigations

HOW TO CHEAT YOUR OWN DEATH

PROLOGUE

Soho, London, 1968

THE NEON LIGHTS OF SOHO BOUNCED OFF THE AUtumn puddles, their reflections half interrupted by the steady droplets of freezing rain. The high-heeled stride of Vera Huntington sliced through one of the deeper ones as she cut her way across the drenched alleyway. Her heels clacked loudly as she quickened her pace, and she threw worried glances over her shoulder as she walked. Once or twice she caught someone staring too intently at her, or a passerby bumped her shoulder, and so she drew herself deeper into the shadows to shake the feeling of being watched.

Finally Vera rounded a corner of Carnaby Street, her attention caught by the warm light of a nearby pub. Her shoulders relaxed as she spotted a constable she was friendly with standing in the doorway, out of uniform and smoking with his mates. He turned to her and smiled, but something in his eyes made her shoulders tighten again. His face was too friendly, too inviting—something was off. Vera's throat constricted as she considered the possibilities. The constable's grin widened, fox-like. Carefully, Vera schooled her features into a sweet but apologetic look, as if to say, *I'd love to join you, but I have somewhere to be.*

After she turned the corner down the next street, she ran.

The glow of Ronnie Scott's jazz club felt like a sign, and she hurried to the door like someone claiming sanctuary at a cathedral. It may have been a sacrilegious comparison, but in 1968, jazz was Vera's religion and Ronnie Scott's was her place of worship.

The music for the evening had already started, but she knew the doorman well enough to bribe her way inside. She'd be safe in there, and she could find Frances. Lately, every Thursday night, Frances would be eagerly perched on a barstool at the back of the crowded club, taking in every note played like it could change her life.

As a society girl, Vera had only recently discovered the delights of listening to a sax bleed out a tune so heart-wrenching it should come with a warning label. Frances had shown her that. Frances had her own London, the kind that included hidden Soho spots that were cool because they were shabby, and Vera never felt freer than when they ran around nightclubs and went to lock-ins at bars together.

She was hit with a wall of sound as she stepped into the venue's main room. Smoke hung above the heads of the seated crowd, who were illuminated by the glow of red table lamps. It smelled of heavy tobacco and weed, of spilled red wine and the sweat of a packed audience.

The flame of Frances's hair in its smart uptwist popped out of the crowd, distinctive even in the low light. She was watching the combo onstage like she'd been hypnotized, and the man to her right was watching her the same way. His suit was expertly tailored, but he wore it in a relaxed way. As though luxury should be quiet; comfortable, even. His dark hair was thick with a slight wave held in place by some kind of wax. He was a throwback to the postwar era, in stark contrast to the men with shoulder-length hair and turtlenecks all around him, whose fashion was the folk music answer to the Swinging Sixties.

"Vera?" Frances's expression was bright as she noticed her friend, but her brows quickly knitted together when she saw a hint of fear on Vera's face, and how tightly she clutched her coat, her knuckles white.

"What's wrong? Has something happened?" Frances asked as she pulled Vera gently by the arm, away from the noise of the crowded bar.

"I got in over my head, Frances," Vera said. Her careful composure started to crack, and tears shook her voice, making it quiver like someone had pounded a fist down on a table near a full glass of water.

"What do you mean?" Frances asked.

Vera shook her head fiercely. "I shouldn't tell you any more," she said. "This is very much a curiosity-killing-the-cat kind of situation, Frances. Believe me, I wish to God I could unlearn the things I found out."

Frances gave Vera a long and considering look. "I can help you, but only if you tell me everything. I can't fix something I don't have all the pieces to."

Vera swallowed hard. "I'm sorry, Frances. I can't risk it." Vera was looking around now, examining the shapes of the people in the club, jumping at the crash of a dropped glass and clutching her bag even tighter.

Frances's expression shifted between concerned and confused. "I . . ." she said, hesitating. "Don't take this the wrong way, Vera, but if you can't tell me anything, then why are you here?"

"I just—I can't rely on anyone in my own social circle. I need . . ." Vera barked out a laugh. "I need more friends in low places."

Frances was quiet. Finally, she said, "And you think I'm the person to put you in contact with these kinds of people?" Her voice was unreadable, and if she was offended by what Vera was implying, she didn't show it.

"Your job at the diner," Vera said, not looking at Frances but scanning the doorway as waiters and waitresses came and went. "You connect with people—all kinds of people. And I know you've made friends while you've been studying here in London . . . friends who might be able to help me out of this horrendous spot I'm in."

"Vera, tell me honestly—is there someone threatening you? Is it your brother?"

"He'll kill me," Vera whispered.

There was a long pause, and a trumpet solo finished to raucous applause. In the hush of the audience, as the musicians drew breath to start their next number, Frances surprised her. This was why Vera had come to Frances for help, this fighting spirit and willingness to get stuck into problems, even when they weren't her own. Even when vital information had been carefully left out.

"What if you got to him first?" Frances said.

CHAPTER 1

THE KEYS RATTLE AGAINST THE METAL OF THE FILing cabinet as I deliver a swift kick to the already dented drawer. Cursing, I step backward. My toes throb, but I give the drawer a second kick out of pure bloody-mindedness. Pain shoots up my foot. I yelp, then let that yelp evolve into an enraged growl out of commitment to my own drama. I already know what's inside—a small square canvas, an early painting my mum did that forms part of a collection that made her famous years ago. I haven't thought about it in months, but a phone call this morning has my mind racing. I need to get my hands on it now.

The drawer is secured with a rotary lock—one that I've known the combination to for months and have opened once before—but after Saxon Gravesdown (the adopted nephew of my late great aunt Frances) angrily took a crowbar to it when he couldn't get it open, the alignment of the thing is so off that it now seems to have clamped its jaws shut forever.

I sink down on the faded rug that covers the cool flagstone

floor in what I now (affectionately and somewhat warily) refer to as Great Aunt Frances's murder room. It's a small antechamber off the main library in Gravesdown Hall—the grand estate I inherited from Frances when I solved her murder—and it houses decades of research into who was up to what in the village of Castle Knoll. A collection of secrets, crimes, coincidences, odd facts, suspicious behavior . . . Aunt Frances cataloged it all.

I suspect that her collection started with only the kind of dirt that might help her identify her own killer, after her murder was foretold by a local fortune-teller named Peony Lane. But Frances started coming across so many lies and sordid pasts that she must have decided it would take years to untangle the relevance of all this information. Evidently, the only thing to do was to collect it all. Like Pokémon, but with crimes.

The windowless room is freezing, and I long to slink back into the library with its plush carpets and roaring fire. There, the flat January light is at least some measure of evidence that a world exists beyond the drawers of cheating spouses and money launderers. But there's a slip of paper in my pocket, one that I've been carrying around with me for weeks. It's had me circling back to this room. To this drawer.

It's one of the last fortunes written by Peony Lane.

And it's mine.

I pull the paper from my pocket for what must be the hundredth time. The single fold in the middle of it is starting to wear thin, so the paper feels fabric soft. It falls open in my palm like a tired set of butterfly wings, and I let my eyes run over the odd block letters of Peony Lane's handwriting. I could recite the fortune in my sleep, but seeing the words written in Peony's own hand somehow lends an extra charge to their presence.

Today I'm concerned with only one line: *Without its beating heart, your family will fall one by one.*

The whole fortune is a puzzle, with this line as the first riddle. I was all set to disregard it when I first read it, and I left it in a coat pocket for weeks. Until this morning, when Mum phoned from our house in Chelsea, where she's been hard at work on a new series of paintings.

"It's past time I got back to my artistic roots," she said. I could hear music dimly in the background, and her echoey footsteps told me she was pacing about in her basement studio. "I have images and feelings buried deep that shaped me as an artist, and this new series is going to pay homage to that."

"That's great, Mum," I said. "I can't wait to see this new series when it launches."

"You'll love it, Annie, and I think you'll love my new apprentice too." The clatter of brushes in turpentine jars sounded, and I could almost smell her paints. I pictured her standing in front of a large canvas, painting in large strokes while trying to keep the phone pinned to her cheek with her shoulder. "Fliss was something of a stray when she came to my door asking if I'd take her on, but she's from Castle Knoll and I've found that talking to her about my life and my childhood there has been very therapeutic."

"Apprentice?" I blinked at this news. Mum has always been extremely private about her work—her whole process is usually shrouded in secrecy. During my childhood among the dust sheets and paint smudges in our run-down Chelsea townhouse, when she was painting she was always in a room of the house locked away, and I knew she was not to be disturbed.

"I know it's out of character for me, but this girl is retraining as a sculptor after a career in law, and we have some mutual acquaintances back in Castle Knoll. Her name's Felicity Rowe and she's only in her early thirties," Mum said. "It's nice to have someone around the house again. Felicity is good company."

"She's living there?" I asked. I tried to ignore the slight twinge I felt, knowing that Mum had taken in someone who she could share her art with in ways she never had with me.

"She needed somewhere to stay, and we've got all these empty rooms. And you'll be proud of me, Annie—I'm taking your advice and remembering to lock the front door these days."

"That's good, Mum," I replied, smiling lightly. Mum is absent-minded in a very typical artist kind of way. She'll remember details from an obscure silent film but forget to file her tax return.

I made a mental note to ask around about Felicity Rowe. Mum has never taken on students before, even when she was a star on the global art scene and was asked to do so constantly. She never gave guest lectures, did very few interviews, and certainly never visited colleges or art schools to talk about her art or her career. She wasn't generous that way; or maybe I'm being too harsh. I think it's more that she views her talent as something fragile, something that—if she lets too many people near—might be punctured. Like a soap bubble—beautiful, but ephemeral.

There was a clatter that sounded like paintbrushes being dropped, and Mum swore under her breath. After a beat I heard her murmur, "Oh, I think I like that there—it's like blood spatter."

"Mum?" I asked. I heard the music from her old radio in the background, but she didn't reply. I imagined her staring at her easel, analyzing the canvas in front of her. When she got into her art, she tended to tune out the rest of the world. "Do you need to go? Maybe painting while talking on the phone is taking multitasking a bit too far." I paused, then added, "Blood spatter isn't your usual style."

"It's this new form I'm experimenting with," she said, and her voice was breathy in an almost enraptured way. "It's getting to the heart of me," she added.

"What do you mean, the heart?" I had the fortune in my pocket even then, and it was like that line pulsed back at me.

"I mean it literally and figuratively. It's a deep study of the human heart, its chambers and vessels, and how, when rendered in paint and shown from different angles, it can be both beautiful and terrifying. There's so much that happens when you look at the heart. You have to face your own mortality and realize there are some things you can control and some that you can't, no matter how hard you might try."

It was then that I felt a sort of imperceptible click in my mind, like heavy clock hands moving one notch closer to midnight. As Mum spoke, the vibrant red colors of the small, square canvas locked away in Aunt Frances's files were all I could think about, and the link between my fortune and Mum's art became impossible to ignore.

I push Mum's voice from my thoughts as I kick the file drawer yet again, but the heat of my frustration has dimmed. My stomach growls, and in a welcome interruption, Archie Foyle's voice floats in from down the hall, along with the smell of fresh bread.

"Beth," I say, wandering into the kitchen. They both look up, Beth in a signature vintage apron over a 1930s tea dress, her arms dusted in flour. Beth is rather timeless and has a knack for making every cooking session at Gravesdown Hall look like a vintage photo shoot.

Archie, Beth's grandfather, has his shock of white curls tucked under a wool flat cap and is snacking on something I can't identify. He's well into his seventies but is the kind of man who never stops moving, showing no signs of slowing down. Both Archie and Beth come and go from Gravesdown Hall at their leisure—they're both former employees of Aunt Frances and live on the neighboring farm—and I like that there's constant company in what would otherwise be an intimidatingly lonely house.

"What can I do for you, Annie?" Beth asks.

"Do you know a woman named Felicity Rowe, early thirties? Apparently she's from around here but lives up in London now?"

Beth thinks for a moment while kneading some dough on the worktop. "Sounds vaguely familiar, but if she was at school here, she would have come after me."

"I remember her," Archie says. Beth and I both look at him, slightly surprised. "Charming girl, sharp too. She went to study law in London after she broke up with her bloke here in Castle Knoll. Childhood sweethearts, they were. You know the type, the couple everyone thinks will get married."

"Well, apparently she's Mum's new apprentice."

Archie's eyebrows shoot up. "Laura? Taking Felicity on as an apprentice? That's a strange one."

"Why?" I ask. Beth stops kneading for a moment, interested in this new turn the conversation has taken.

"Well, isn't Laura best friends with Reggie Crane? Detective Rowan Crane's dad?" Archie asks.

"She is," I say. "Why would Reggie have an issue with Felicity Rowe spending time with Mum?"

"Well, Fliss is persona non grata in the Crane family, after things fell apart with Rowan. Broke his heart, she did."

I blink in surprise. Of all the hearts in Castle Knoll, Detective Crane's is the last one I expect to hear about being broken. Beth and Miyuki, her wife, might be my closest friends in the village—they never make me feel like an outsider, even though I only moved here from London last summer. But Crane and I are . . . I don't know quite what we are. Friends, certainly, but there's also an element of mystery in how we interact. We're both holding things back, but in that way that you do when you only want someone to see the best of you. With Beth and Miyuki, I ramble on about whatever pops into my head over dinner once a week, and have no qualms about letting loose the less attractive laugh that only escapes after one too many glasses of Shiraz.

And while Crane is someone who has helped me out of more than a few scrapes, he's also been the person who has stood by and encouraged me as I work through the facts hidden in Frances's file drawers. And we make quite a successful team—together, we've solved four murders. Being the local detective, Crane understands my need to get to the truth when something is afoot, and he seems to actually appreciate my sideways approach to figuring things out. The fact that he's only just over thirty, quietly handsome, and unattached adds a bit of electricity to our interactions.

But one thing Crane and I have never had is a conversation about deeply personal things like falling in and out of love. Quite frankly, I find it far easier to talk about murder. And I suspect he'd agree.

"So let me get this straight," I say carefully to Beth and Archie. "Mum has—out of the blue and quite uncharacteristically—taken on Detective Crane's childhood sweetheart as her new apprentice? Probably to the chagrin of her best friend, Crane's dad? I mean, that sounds like dusting off decades-old village drama."

One side of Archie's mouth tugs downward in something resembling a wince. "There was more to it than that," he says. "Though I'm not one to spread gossip—"

"Yes, you are," Beth cuts in lightly.

"All right, that's fair," Archie says. "But there's something you should know, Annie. When Fliss ran off to London, not only did she break young Rowan's heart but she also stole quite a lot of money from the Crane family. Money they never got back, taken in a way they could never prove. She's wily, that Felicity, and extremely clever."

The conversation lulls after Beth hands me a couple of slices of bread, still warm from the oven. I take them back to the file room with me, and the butter melts while I go back to work trying to open the stubborn drawer. I twist the rotary lock on it again and again, while pressing the metal of the drawer inward with the other hand. Finally, I give the handle a decent tug and the drawer opens.

I reach in and take out the small canvas nestled inside. It's only about thirty centimeters square, but as soon as I see the image, I know—I feel it in my bones—that something's coming. That Peony Lane's fortune is already intertwining with the events playing out around me. I shudder.

Without its beating heart, your family will fall one by one.

The visceral nature of the painting is as I remember it,

but looking at it now I can make out the very clear shape of a human heart, under the layers of artistic license. I can't decide if Peony Lane's fortune only feels important because I've suddenly been faced with a few things I can't make sense of. Her fortunes work that way sometimes—you never know if they're actually coming true as strange things unfold around you, or if your brain is looking at the strange things and assigning them significance because of the fortune.

When my phone pings, I start and nearly drop the painting. It's a text from Mum.

You there?

I squint at my phone. An ellipsis bubbles up at the bottom of the screen, so I wait for her to finish her thought before replying. It's classic Mum to not say everything all in one go.

Don't freak out. But something bloody's been left on the doorstep.

Another ellipsis dances about. I don't wait for her to say more; I start typing furiously.

What do you mean, something bloody? I fire back.

I'm not sure, she says. *A piece of an animal, maybe? It looks like an organ but I can't figure out what. A liver?*

A photo pings through, and I open it. I fumble a little before zooming in on a shiny red lump that's sitting in the *o* of the *Welcome* written on the front mat.

"Or a heart," I murmur to myself, my throat dry.

I won't lie, Annie, I am a bit concerned about this, she types.

Worry lines creep across my forehead as Peony Lane's words ring in my ears. *Without its beating heart, your family will fall one by one.*

And now there's a heart on Mum's doorstep.

Could this be a warning?

Or a threat?

One thing's for sure: I've long stopped believing in coincidences.

With shaky hands, I wrap the painting in clean tea towels to pack into my bag. I'm already moving before I send her a final message. *I'm on my way.*

CHAPTER 2

September 20, 1968

"REGISTRATION WAS A WEEK AGO," THE STERN-FACED woman at the reception desk said.

I'd known this, of course, but somehow I thought that when I turned up at the psychology department at University College London a week late, they'd make an exception for me. Perhaps I'd expected my enthusiasm would charm them—it had been oozing from every pore since I'd packed my suitcase and made my way to London. This was the fresh start I needed. No more thinking about murder—whether my own or anyone else's. I was going to learn about people, what keeps us going and how our minds work.

"I'm so sorry," I said. "I needed to work for an additional week to be able to cover the cost of moving here. I'm Frances Adams. I applied for the scholarship for women from rural areas." I said this hopefully, as if she could somehow magically create a second scholarship for me since I'd missed out on the first.

Her lips thinned with annoyance, and she removed her reading glasses so that they made use of the chain around her neck. She was one of those stout older women you'd have wanted as a neighbor during the war. I could imagine her sheltering people in a carefully dug and well-stocked bunker in her garden, the walls lined with jars of preserves and a ham radio taking up a corner. The plaque on her desk announced her as Betty Braithwaite, office manager.

"I'm aware you applied for the scholarship," Betty said, "and you didn't get it." She took in my worn shoes and my faded baby doll–style dress. I'd bought the navy fabric as an offcut and sewn it myself, then made a matching blazer using some nautical buttons off an old fisherman's jacket I'd found in our attic in Castle Knoll. In Dorset I was seen as rather fashionable, with my ability to copy the latest styles from the magazines. In London I just felt like a child playing dress-up.

Betty sighed. "Where have you come from, then?" Her eyes darted to my battered suitcase, and I tried to stand in front of it to disguise the stupidity of my decision to come straight to the university, rather than find somewhere to live first. I'd thought that someone here could point me in the direction of university housing, if it existed.

A man of about my father's age hurried in—a Black man with white stubble and wire-framed glasses. He was wearing a tweed jacket and everything about his appearance telegraphed professor.

"Professor Dane, I'll be right with you," Betty said, "as soon as I can sort out Miss Adams here." She shuffled papers on her desk and sighed as if she was weighing a heavy decision.

"I did send a telegram to the department about my delayed arrival," I said. I felt she might, at any moment, tell me they'd given my place to someone on a waiting list when I failed to turn up on time.

"Miss Adams, what concerns me is how you plan to fund the rest of your education, if covering the cost of moving here was such a hard-won achievement," Betty said.

I could feel the eyes of the professor on me, though he looked friendly and I didn't feel judged by him. "I'll get a job, of course," I said.

"Your work here will be very time-consuming." Betty picked up her glasses on their chain and positioned them at the end of her nose. She examined a form on her desk, which I imagined had nothing to do with me. Perhaps she wanted to give the impression of being very busy. "I'll tell you now that waitressing while trying to study will have you exhausted and unable to keep up by the end of your second week."

I squared my shoulders and gave Betty my best level stare. I no longer had the impression of her sheltering her neighbors during the Blitz. I imagined her in front of her bunker, deciding who was worthy of sharing her space.

"The variety of skills and viewpoints of students will be greatly diminished by placing administrative barriers on the working classes," I said. I admit I was trying very hard to sound clever enough to belong there, but I also meant it. I might be the child of people who run a bakery in the countryside, but I knew I had as much of a right to be there as someone who came in wearing nice shoes and had pockets full of cash.

Betty looked at me over her reading glasses. "I didn't realize we had a junior Marxist on our hands. The sociology department is in the next building," she said curtly.

I heard a cough from behind me. Betty and I turned to the professor, having forgotten he was there.

"Betty, what exactly is the issue?" he asked. "From what I gather, this young lady has been granted admission to one of our courses, has been working to cover the expenses, and also notified the department of her need to register late. Can you simply complete her registration, hand over her timetable, and leave her to sort out her personal finances as she sees fit?"

I felt nicely vindicated, with a member of the academic staff coming to my defense. I was nearly brave enough to ask Betty what she had against waitresses, but I held my tongue.

Betty sighed loudly but shuffled out a form from her stack. "Sign here," she said. There was more sifting of papers, and a timetable was placed on the desk between us. "This is the schedule for the introductory lectures. You'll notice they're peppered throughout the day, and attendance is mandatory. Too many absences and you'll be removed from your course."

"Thank you," I said. I hated to ask the woman about housing, but it had to be done. "You don't know if any rooms are still available in university housing, do you?"

Betty scoffed, but the professor stepped forward and put up a hand between us. "There are a few boardinghouses near the university that are women only. I'd recommend trying one. Here." He pulled a flyer from a nearby bulletin board and handed it to me. "This one is reputable. I have a few female students staying there and I've heard the rooms are clean and affordable, if a bit sparse."

"Thank you so much," I said, and gave him a genuine smile.

"I'll walk with you," he said, and gave Betty a stern look.

I picked up my suitcase and nearly laughed as Betty called, "If you get arrested at one of those protests about the Americans in Vietnam, the university can expel you!"

I followed the professor along the hallway, and he chuckled. "I'd say not to mind Betty, but in all honesty, I think rubbing her up the wrong way is a sign of good character. I like to see people push back when someone's making an unfair judgment. I get my fair share, as one of the few Black members of staff in the department."

"I hope Betty doesn't make too much trouble for you," I said, because I didn't really know what else to say.

"Oh, she's the least of my worries," he said, and smiled in a world-weary way that made me feel unexpectedly sad. "But enough of that. Let's see which lectures they've put you down for in your first term." We stopped walking, and I handed him the piece of paper Betty had given me.

"I'll admit to being slightly upset that I didn't get to choose," I said.

He looked at my timetable, and his brow furrowed. "Yes, I see what you mean. Have you looked closely at this list yet?"

I took the paper back and examined the titles. Some sounded just right, like Introduction to the History of Psychology and Research Methods. But three others showed a trend I didn't like. Introduction to Child Psychology, Early Childhood Development, and Behavioral Management of Children.

"I'm drawing a rather unfair conclusion here," I said.

"Your conclusion isn't unfair," Professor Dane corrected me. "But the class assignments are. Here." He took the paper back from me, reached into his tweed blazer, and brought out a pen. "Do you have any special interests? Neuroscience or linguistics or something like that?"

I shook my head. "I'm only just beginning to discover how much is out there, in terms of ideas and fields of study. I want to learn about people," I said, and flushed because that answer seemed feeble. The truth was, I just wanted to change my life. I was stagnating in Castle Knoll, fixating on the fact that a fortune-teller had predicted my murder, and I was helpless to get any answers beyond that. To make matters worse, uncovering the truth behind the murders of other people had become something of a habit recently. Murder seemed to follow me everywhere, and I was ready to turn over a fresh page.

"Well, in that case, let's sign you up for a better range of lectures and seminars to give you an idea of the directions you can

take in psychology. How about one of mine? Not that I'm trying to bias your trajectory," he said, and smiled good-naturedly.

I laughed. "I'd be happy to take anything you teach. It'll be nice to see at least one friendly face when I'm struggling to keep up with all the information flying at me."

"Wonderful," he said. "There's one that's not entry-level, but if I sign off on you joining, no one will argue." He crossed out several courses and wrote new ones in.

"I'm keen to dive into anything, really," I said. The same excitement I'd felt when I'd left Castle Knoll was bubbling up again. "What's the lecture called?"

"Understanding the Homicidal Mind," he said. "It's fascinating. My specialty is in the exploration of why people kill."

"So you . . . study murderers," I said cautiously.

"It sounds dark, I know. If it's not a direction you're keen to go in, I won't take offense."

"Oh, it's not that," I said. I took a long breath, realizing that no matter where I went, I couldn't outrun myself. "It sounds perfect for me. Sign me up."

CHAPTER 3

I'M PACING THE ICY FRONT STEPS OF MUM'S HOUSE IN Chelsea, having first checked that the space is free of any suspicious animal remains. Also, I've remembered a rather significant detail in her romantic life that's left me not wanting to ring the bell. Laura Adams may be good at a lot of things—creativity, taking chances, having fun—but one thing she's never been great at is learning from her mistakes. She'll eat too many churros before going on a roller coaster, or overpay for a fake antique in Bali, only to do it again when she's presented with the same choice a second time. Or a third.

It was naive of me to think that this pattern wouldn't extend to the men she dates, but when I heard that she'd recently let my dad back into her life—the man who supposedly conned her out of most of the money she made when her art blew up in the nineties—I was surprised.

Before I moved to Castle Knoll, I'd spent my life in Chelsea with just Mum, in the posh-but-crumbling townhouse that Great Aunt Frances let us live in after Dad left. I was only a baby when that happened, so I have no warm, fuzzy memories to cling to, no hope that one day he might come back. I never found myself wishing I had a dad because I never thought of Mum as not enough. She's rather eccentric and is, quite frankly, a train wreck administratively, so I simply learned how to do things like register myself for school and keep records of my vaccinations. And all that time, she taught me that life can be a series of small adventures whenever you want it to be.

We'd put on fake accents to get free drinks, play a game where we raced across London to see how far we could travel without paying for public transport, then have a competition to see who was better at talking her way out of the fines (Mum).

Does this make us close in the way that some of my friends are with their mums? I'll put it this way: I'd never hesitate to call her if I needed someone to bail me out of prison. If I needed a kidney, I know she'd offer to give me both of hers before she remembered that you need at least one to stay alive. But would I come to her in need of financial advice? Absolutely not. Career help? Hard no. Relationship advice? Hell would need to freeze over for me to even consider that.

I let my finger hover over the bell, then think better of it and pace again. It's cold out here. I need to make a decision soon.

My fortune plays in my head on a loop:

Without its beating heart, your family will fall one by one. Beware the heart kept in darkness. It will be death's catalyst if brought into the light without its proper name. Following footsteps can lead to bad places—tread lightly, or not at all. But it will be your own heart, if left unguarded, that's ripe for the knife.

The words have left me unsettled, but I'm not about to go all Aunt Frances with it. I could read that final line as a prediction of my own murder if I wanted to, but it could mean a variety of other things. It could mean something will leave me brokenhearted if I let myself be too vulnerable. It could mean pain, but not necessarily death.

I look at the tattered welcome mat under my feet and try not to remember the animal organ sitting there. I wish Jenny were here, but I can't rely on my best friend to shepherd me through every unpleasant thing. She's off on a monthlong work trip to New York, so navigating the unsettling words of Peony Lane is completely up to me this time. I take a deep breath and push the bell. Really, the person I'm avoiding isn't my mum. It's my dad. Having never met the man, I find I'd like to keep it that way.

"Annie, hi!" The door bursts open, and Mum is pulling me inside. Her blond curls went gray a few years back, and she wears them long and rather wild, held loosely away from her face by a variety of colorful scarves. Today, she wears one that's bright yellow and looks like hand-dyed silk. It's folded like an Alice band but knotted just under one ear so that the tail flows long over one shoulder. She looks far more fashionable than I ever manage.

She notices my eyes darting around the hall, and a stern look passes over her face. "He's not here," she says. "But you can't avoid him forever."

"I do love a challenge," I mumble, and she rolls her eyes.

"Honestly, Annie, you've never been resentful about him not being around when you were growing up. Why start now?"

"It's the whole criminal element, actually," I say evenly. "I'd like to keep the con men in our lives to a minimum."

"We've been through this," she says. "He didn't realize the investors who took my money were a Ponzi scheme. It was someone he met through work who seemed reputable."

"Then why did he run?" I cross the kitchen and step carefully over what looks like a fresh splodge of paint—or possibly congealed scrambled egg; the color and consistency seem about the same—and poke at the open containers of takeaway balanced on the cooker.

"It's more complicated than that," Mum says. She raises an eyebrow and I instinctively back off—we're veering dangerously toward sharing feelings and relationship woes.

"Fine," I say, putting my hands into the air. "I'm not here about that. It's the animal part on your doorstep that's rattled me." I run a hand through my own blond curls, then give up when I hit too many tangles. "Maybe we should have called the police. Has anyone suspicious been hanging around lately? Anything else weird you've noticed?"

Mum blinks at me for a moment, like she's not following, and then her features soften. "Honestly, Annie, it was just a random occurrence." She waves a hand to indicate how little she cares, but her eyes dart behind me briefly toward the door. "I've decided it's nothing. Really." She gives me a thin smile—evidence enough that my trip here wasn't for nothing. She's worried.

She crosses over to the takeaway boxes and busies herself shuffling them into stacks. There's a silence and I watch as unease grows in the pinch between her shoulders. "Can we change the subject, please? It must have been half-eaten prey left behind by some fox or cat, nothing more." Finally she turns to face me, exasperation plainer on her face. "But I'm flattered that you came to visit. You're overdue anyway." She smiles again, this time more warmly.

I sigh. "Okay, fine, no more talk of dead animals."

"Or suspicious characters hanging about," Mum adds, one corner of her mouth lifting. "When I need a detective, I'll ask for one."

"Fair enough," I say. "In that case, I'm extremely interested in the gossip about this new apprentice you've taken on. Did you know she's Rowan's ex-girlfriend?"

Mum doesn't bite—or not in the way I want her to. She offers no backstory about Felicity Rowe, gossip or otherwise.

"Oh, Felicity!" she exclaims. Her expression shifts instantly as relief at the change of topic washes over her face. "You'll love Fliss, honestly. She's so vibrant and interesting, always coming up with ways to get out into the world and push boundaries. She just gives off, I don't know, an *energy*."

"So does plutonium," I mutter.

Mum either doesn't hear or chooses to ignore me. "It's been something of a revelation being the person who has knowledge to share when it comes to navigating the art world," she continues.

"What's her art like?" I ask. I'm trying to ignore the uncomfortable feeling I get when I hear Felicity described as vibrant and interesting. I may be the one Mum relies on to keep the water running when she's forgotten to pay the bill, but when it comes to the more colorful aspects of her life, I can't keep pace with her. What must it be like for her to finally have someone who injects just as much creativity and vibrancy into a day as she does? Someone who isn't just along for the ride, but designs the roller coaster?

My thoughts shift to Rowan Crane. I'd thought that, around him, I was the exciting one. But what if that's all in my head? His past includes falling for someone like Felicity (who I'm starting to think of as a vivacious femme fatale), while all this time I've just been ordinary old Annie, meddling in his cases and not being nearly as interesting as I think I am.

"Her art is, well, it's in progress," Mum says.

There's something in her voice that makes me pause, something she isn't saying. "You sound like her art might not be to your liking," I say cautiously.

"That's not what I said," Mum replies, and her voice is clipped.

I startle at the quick change in her tone. "Well, why did you take her on as an apprentice? She's not a painter, right? You said she was a sculptor," I say.

Mum looks at me for a beat too long. "That's the second time you've asked why I took her in. Why is it so strange that I want to help a fellow artist?"

"Aside from the fact that you've never done it before?"

"Well, I'm doing it now. And I have my reasons," she says. "So we'll just be leaving it at that." She speaks with a forced breeziness, but her tone sounds final.

Now I'm fully convinced that something strange is going on in the arrangement Mum has with Felicity. I'm worried maybe she was coerced into taking her in, or she's being manipulated. What apprentice needs to move in with their mentor?

"Is Felicity around?" I ask. If curiosity is going to eat me alive, I might as well kick off the banquet. And it would be one way to get some answers, if only through observation. "I'd love to meet her."

Mum takes a pair of chopsticks and dips them into what

looks like cold chow mein. "I haven't seen her since last night," she says, her mouth half-full of noodles. "We were at a gallery opening in Marylebone and she was chatting all night with a really good-looking man who was a buyer for a collector. Sadiq, I think his name was. My guess is she stayed the night with him. She's irresistible like that, always making conquests." Mum puts the now-empty container on the table, and I stare at it, trying not to think too hard about Felicity's irresistible ways.

I busy myself with collecting the takeaway cartons, annoyed that I feel like a teenager again. "Is there a bin bag?" I ask. "I'll clear all this up." As I look around the kitchen, I notice rubbish has accumulated on worktops, and recycling is teetering in a pile in the corner.

"Oh, Fliss used them all the other day. I think she must have needed them for a project or something. She grabbed the whole roll, and I haven't been to the shops to get more yet. Here." She hands me an empty Tesco bag. "You'll have to go to the skip around the corner. The main bin's full."

I sigh but dutifully fill the bag with as much kitchen detritus as I can force into it. The freezing air is welcome as I emerge onto the doorstep. It's funny how quickly the comforts of this familiar house can wear thin. Being away from the paint splodges and accumulated chaos had me romanticizing everything, but ten minutes at home and I see them for what they are—the evidence of someone who, while she's always been the adult in my life, is in need of looking after.

I trudge down the steps and turn right, rounding the corner that the house sulks on, and walk to where the fence of our property ends. A small alleyway ends abruptly with a brick wall that separates us from the back of a block of flats.

A large metal skip sits against the wall, its black plastic lid keeping the rats out. I inhale sharply as a large orange tomcat slinks out from underneath, and I think again about the bloody present left on the front step.

"Were you the culprit?" I ask the cat. It winds around my ankles and then wanders off, perhaps in search of scraps somewhere else. Normally I like to pet the neighborhood cats, but today I stride over to the bin and throw back the heavy lid.

I have to stand on tiptoe to heave the Tesco bag over the edge, but as I'm about to let go of it, my focus lands on a rippling fan of red hair. My eyes trace the hair to the roots, finding it attached to the porcelain skin of a body splayed inside the skip. Distantly I hear the crumple of the Tesco bag as it drops to my side. My hands shake as I struggle to get my phone out to dial the police. Each breath is strained and my head swims. I try not to look but can't help noticing that her eyes are open and glassy. When I close my own, all I can see is bloodstained clothes and the gaping crater in her chest. I swallow hard at the implications of that.

I dial 999 and somehow get out the basic information. "I've found a dead girl in a skip . . . There's so much blood, and I think her heart is missing . . . Where? Chelsea, Tregunter Road . . . No, her *heart. I think it's missing.*" The voice at the other end of the line barely registers in my mind. I think I'm arguing with the emergency operator, but then I'm sitting in the alley, and I've hung up. I'm trying to look anywhere but at the skip as the orange cat returns and rubs against my shins.

This is clearly the body of Felicity Rowe. I'd googled her name on the train out of the morbid curiosity of wanting to know what an ex-girlfriend of Crane's looked like. I found some of her social media accounts, and a rather empty web page devoted to her sculptures that simply said, "Watch this space."

She was pretty in a quirky way, with the kind of pixie pointed chin and double-bun hairstyle you'd see among Mum's crowd. She wasn't who I'd picture with Crane, but then, we all looked different as teenagers.

But now the image of her lying dead in a skip is superimposed over the smiling Instagram pictures I'd seen earlier. With every breath I'm taking, the scenario beats against my skull—the blood, the glassy eyes, the odd angles of her arms and legs.

She was lying on a pile of bin bags, which wouldn't have been significant normally, given that she was in the bin. But the flimsy plastic had torn in places, and bright canvases were showing through. A stack of them.

They were painted in an unmistakable style, a style I'd know anywhere.

I put my head between my knees and breathe. As I try not to faint from the shock of the whole grisly scene, my brain does what it seems to do best lately. It absorbs a shocking discovery, and out of the information gathered, it forms a question. And then the awful event breaks itself into two pieces—the tragic human element of a murder scene takes backstage, because it has to. If it didn't, I'd melt into a useless puddle of a person.

That question then drives my ability to process all that I've seen. In this case, the question is: *What is the heartless body of Felicity Rowe doing on top of a huge collection of Mum's paintings?*

CHAPTER 4

September 25, 1968

PROFESSOR DANE'S LECTURES PROVED EXTREMELY POPular. The lecture theater was packed, and while most of my fellow students were male, there was a smattering of women enrolled in Understanding the Homicidal Mind.

As Professor Dane lectured, I could see why the room was so full. He was engaging, funny, clever, and warm. His subject matter was dark in a way that drew people's curiosity, like the need to turn your head and observe the scene of a crash. There was something morbid in all of us sitting there, eagerly taking notes. What was it we hoped to get from this lecture? Was each of us going to learn enough about why people kill so that we might stop it from happening? Or did we just want to sit there in the confidence that we weren't the evil ones, no matter what petty sins we had committed?

For me, there was a draw in the fact that the crimes we were studying hadn't happened to me. Perhaps the more I learned about these things, the less likely it would be for me to fall victim to something so horrifying. A false comfort, surely, because there was one staggering common factor in the case studies we looked at.

The victims were most often women.

But I was already learning to think like a student, to question the datasets in front of me. If we were looking primarily at cases where women were the victims, perhaps this was because Professor Dane, consciously or not, chose stories to fit that particular pattern.

"One of the most significant factors murderers often share," Professor Dane was saying, "is a tendency toward antisocial behavior. Now, when we say antisocial, we don't always mean the people who can't have proper conversations or don't make friends easily. Antisocial behavior can apply to some very charming individuals. Other traits that may indicate an antisocial person include a lack of empathy, the feeling that rules don't apply to them, and the ability to stay detached from their own actions. They may also feel the need to exact revenge on anyone they believe has wronged them."

I took notes furiously, making lists and including my own questions in the margins. Next to lack of empathy, *I wrote,* What makes one empathetic? Is this innate, or is it a learned behavior? Is it possible for someone to lose this ability due to trauma or past experience? *I wished I could ask but I wasn't brave enough to raise my hand.*

The student next to me raised his hand, and out of the corner of my eye, I caught blond shoulder-length hair and an overpronounced chin.

"Yes," Professor Dane said, and pointed to him. "It's Max, isn't it?"

"It is, sir," he said. "I was wondering"—he paused, and I felt his eyes slide my way in the tiniest of movements—"what makes

one empathetic? Is this innate, or is it a learned behavior? And is it possible for someone to lose this ability due to trauma or past experience?"

I looked up from my notes and didn't bother to hide the shock on my face. I took my notebook and clutched it to my chest, suddenly territorial. I was outraged, certainly, but I also felt a strange sense of exposure. As if, simply because of my proximity or my demeanor—my obvious inconsequence—my work was there for the taking.

"What fascinating questions, Max," Professor Dane said. "I sense you have a great talent for getting to the heart of the subject matter." Professor Dane talked about empathy for a while, but I couldn't focus on what he was saying. I was too fixated on the student next to me, Max. He leaned back in his seat as the professor went on. The side of his mouth twisted upward slightly when I turned to regard him. Instinctively I knew that he was enjoying this.

I took a long breath, and slowly my outrage shifted to something more manageable, as I realized I was in familiar territory. I might have felt small and adrift under the bright lights of London, and inadequate among people I was certain were cleverer than me, but I had experience dealing with entitled men.

My hand shot into the air before I could talk myself out of it.

Professor Dane's eyes found me and crinkled kindly as he acknowledged me. "Frances, you have a question?"

"Yes, sir, thank you. I was wondering about power." I tilted my chin and tapped my pen against my jaw, as if I was deeply considering something just out of reach. In reality, I was taking in Max's shift in posture now that I had the floor. He'd straightened his shoulders and was bouncing one leg slightly. "The antisocial behavioral traits you've mentioned all seem to have that in common," I continued. "For example, individuals who think rules

don't apply to them could be assuming superiority over others, even if in reality that superiority might not exist."

"Is there a question in there?" Max interjected.

I turned to him and raised an eyebrow. "I'm getting to it," I said calmly, as if he were a child pestering me for sweets while I was talking to other adults. "My question is, how much of a sense of personal power must someone have for their empathy to completely erode?" I looked Max squarely in the eye.

"By your logic," Max said, keeping eye contact with me, "we could equate murder with a sense of entitlement. But every person of wealth and power in London isn't a killer."

"But a sense of entitlement must be present to kill," I countered. "Because isn't murder the worst kind of theft? Stealing someone's future? If an individual feels so superior to others that they can take their life, not just their possessions, or their ideas"—Max finally broke eye contact and huffed, and I could see him trying to unpick my words in his head—"then perhaps in looking at what makes a murderer, we should also look at what makes someone feel that particular kind of power."

Several people in the class murmured their agreement, and more hands shot into the air to join the discussion. My point had resonated with the other students, and with Professor Dane, and a lively debate began. A lot of people acknowledged my point before they added their own views, but the one thing that gave me the most satisfaction was watching Max sit there silently, with no thoughts of his own to contribute.

The lecture continued, and though I received compliments from Professor Dane on my arguments, I was still shaking as I left the lecture theater. Whether this was out of anger with Max for his arrogance or due to leftover nerves from having spoken my mind in front of a hundred other students, I couldn't tell.

As I moved to the exit, I noticed Max was perched on the back of one of the chairs at the rear of the hall. He wasn't facing me but was animatedly talking about ego and id to a small group of students, holding court as if this had been his lecture all along.

"Don't spare a thought for Max Torrence," said a girl next to me. I brought my expression under control because she must have noticed the intensity of the glare I was throwing at him. We were walking up the center aisle toward the doors, but it was taking a while to get there because of the crush of people leaving.

"You know him?" I asked.

"Everyone knows him," she said, and her expression was tight. "And bravo, by the way. You had the measure of him in those comments you made—his family are extremely important to the college. His mother is an heiress—you know, the serious kind of money that spans generations. And his father is head of the Department of Psychology. I think Max assumes he's in charge simply by association."

I winced. "Was it that obvious that my comments were directed at him?"

The girl shrugged. Her hair was a plain sort of brown, and she was dressed in a twinset of neutral colors. She wasn't someone I'd have noticed if she hadn't been one of the few other women in the lecture. "I'm Elaine," she said. "I've seen you at the boardinghouse. I rent a room there too."

"I'm Frances," I said. "I'm sorry I haven't introduced myself. I've been a bit overwhelmed since moving here. It's my first time living in London."

We spilled out with the rest of the students onto Gower Street, the deep red brick of the university building at our backs. Suddenly a black car pulled up in front of us, and one of the back windows rolled down.

"Max!" The bleached-blond bouffant of a girl a little older

than me emerged from the window, and she looked right through Elaine and me. "Over here!"

Max shouldered me aside, throwing a last-minute smirk over his shoulder before opening the back door of the car and getting inside.

"His girlfriend?" I asked.

"His sister," Elaine said. "Vera Huntington. She's a socialite, but the annoyingly cool kind." Elaine pulled out a packet of Embassy and held it my way. "Cigarette?"

I shook my head, and we started walking back toward the boardinghouse.

"Anyway, Vera's good for a laugh but her idea of fun could get anyone into trouble. She's married to a famous heart surgeon nearly twice her age and gets bored easily," Elaine said.

"How do you know all this?" I asked.

"Max and I used to go out," she said, rather grudgingly. "We're both second years, so this was last year. I know it might seem impossible he'd go for me—he's good-looking and popular, but he likes his girls plain and a few rungs down on the social ladder. What you said about power"—she inhaled deeply and let out the smoke from her cigarette in a long stream—"that was spot-on."

"I'd never call you plain," I said, feeling slightly uncomfortable. I wasn't used to people being so open, but London girls were probably used to straight talking and speaking their minds. I supposed I should think of it as a refreshing change from the secretive residents of Castle Knoll. "And he's not that good-looking," I added. "He's got a chin you could moor a boat to."

A laugh erupted from Elaine, and she stopped and put a hand on my shoulder. "I like you, Frances, you're all right. Even if you are a bit green."

I smiled, not sure what to make of that. "What happened

with you and Max, if you don't mind me asking? He didn't break your heart, did he?"

"It was the other way around, surprisingly," Elaine said. "And after Professor Dane's lecture just now, I might have to suggest Max goes on a government watch list."

"He does seem like someone who'd tick quite a few of those antisocial-behavior boxes," I said.

"Well, I'll be sure to watch my back," Elaine said, and she gave me a flimsy salute, as if the conversation was all just some big joke. "Because there was another item on the antisocial list I could just see Max ticking off. He certainly likes to get revenge on anyone who's wronged him."

"Remind me to stay out of his way," I replied.

"I just did," Elaine said, and her expression wasn't playful anymore.

CHAPTER 5

October 16, 1968

I DID NOT STAY OUT OF MAX'S WAY.

In my defense, this was because he made quite a habit of getting in mine. I was always early to lectures, but much to my chagrin, so was Max. Elaine sat on one side of me, and annoyingly, Max repeatedly took the seat on my other side. I constantly felt like my notes were under scrutiny and that at any moment the words I was writing might be heard coming out of his mouth in the form of a question or comment. He didn't attempt it again, but the threat was always there.

I got a job at a diner in Soho—a cool spot in the style of those American burger places you see in films—waitressing and cleaning up after the hordes of people my age who frequented the shops and clubs there. I learned more about life and art and music in my first few weeks working there than in all the other weeks of my life combined. It was called Benny's, and I got lucky with how hip the scene was there. Benny, the manager, was an American who pretended to be from Chicago but was actually from Oklahoma. He walked with a swagger and talked about Motown Records and said things like You dig?

I'd walked in on a whim asking if he had any positions to fill. Benny looked me up and down, then said, "Sure, kiddo. You're pretty enough to fit in but not such a knockout the modeling scouts will snap you up, like the last girl."

I decided not to be offended. I needed the money if I wanted to eat and have any kind of social life. And thankfully, Benny was one of those harmless fatherly types. All the waitresses said that if you were in a tight spot, Benny would help you out of it.

It turned out that Elaine's room at the boardinghouse was down the hall from mine, which made falling into a friendship happen all the faster. Not a day went by when she wasn't knocking on my door to borrow some pencils, or I didn't go see her to ask her opinion on a chapter from a textbook.

But the best times were the random evenings when I'd come back from the diner with paper bags full of leftover chips, and we'd picnic on the floor of my room, washing down the salt and grease with swigs from a bottle of cognac. Elaine refused to explain where the cognac had come from, so I stopped asking. Often our conversations were about men, and somehow she always managed to circle the conversation back to Max.

"The best thing you can do," I said one evening, "is find someone new to go out with." We'd been studying until the booze started to make our thoughts run together nonsensically. I reached over and took too large a sip from the cognac, which caused a coughing fit.

Elaine good-naturedly snatched the bottle away from me. "You mean, to make Max jealous?" she asked. Her expression shifted from relaxed to energized, like plotting was just the thing to give her a new lease on life.

"Don't be ridiculous," I said, stretching my legs across the worn rug that came with the room's sparse furnishings. "Go out

with someone new just to . . . you know, live your life." I gestured grandly in front of me, like a sloppy orchestra conductor.

"Oh, that." Elaine giggled. "Life, eh? Good advice, Frances, you should be a therapist."

"Don't tease," I said, "I'm already stressed about my future . . ." I trailed off. "Anyway, I think you might be fixating on Max too much."

Elaine took a finger and dragged it through the leftover salt from the chips. We'd torn the paper bag open down the side and along the bottom, so it could lie flat and we could attack its contents properly. She licked her finger and looked at me with a different kind of mischief.

"And who are you fixating on, then?" she asked. "There's got to be someone. A nice fit farmer back in that village of yours? Or a bloke from the diner?"

I felt an involuntary flush to my cheeks as the image of Ford Gravesdown flooded my mind. I knew he was in London, of course. He was staying in his Chelsea house while his nephew, Saxon, was at boarding school. What he was doing with his time was a mystery to me, however.

I'd had several invitations to see him, but I'd responded politely and declined each one. The on-again, off-again nature of our relationship would distract me from finding my own way here in London and focusing on my studies.

"There is someone, isn't there!" Elaine exclaimed. "I knew it! Let me guess, he's an apprentice at your family's bakery, and you fell in love one spring over hot cross buns." She giggled again, which grated on me. There was an edge of teasing, but I felt like she might descend into full mockery if I wasn't careful in how I responded.

I shook my head, trying to clear my thoughts. I was likely just being paranoid. I'd spent so much time looking at the people around me as suspicious that I lacked the proper skills to maintain friendships. Namely, trust.

I missed the intensity of Ford's gaze when we were conversing about some puzzle or a complicated dynamic between people. I also missed his steady hands and the light smell of expensive Scotch when he leaned close to me, but I was trying to tuck away those thoughts. I wanted to be wary of Elaine, but I also wanted a proper friendship for once, where no one had ulterior motives.

I pointedly ignored comments about the imaginary bakery boy. "There was someone, an on-again, off-again situation, but it's over for now," I said.

"On-again, off-again," Elaine said, her voice vaguely singsong. "That's something I could never do. I don't have time for inconsistent men." She looked at me, and there it was again—only the tiniest hint of it, but it was there. A look that said, You see? My choices are above yours.

Which had prickled at me, until last week, when she went and contradicted herself beautifully.

One day when I was working, Elaine came into the diner with Max's sister, Vera. I'd yet to meet her, but I'd seen her often—since she was always there after class in that black car, shouting for Max.

"Ever been to an art auction?" Elaine asked. She was sitting across from Vera in one of the booths, which were upholstered in red leather. The lights in the diner were just dim enough that you couldn't see the cigarette burns that peppered the leather like trashy constellations. "Glitz and glamour and all that?"

Vera was quiet but smiled at me. I was wearing white go-go boots that I'd bought with my first wages, and a black-and-white checked dress I'd made myself, copied from a girl I'd seen at La Chasse a few nights back.

One thing I'd learned quickly in London and hadn't known in Castle Knoll was that being cool was its own social status. For ages I'd thought that wealth automatically equaled culture and superiority, but I was finding that expensive taste did not make for an interesting person.

Vera watched me coming and going, cracking jokes with the kitchen staff, talking about books with the students on their third cups of coffee, and singing all the words to the latest singles as they blasted from the radio. Whatever she saw must have interested her. Otherwise, why keep such an eye on me? Maybe it was the quiet confidence I exuded as I worked. It was new to me, this life, but I'd found my rhythm.

"Art intrigues me," I said. "Are we talking modern art? Like Warhol or Rothko?" It was slightly vain of me to name-drop artists like this. I couldn't have pointed out a Rothko to save my life, but I'd heard those names mentioned by customers as they smoked and tried to be more interesting than the person sitting opposite them.

"This is more of the boring kind," Vera said. Her voice was high-pitched and sweet, a contrast to how she yelled for Max from the car. She had a habit of letting the ash on her cigarette get as long as possible before tipping it into the ashtray, and I liked that. It made me feel my conversation was so interesting to her that tending to little things like cigarette ash was completely inconsequential.

"My husband is a collector of classics," she continued, exhaling smoke over her shoulder and blinking slowly. "It's an investment rather than a passion." She rolled her eyes as she said this, hinting at an appreciation of art that went beyond money. "There's a party hosted by one of his acquaintances, a silent auction at a private home in Knightsbridge. I told him that, after the frightful bore of the last one, I'd better be able to bring some friends with me. He agreed, but only if my friends are accompanied by respectable dates."

"Single women coming alone to events is considered gauche in the old-fashioned world of Dr. Huntington," Elaine said, and let out a cynical scoff. "And conveniently, Max and Elaine are on again, rather than off again."

I clenched my jaw to keep it from dropping, but my brows lifted in surprise. "I thought that was something you said you could never do." I put fake innocence into my voice, hoping it would remind her of our earlier conversation. It was walking an edge of mockery I didn't usually tread, but I felt like Elaine needed to be reminded of her own hypocrisy.

Elaine tossed her hair and ignored my comment, as if anything she'd ever said about Max was a figment of my imagination. "Can you find a date who at least owns a suit?"

I narrowed my eyes at her. Her baker-boy comments from the other night gnawed at me anew. When she'd asked if there was a man in my life, she'd speculated about a farmer or another diner employee. Even though we rented rooms in the same boardinghouse, it seemed she was a snob.

I smiled at Elaine, a grin that showed I was ready to meet her challenge. "Of course I can," I said. "I know just the man."

And that was how I found myself ringing the bell of the Chelsea townhouse of Rutherford "Ford" Gravesdown. A house I'd avoided ever since my arrival in London because it was full of bad memories. More specifically, it reminded me of the last time I was here—to drop off a friend who was never seen again, and whose disappearance pressed upon me like a lead weight.

But what surprised me as I stood there waiting for the door to open wasn't the bad memory of an unsolved disappearance. It was the desire to be back in the world of Ford Gravesdown, where mysteries were plentiful and relationships were complicated.

It was interesting, and fun, and just a little bit dangerous.

CHAPTER 6

MUM SPENDS MOST OF THE TIME THE DETECTIVES are here in tears, or pacing and trying to find things that belonged to Felicity, like they're clues that could help. She'll dart to the hallway and return with shaky hands holding a hair clip, or a sweet wrapper, insisting someone catalog and investigate it. I watch grief war with fear as she tries to describe Felicity's personality, recent movements, and potential enemies to the investigating team, until finally the police leave.

We sit for a long time in silence in the kitchen, as the sun goes down. Eventually she picks up her phone, looks like she's about to make a call, then glances at me and sets it down again.

"Please don't phone him," I say wearily.

"Phone who?" Mum asks, but she's not fooling anyone.

"Sam."

"Do you mean your father?"

"I'm not calling him Dad. I will forever refer to him as Sam," I say. "Or Mr. Arlington."

"Annie, you're being a bit unfair," Mum says.

"I've just found a dead body. I don't want to have to deal with the weirdness of confronting an absent father in the same day."

"I didn't call him or even text him," Mum says. But she gives me a reproachful look. "You might think about me, too, Annie. Fliss was my friend, and now she's gone. Having Sam here would help me feel better."

I try to ignore the implication that my presence does not contribute to Mum feeling better. I look at her and see that she's still shaky. It's one of those moments when I wish I was warmer as a person, the kind of comforting presence that makes cups of tea and gives hugs. But it would be strange for me to suddenly hold Mum's hand. Or am I just making an excuse not to? I don't know what to do, and I feel like a bad person for not knowing.

"I'm sorry," I say. I shut my eyes for a moment. "This must be hard for you."

The silence stretches out between us, and Mum sniffs.

"I want to help," I say eventually. "And we both know that the way I tend to do that is through working things out. I'm just . . . apologizing in advance if this isn't the properly sympathetic way, but I know you told the detectives that the last time you saw Felicity was at that party last night. Was there anything else significant she might have said or done that you didn't remember to include in your statement?"

Mum gives me a harsh glare. "Are you implying that I'm keeping things from the police?"

"No," I say. "I just thought that—"

Mum cuts me off. "You thought that you'd just bulldoze your way into information, disguising your investigative strategies as a heart-to-heart."

"That's not what I was doing!" I say, my voice rising. "I already tried to explain, it's my way of helping!" But her words hit a little too close to the truth, given my need to understand what's happened here. I want to feel more in control of the chaos of finding a body, and answers will do that for me. "I just want to know who Felicity was and what was so special about her!" I say, which is entirely true, even if it's an abrupt change of subject.

"No, you don't. You're angry I didn't share all my reasons for taking her on as my apprentice, and you're trying to push for that now. It won't work," she says curtly.

The front doorbell rings, and I wince. I get up to answer it, wondering if there'll ever be a way I can communicate with Mum and not make her angry.

When I open the door, Detective Crane is on the other side, blinking a little, like he's startled that the door actually opened after he rang the bell. He looks tired and runs a hand through his dark hair in a quick frustrated motion.

My mouth has fallen partly open in surprise, but I close it quickly because I don't want to make him feel like he shouldn't be here. In truth, I'm happy to see him. *Happy* is the wrong word, possibly. I'm relieved. And I feel a bit safer.

"Annie, hi," he says. "I came as soon as I heard about Fliss. Well, actually, I started driving before then, because . . . I mean, can I come in?" He's rambling, which isn't like him. He's usually got a calming presence, the type of person who's in the right job because he's unflappable around things that unsettle most people. Dead bodies, dangerous situations—Detective Crane is the person you want taking charge while you breathe into a paper bag in the corner and try not to vomit.

I want to ask him a thousand questions—how he heard,

and what he means about starting to drive here before he got the news. But as I lead him along the wide hallway and into the kitchen, I glance behind me and take in the hunch of his shoulders and the fact that he seems to be making himself smaller. I think back to what Archie told me before I left Castle Knoll—Felicity Rowe broke his heart some years ago. Whether or not she also stole from the Crane family, there's painful history there. And he and I have never been on the kind of terms where he'd tell me about it. We communicate in the language of murder investigations.

It's a pattern I didn't mind until now, but only because I like any kind of communication with him. I don't want to sit next to him and suddenly break character and jump in with something like, "What happened between you and Fliss? Did you love her?"

Mum has disappeared to her basement studio. I can hear the mellow singing of Phoebe Bridgers drifting from below, so I imagine she's processing all that's happened in her own way. I try not to think about how the loss of this woman I've never met is hovering between me and Mum, and me and Crane. And then I feel like an insecure teenager because all of these thoughts are really about *me*. What is it with coming back to the house I grew up in that makes me feel like I'm seventeen again?

I resolve to break a few cycles, as soon as I figure out how. I fill the kettle and use a long match to light the ancient gas burner on Mum's cooker.

"Coffee rather than tea, right?" I ask. "I can do decaf, since it's late."

"I won't sleep much regardless, so you might as well make it a strong one," he says, and the tone of his voice is weary but grateful.

He sits down in one of the rickety kitchen chairs that face the large window above the sink, which overlooks the garden. Since there's a lower ground floor to this house, the garden stretches out in a tangle about twenty feet below, and we have a view over the fence and into the rear alley, where the white forensic tent around the crime scene is located. He's staring at it like if he blinks, evidence will be lost and evil will endure.

I go through the motions of making two cups of coffee in the cafetière, and it's only when I set one in front of him that his concentration breaks. "Oh, thanks," he says.

I'm suddenly not stuck at seventeen anymore; I feel like I'm the adult here. There are questions I can ask, gently, to help shake loose whatever is weighing on him.

"Did you come here straight from Castle Knoll?" I blow on my coffee a little, then take a long sip.

Crane nods, then meets my eyes. Now that I look closer, I can see grief under the exhaustion. I feel a pinch in my chest, because I don't want him to be hurting but also because it means there was something lingering and deep with regard to Felicity.

"I could have stopped it," he says, and his words sound thick, like he hasn't used his voice much recently. "I mean, I think I could have. Fliss phoned me several times. Yesterday, and the day before. I didn't answer," he says, looking down into his coffee. "Her messages were strange, but I didn't call her back. She hadn't phoned me in ten years. I should have realized something was wrong just from that."

"Do you feel like sharing what she said?" I ask. "I'm trying to understand her role here, in Mum's life and in her art. I rushed up here because of something Mum said on the phone that made me worry, and . . . I don't know, I started to feel like something was off and I needed to be here. And now that this has happened to Felicity, I'm a bit rattled to find my instincts were right."

Crane's eyebrows lift, concern etching its way into his slightly rugged features.

"What was the thing she said on the phone?" he asks. "The thing that got you worried enough to come up here?"

I tell him what Mum found on the step. "She sent me a picture she'd taken on her phone. I'm no animal anatomy expert, but I'm almost certain it was a heart. And now, I just . . . What's the likelihood it was left by a cat? It seems so deliberate, especially with the way . . ." I trail off and shut my eyes for a moment.

"Especially with the way Fliss was killed," he finishes. "I tried to get some details from some of the people at the scene before I came up here. They aren't supposed to talk about any of it with me if I'm not assigned to the case, but when I mentioned I might have been the last person she contacted, one of the detectives shared her preliminary observations. We'll know more, of course, when the autopsy is performed." He sips his coffee, and his eyes dart to the window again, but only for a fraction of a second before they're back on me.

"But to your question about the animal heart," he continues, "I don't think that was done by a cat, given how you've described it. This is just conjecture, of course, but I don't think cats are that specific in how they leave their little gifts."

I open my mouth to add something, then pause, struggling with how to word it. "There's something else. It's probably nothing, but—" I stop, feeling almost silly making connections where there may be none, but then barrel onward. "I don't want to be the person who has to bring Aunt Frances into everything, but something I read in one of her diaries has some eerie parallels to the way Felicity was killed."

Crane's eyebrows lift. "Someone Frances knew died in a similar way?" he asks.

"I mean . . . yeah. But it was back in 1968, and the person who did it was caught, tried, and found guilty," I say. "It was a socialite named Vera Huntington that Frances was friends with briefly, and she was found with her heart cut out."

"Who went down for it?" Crane asks.

"Her husband, a famous heart surgeon of the time. It's been too many decades for anyone involved in that case to be active again, but . . . a copycat maybe?" I'm clutching at straws, but I can't ignore the similarities between the Huntington murder and the way Felicity died. "Those messages Felicity left you, did she mention being threatened, or feeling watched?" I ask.

"No," he says, looking at his hands. "If she had, I'd have called her back or come up sooner."

"Hey," I say, and reach across the table to rest my hand on his arm. "This isn't your fault, you know. You not calling her back didn't cause this."

He inhales and gives the barest of nods. "I honestly thought . . . I mean . . ." He looks awkward for a moment and leans back in his chair, pulling his arm out from under my hand. "Felicity and I nearly got married when we were still at university. I'm glad we didn't—we were bad for each other in so many ways—but it was her who did the leaving. And me who did the waiting for her to come back. Which she never did."

I'm sitting very still, like if I move too quickly, he'll bolt like a startled stallion. He's never talked about anything so personal with me before—there's never been a need. The cynic in me is thinking he's only doing so now because it's relevant to the crime-related questions we're asking. It's not that he wants to share pieces of his life with me, just so that I can know him better.

He rubs a hand across his jaw, where his normally short beard is looking a little longer than usual. He looks at me as if he'd forgotten I was here, and his expression shutters. "Anyway, her messages were short, but she kept saying, 'I made a terrible mistake.' I didn't call her back because I thought she was talking about me—about us. It was petty of me to ignore her, and stupid to think that events from ten years ago were suddenly important to her. But now"—he sighs and leans forward again—"I think maybe she actually was reaching out for help. She just didn't use those words. That her mistake was something recent, something to do with her life here with your mum and their whole art scene, that she knew was catching up with her."

"I can try to ask Mum again, about what she and Felicity were up to, and for any details about the last few days she might not have told the police," I offer. "But she got angry with me earlier and shot my questions down. I'll have to wait a day or two for her to cool off. She gets like this sometimes."

"A day or two might not be time we have, if there's an important lead to chase," he says. I can tell he still feels guilty, and much of his need for answers might be tied up with those feelings. And, honestly, if solving a murder helps Crane chase away old ghosts, I'll step out of my comfort zone to get him there.

"There's something I can try," I say. "Someone I can talk to." I pick up my mobile and find Beth in my contacts. She answers on the third ring.

"Annie, you miss us already? I told you, London smells bad after too much time in the countryside. Like backed-up sewers and deep-fat fryers," Beth says cheerfully.

"As much as I wish I was back in Castle Knoll, I've got some business here that's going to take longer than I thought." I hold my breath for a moment, considering how much to tell Beth about Felicity and finding her body. Finally, I decide not to go into it right now, because I want to stay focused on Crane and what I'm dealing with when it comes to Mum.

"No worries. I can look after the house while you're gone, and Granddad will make sure the fridge gets raided on a regular basis so that nothing in there gets wasted," she says.

"Thanks," I say, and smile weakly. "There's one other favor I'd like from you, if you don't mind?" My eyes dart to the stairs leading to the floors below, where Mum's music is still going strong. I don't want her to overhear, because I don't want her to know the lengths I'm going to for answers when she won't give them to me.

"Sure, what do you need?"

"You know where the keys to Frances's files are, right? I keep them in that little ceramic cat statue in the library. Can you go into the filing cabinets and get the one for Sam Arlington? The first piece of paper in his file is contact information that a private detective dug out for Aunt Frances a while ago. I need Sam's mobile number, please."

CHAPTER 7

October 18, 1968

THE HOUSEKEEPER ANSWERED THE DOOR, AND I IMMEdiately started to feel ridiculous for being there, given that I'd declined all of Ford's previous invitations to meet for dinner or drinks or the theater. It wasn't that I didn't want to see him, but more that I knew deep down that if I'd arrived in London and started socializing with Ford, he'd quickly become my entire *social life, and I'd never find my own way in London like I wanted to.*

Or perhaps that was just what I was telling myself so that I avoided any more romantic tangles. Because Ford and I have a strange history. I met him almost two years ago, trespassing on his sprawling estate with my friends in Castle Knoll. One of them—Emily—was trying to seduce him to gain power and money, and ended up vanishing without a trace.

In the process of investigating her disappearance, I was quickly drawn into Ford's world of chess moves and expensive whiskies, and I found out that he was a complex man of many attractive traits alongside his many flaws. He inherited the estate at only twenty after the rest of his family died in a car crash. Then, after a troubled few years as a societal rake and cavalier partygoer, he became something of a recluse. By the time I met him, he was holed up in Gravesdown Hall trying to bring up his nephew, Saxon, while being pulled apart by his own inner demons.

It may seem like the most terrible of decisions, but in the fallout of what happened to Emily, I found myself drawn to Ford. There was a time when he and I were romantically involved, but in a rather formal way. I think he didn't want me to feel like just another of his conquests, so our relationship consisted mostly of fancy dinners and rather chaste kisses, until I broke up with him in favor of a whirlwind romance with the ramshackle but more exciting (or so I thought at the time) Archie Foyle.

My relationship with Archie burned brightly but soon ran out of fuel. It was less what Archie did that drove the separation, and more that I was coming to know myself a bit better. I felt justified in turning down Ford's recent invitations because I didn't want to fall into that pattern a second time. I thought I'd learned my lesson well.

And yet here I was.

I tried not to feel self-conscious about my white go-go boots or the fact that I smelled like the chip fryer from work. The old Frances might have let that get to her—Castle Knoll Frances. This was London Frances. The Frances who could happily jump between lectures at the university, the clatter of the diner, and the glitz of a party in Knightsbridge.

The housekeeper led me through the wide hallway, the crystal chandelier glittering overhead, to a drawing room with wood-paneled walls, a large marble fireplace, and tall windows. A fire roared, even though it had been particularly mild that week.

Ford was standing over a record player, looking at the liner notes as the music played. "Hey Jude" by the Beatles had been dominating the charts to the point where I was sick of hearing it, so I was pleasantly surprised to hear "White Room" by Cream.

I noticed that Ford still kept his dark wavy hair slightly waxed, a look that should have felt old-fashioned but instead seemed timeless. Like he didn't bother so much with trends he felt wouldn't suit him. I nearly laughed as I tried to imagine him with the goatee and long hair the hippies at the diner were currently sporting. But tonight he wasn't embodying that timeless image completely. Instead of listening to a recording of Wagner or some philharmonic performance, he had the guitar stylings of Eric Clapton reverberating around the cherrywood of the room. He glanced up at me as the lead vocalist belted out the chorus, his expression warm but cautious. He turned the volume down on the hi-fi and the song felt muffled due to the sudden drop in sound.

"Frances," he said. He had that knowing tone in his voice, as if to him, my presence was always inevitable. "How pleasant to have you finally turn up."

Those words felt almost like a warning shot, and I wasn't going to ignore that. Max from my psychology course may have issued me with a challenge that first day, and I may have handed him his hat straight back, but it was Ford who first taught me how to spar with words. Or perhaps I'd always had a knack for it, and it was simply he who helped me sharpen my sword.

"Hello, Ford," I said, giving him a careful smile. "Forgive me for assuming you'd understand my need to focus on my studies here in London. I did, after all, give you a thorough explanation by post when I declined your invitations."

The look in his eyes took on a familiar sparkle—it was the look he got when he fell into his usual habit of treating me the way he would any other woman, only to have me remind him that he shouldn't treat any woman that way.

"To what do I owe the honor, then?" he asked.

The complex knot of my motives and his expectations started to grow tighter in my mind. It was like doing mental math—I'd chastised him in the past for toying with me (and my friends) simply for his own entertainment, and now I was doing the same thing. Well, not exactly the same thing, but I was still using him. I needed some form of armor if I was going to walk into this party in Knightsbridge, and I hated to admit how curious I was about the whole scene. I wanted to go, plain and simple. And I was not above asking him to be my date, so that I might arrive on the arm of a titled aristocrat and shock Max and Elaine into silence.

"I've come with an invitation," I said. "You've every right to turn me down, and you may already be busy . . . but I was wondering if you'd accompany me to a private art auction in Knightsbridge." I smiled sweetly and realized that if he did turn me down, I wasn't sure how I'd feel. I looked at him standing there, in his casual shirt with the top button undone, his stance confident but relaxed, and those regal cheekbones and dark brown eyes looking like something someone wished into existence . . . Was I using Ford to go to Vera's party, or was I using Vera's party to decide to finally go out with Ford?

He raised an eyebrow, but he was clearly intrigued. "And why have you suddenly decided that you can be distracted from your studies by going out with me? Please tell me there's more to this than simply dressing to impress some wealthy new friends you've made on your course."

I felt my lips press into a thin line, because it had only been five minutes and he'd got the measure of me. Why did I really *want to go to this party? Aside from my sudden realization that I needed an excuse to see Ford, but on my own terms.*

Ford saw me hesitating, thinking, and chose that moment to take a few steps toward me. He stopped just short of an arm's length away, but the distance still felt intimate.

"Come now, Frances," he said, and his voice was on the playful side of chiding. "We know each other better than to pretend

that superficial motives like keeping up appearances are of any consequence. You're clever. I'm clever. And we're both easily bored. Something tells me you've settled into London life—taken in the interesting sights and sounds, made friends and had some fun—and now? You're restless. You're restless for someone who understands the way your mind works, for someone to navigate this maze with you at your more accelerated pace."

I met his eyes, and there it was—the pull that had always been there, that I'd told myself had faded when I was spending time with Archie last winter.

He continued, not breaking my gaze. "I know you're restless, because I can see it. I feel it, too—it's lonely being the person no one can keep up with but no one really notices. So I'll ask you again. Why do you want me to come to this party with you?"

I thought about what I'd said in my lecture on Understanding the Homicidal Mind. About how the willingness to kill comes from personal power. The entitlement one must feel to be able to take a life.

"On my first day at the university I made a powerful enemy," I said. "And rather than staying out of his way, I find myself needing to circulate more in his world to learn how he functions. There's a sort of comfort in feeling prepared, in not shrinking away but meeting him on his own playing field."

"Ah," he said. "A 'keeping your enemies close' approach. I can certainly relate to that."

I smiled, because it was nice to feel understood. For the past two years—since the fortune-teller Peony Lane had predicted that one day I'd be murdered—people close to me had been judging my faith in that fortune in a variety of ways. Dismissal, or pity, or expecting it was a phase that would pass. But not Ford. It was just as he said: He related to my way of thinking.

"So you'll come?" I asked.

"I don't see why not," he said. "Out of curiosity, what is this enemy's name? The one who gets you invited to private art events in Knightsbridge?"

"His name is Max," I said. "Max Torrence. But I was invited by his sister, Vera Huntington."

Ford's soft expression grew taut, and he nodded. I had a vision of Sherlock Holmes, internally calculating details and observations. Plans were being made; games were afoot.

"You know them?" I asked cautiously.

"Our fathers were friends, if that tells you anything."

"That tells me plenty," I said, and my voice was serious. Ford's late father was a terrible man, his brother and his wife equally so.

"Good. I don't want you to underestimate them," he said. "Not that you would." He gave me an approving smile. "I don't know Max or Vera," he added, "but the Torrence family's wealth is formidable, which means their sense of power and entitlement will be equally so. I'm glad you've got the good sense to go in prepared."

"Well," I said, "I know when I'm in over my head, which is why I'm here."

"Regardless of what brought you here, Frances," Ford said, taking another small step toward me, "I'm glad you came."

CHAPTER 8

I DON'T KNOW WHAT I EXPECTED OF SAM ARLINGton, but it was not that he'd want to meet at a restaurant in Mayfair that has a Michelin star. When I phone him, his voice is cheerful, and he very quickly invites me to lunch the next day at a place I'd heard of when I'd lived with Mum but could never afford to go to.

His immediate willingness to meet makes me suspicious, but then I worry I'm overthinking this. Mum has been trying to get me to reconnect with him for weeks, so if anything, he's probably jumping at this chance just to make her happy. But how do I know he's that kind of guy? I honestly don't. I can't let my guard down around him. If he wins me over, he may just con me, the way he did Mum. And at least one of us has to stay vigilant until we can suss out his intentions.

"I'll book a table for two," he says, and is halfway through praising their grilled monkfish when I cut him off.

"For three," I say. "If you don't mind."

"Oh, that's right. You've got a fella," he adds brightly.

I feel an unmistakable inward cringe. I've only acknowledged him as my dad for a minute and a half of this phone call, and already he's making awkward comments about my dating life. I also pause to wonder what Mum has told him about Detective Crane. She's clearly overinflated our relationship, but I have no idea why.

"Would love to meet your fella. Bring him along," Sam says, as if it was his idea to invite Crane rather than my insistence.

The repetition of the word *fella* is helping me form a mental picture of Sam, and it includes loud talking and a tendency toward uncomfortable political views.

I pause in front of the restaurant, my hand hovering over the brass handles of the ornate wooden doors, with Crane at my heels. I realize I wouldn't even recognize Sam today—I haven't seen any recent pictures of him, even though Mum's dating him again. To be fair, she's never been the print-out-and-frame-photos kind of person, and I've given her nothing but pushback every time she mentions him. But walking into a restaurant and scanning the room for him suddenly feels extra uncomfortable.

"Having second thoughts?" Crane asks quietly. "I can understand if you are. Meeting your dad for the first time can't be easy."

I turn to face him and feel my expression twist a little with conflicting emotions. "This is going to sound a bit strange," I say, "but it's actually as much what I'm *not* feeling as what I am. I should be nervous, or energized by some anger, or simply excited and curious. But I'm none of those things. And I'm working *hard* to be none of those things. Because any of those emotions are cracks in my armor that he could get his fingers into. And he proved a long time ago what kind of man he is."

Crane puts his hands into his pockets and keeps his gaze steady. It's a stance he uses when he's trying to seem non-threatening, and this annoys me.

"You don't have to do that thing," I say.

"What thing?" And he looks down for a beat, then up again, another of his *I'm just a relaxed guy, you can talk to me* moves.

"The thing where you school your body language to set someone at ease because you want to keep them talking. I've seen you do this when you question suspects, and I'm not a suspect."

"Remind me never to play poker with you," he says.

"I'd like to see you bluff," I reply.

"I wouldn't, if I was playing against you." He removes his hands from his pockets, but reluctantly, like it's challenging every instinct he has. He fidgets with his watch now that he doesn't know what to do with his hands. "I imagine you already have a list of all my tells in a notebook somewhere," he adds.

"I'm adding the watch fidget to the mental tally as we speak."

His hands fall abruptly, and he crosses his arms. "You don't have to do that thing either," he says.

"What thing?" I tilt my chin and look at him sideways.

"The thing where you avoid saying what you're feeling by being hyper-observant of other people's habits."

"I just told you my feelings!" I say. My voice is only mildly exasperated, because this little verbal tennis match is easing the tension between my shoulder blades. "You know—that thing just now where I was saying I'm struggling to feel anything about my dad?"

"That's not the whole story, though," he says, and his eyes

lock on mine in a way that feels new. "There's something under the surface that you're grappling with, and I can tell because you were playing with your necklace in the car on the way here, then talking far too much about random things you noticed as we drove by them. How there seemed to be more pigeons than normal out today, and that a new ice-cream van was parked at the end of your mum's road."

"The ice-cream van could have been someone watching the house!" I say. "That would be *great* cover for someone engaged in surveillance. And I don't play with my necklace."

"You might only have a mental tally of my nervous habits, but I have an actual list of yours," he says, a light smirk on his face.

I don't even try to hide my shock. "What—like . . . you've written things down? About me? I don't know if I should be flattered or alarmed. Is this in a police-surveillance sort of way, like when I was a suspect in Peony Lane's murder?" I don't enjoy reminding him of this, but the association just sort of slips out. In the autumn, the fortune-teller who originally told Aunt Frances that one day she'd be murdered ended up dead herself, feet from where I was sitting, making me look horribly suspicious at the time.

Crane flushes, and I can categorically say that this is the first time I've *ever* seen him do this. True, his face is half-covered with an unintentionally trendy beard, making the red of his cheeks a little less obvious, but it's there.

"It's more a sort of . . . quirk of mine," he says, and he looks genuinely uncomfortable. He's clearly regretting letting this juicy little fact slip out, so of course I have to pounce on it.

I grin. "Like, you keep a journal? Have you secretly been Aunt Frances all along, cataloging everyone's movements and trying to find out their secrets?"

He runs a hand through his hair, his eyes darting to his shoes again. "I don't keep files like Frances, but I do have a set of notes and observations in a style of my own. You'd find it abrupt, and probably hard to follow."

"Okay, I know you're trying to minimize your passion for journaling by making it sound boring, but this is only intriguing me more," I say, and my grin deepens.

"It's not a passion," he adds hastily. "And because I know this is the next thing on your mind, no—you can't see my journals."

Thankfully I have enough self-respect not to let my face fall into a full-on pout, but the twitch in my mouth is there nonetheless.

"But look at that," he says, smiling a little mischievously. "I shared something you didn't know about me. So in the spirit of that, maybe you'll tell me what's really underneath the 'I'm struggling to feel much of anything' response to going inside the restaurant and meeting your dad?"

I huff, but there's not a lot behind it. "Fair," I say. I pause, prodding at my feelings. "I think it's less about my dad and more about my mum. She raised me, so she's the one who matters. She wants me to meet Sam and get to know him. I've avoided doing so because I don't want to change the dynamic I've got with her.

"And yet here I am walking into a meeting that I arranged with him behind her back. Is it in the service of doing something because it's important to my mum? No. It's not. I've chased my dad down and am ready to see him because of *a murder investigation*. What kind of person does that make me?" My voice wobbles a little as I ask that, because it's not great to speak that truth aloud. "The kind of person who won't face tricky family things for someone she loves but will do it when there's a puzzle to be solved."

Crane puts a hand up. "Okay. First, Fliss's murder isn't going to be reduced to just a puzzle," he says, and he moves his hand to my shoulder as I open my mouth to defend my poor choice of words, but he rushes on. "But I know you didn't mean to do that. I think you need to give yourself a bit of grace here, Annie."

"But it's worse than that," I say shakily. "It's like I'm using a meeting with Sam to investigate *her.* Because I know there are things Mum isn't telling me. That's the kind of relationship we have."

Crane gives me a minute to steady myself, and I try to hide how furiously I have to blink to keep the sudden water in my eyes from spilling over.

"I can't really offer any wisdom," he says eventually. "But I don't judge you for any of that. I know a lot about what that feels like."

My eyebrows lift in surprise, and I regard him slightly differently. Crane's dad, Reggie, is Mum's best friend. They see each other a lot—Reggie drives a cab for a living and whenever he takes someone to London he meets up with Mum. She helped him through a difficult time a few years back, when he was in the closet and not sure what to do about wanting to leave his marriage. He did leave, eventually, and he might even be dating a new guy here in London. But I've never wondered what Crane's relationship with either of his parents is like. I instantly feel a bit bad about that.

And it's like Crane can tell, because he gently grabs my elbow and gives me a sad smile. "Let's go inside and do what we do best."

"You mean I'll make nervous conversation while being internally snarky, so that my conflicted feelings have some minor outlet while you sit there stoically?" I ask.

He laughs. "Yes, that's exactly what I mean."

WHEN CRANE AND I walk into the restaurant, we're led to an out-of-the-way table where a lanky man with blond hair sits in a cream linen suit. That alone makes him seem like he's dressed for a role he doesn't know well—it's January in London, and he looks like he should be on a boat on the French Riviera. I notice a fake tan as we get closer and tell myself I'm being observant rather than judgmental. This is a lie. Of course I'm being judgmental, but I want to believe this is out of protectiveness for my mum. And it could be? What someone is wearing and where they choose to eat might be nothing to her, but to me they are all part of figuring out who someone is. But I'm forced to admit that there's a petty pleasure in my internal judgments right now, and I'd need a good therapist to riddle out why that is.

I have thirty seconds or so to observe Sam Arlington as Crane and I cross the restaurant to where he's seated. I've only ever seen a couple of older photos of him, and they were ones Mum didn't know I'd snooped and found. She really did erase him from our lives when I was a baby. But once when I was about ten, I read *A Little Princess*, then *The Princess Diaries* and a few other books where long-lost dads came back and turned out to be a winning combination of wonderful/wealthy/famous/royal, and I started digging around trying to figure out who he was. This wasn't because I wanted a real dad; it was because I wanted to live in a fairy tale. And I found a couple of photos of Mum's early art shows, where she and Sam were beaming and drinking champagne in galleries with her work hanging in the background.

The man sitting in the restaurant today is a vague replica of the man in those photos, but only in the way that your brain tries to fill in gaps from things you see blur past a train window.

"Annie," he says. "At long last." He holds out his arms almost theatrically, and I have a moment where I'm not sure what to do. Do I leave him hanging? Or do I accept the hug he's offering, because after all he is my father, and that's a relationship that should be closer than a stiff handshake? I go with the hug, but I allow myself to feel a bit weird about it.

We sit, Sam on one side of the table and Crane and me on the other.

"Well, this is nice," Sam says, and signals for the waiter. He orders a bottle of champagne without asking us first and rattles off some recommendations from the menu in a way that makes me think he wants to show he knows it by heart. "I'm glad you're finally ready for us to get to know each other," he continues. His eyes dart to Crane for a second, almost as if he wants to point out that I've made it awkward by including him. "What changed your mind about wanting to meet me, if you don't mind my asking?"

It's exactly where I want the conversation to go, actually, so I'm glad of his question. No small talk, no "What are your career goals? What have you been up to in the last twenty-six years?" and mercifully nothing about Crane as my hypothetical "fella." And I suppose that if I've faced the harsh truth of being emotionally distant amateur-sleuth Annie, rather than "It was important to Mum so I thought I should make an effort," I may as well own it.

"What changed my mind?" I take a moment to sip the champagne that's poured for me. "It was the murder of Felicity Rowe, actually."

Sam's brow creases with a hint of confusion, but he leans forward. "It must have been terrible finding her body like that," he says. He hesitates, then adds, "And it's a horrible thing to have happened."

I take note of his immediate interest, and the fact that it only occurred to him to mention how horrible the situation is as an afterthought. Most people would have expressed their sympathies and then tried to change the subject. It's yet another element of Sam I wasn't expecting, and it has me wanting to uncover who exactly this man is. I cringe to think we may have just found our first square foot of common ground.

"Did you know Felicity?" I ask. "I assume you must have been spending quite a bit of time at the house in Chelsea, seeing as you and Mum seem to have rekindled things."

I feel Crane's posture shift and resist the urge to look at him.

Sam gives me a broad smile. He reaches for his champagne and necks half of it in one smooth move. "Couldn't get anything out of Laura, could you?"

My eyebrows shoot upward and I realize it's too late to appear nonchalant. But Sam isn't offended. If anything, he looks strangely relieved.

"I hear you've quite a knack for solving crimes," he continues. "And I for one would be happier if we abandon all pretense and talk frankly."

"I mean, this does feel a bit like pretense to me." I gesture around the restaurant.

"Oh, this? No, this is all genuine. I love the finer things in life." He sits back in his chair in a way that's so relaxed he could have been in his own sitting room. "What I mean is, I'm actually *relieved* you didn't decide to meet me because you're looking for some fuzzy father-daughter time you feel it's never too late to have. You've come to me because you think I might have information that could be useful to you, and I respect you for that. I'm pleased to see you take after me in the shrewdness department," he says.

"That's taking it a bit far," I say. *Shrewd* is not an adjective anyone feels happy to have attached to their personality. But, more than that, I don't like that he's immediately recognized the same common ground as I did. Within the first two minutes of us knowing each other, I feel he's seen right through me. In some ways I'd prefer the made-up image I had in my head after talking to him on the phone—the man who'd make dated references to movies that were never good to begin with, and refer to people's wives with phrases like *the ole ball and chain*. But then I suppose he's not that generation. He doesn't look older than Mum, meaning he's probably in his early fifties, so Gen X rather than boomer.

"Well, regardless, I'm pleasantly surprised that you insisted on bringing your detective and you're straight out the gate with questions about Felicity. Because I have questions about her too," he says. "So I say we invite the detective to finally be part of the conversation, and the three of us share what we know."

I look at Crane and feel a comforting sort of pulse when I see my own feelings reflected on his face. This is going a little too well, and Sam's just a bit too eager to join forces.

Crane clears his throat. "You probably already know

everything we do," he says. "Assuming Laura told you the details about how Felicity was found, and how it appears she was killed."

Sam's expression turns ashen. "Missing her heart, apparently," he says, his voice softer now. "Horrible way to go."

There's a moment's silence, because it truly is an awful thing to have happened. It feels only fair to let that sit for a beat.

"There's something about the crime scene that I find to be of particular significance, though," Crane says eventually. "Her body was found on top of a stack of canvases that had been wrapped in bin bags, like they were being thrown out anyway. But Annie recognized the style of these canvases as Laura's early work. And Laura had told Annie earlier that Fliss had taken the roll of bin bags because she needed them for something. The same brand that the paintings were wrapped in when her body was found."

"So, it looks likely that Felicity took the paintings, wrapped them in bin bags to disguise what they were, and put them in the skip," I add.

Sam's expression changes then, shock clear on his face. "This is something Mum failed to mention to you?" I venture.

"Yes," he says flatly. There's a sternness about him now that's something of a surprise—it's like Sam can be any character he wants, and each character is only a breath away. Carefree older man with expensive taste had turned briefly to long-lost father who just wants a hug, then became the cynical but straight-shooting guy who wants in on a murder investigation. Now there's seriousness in his anger with Mum for not telling him everything. This latest revelation of his character makes me feel like we're getting somewhere.

"You sure they were Laura's paintings?" Sam asks.

"They're in Evidence at the moment," Crane says. "They need to be analyzed forensically, along with everything else that was in that skip. So at the moment it's Annie's memory we're relying on for that fact, but—"

"I'm nearly positive," I interject. "The corner of one was sticking out, and I recognized her signature—the messy initials she always paints on the bottom right side of each piece. The sort of sideways *LFA*, for Laura Frances Adams." I can picture it in my mind easily. Mum always signs her paintings in the same way, so distinctive yet almost as an afterthought, like slapping her initials on a piece is the thing she cares least about.

"Can you tell us what you knew of Fliss?" Crane asks. "How she came to work with Laura and what their friendship was like?"

"I wish I could," Sam replies, "but I didn't have a lot of insight into their friendship. But there's something more significant that might help. Well, it's a theory of mine, but I'd like your take on it. For Laura, because I think she needs our help—whether she wants it or not." He leans back in his seat as some starters arrive, and I find I'm not even bothered about the fact that I don't remember ordering any of it. I simply take what looks like a scallop and try not to let the delicious flavor distract me as I listen to what Sam is saying.

"What theory?" I ask when I've finished chewing.

He takes a deep breath. "How much do you know about the reasons your mum and I split when you were a baby?"

I blink back my surprise, because that wasn't a direction I'd predicted this conversation taking. But I'll admit, I'm extremely curious. "She said you convinced her to invest the proceeds from her art sales in a fund—the millions she made when she first became a household name—but that it turned out to be a Ponzi scheme, and she lost everything."

Sam nods slowly. "I wondered if she'd tell you something like that." He sighs and bites his lip, thinking. Finally, it's like a decision is made. He leans forward and drops his voice, even though the tables around us are empty. "What I'm about to tell you . . . it's delicate information. I think Laura chose that Ponzi-scheme story because it's a lot simpler than what really happened."

"Wait, are you saying there was no Ponzi scheme?" I ask. I'm loath to believe this man—who swooped back into Mum's life just after I inherited the family fortune, and who sits with a fake tan at a gourmet restaurant and orders for the table without asking the other guests what they want—over the word of the woman who raised me.

"Years ago, around when you were born, we lived in Frances's house in Chelsea." Sam takes on a storytelling tone, though he keeps his voice low. "And though these were happy times, we were pretty skint, to put it lightly. I was working odd jobs, and your mum was trying to get her art into the hands of more serious brokers and shown at better galleries so that she might have a shot at a big career. She had potential; everyone around her knew it.

"Rattling around in that big, neglected house . . . When we moved in, it had the air of an abandoned fancy home. It was like Frances and her husband just locked it up one day, with all their things inside, not caring about what was left behind. When Frances told us we could live there, she didn't seem bothered about what we did with the things we might come across."

"Wait," I interject. "I thought Frances let Mum move in

with me as a baby, after you left. That she let us live in that house as a way to help Mum out, as a newly divorced single mum."

Sam looks taken aback for a moment, but then simply says, "Well, if Laura saying it like that helped her feel better about the past, I suppose it makes no matter. But I *did* live there with the two of you at the start, and that's important. Because while I was there, I found something in the house that was very valuable. A few somethings, actually."

"Like what?" Crane asks.

Sam gives him a calculating look—one that shows he hasn't forgotten that Crane is with law enforcement. Sam is surely remembering that any details he reveals about old crimes could possibly come back to haunt him, should Crane decide to make life difficult. "Let's leave those details out for now, shall we?" Sam drains his champagne glass. "The problems arose when I sold these items for a very large sum. So technically, Laura did amass quite a fortune all of a sudden, but it was because of what I did, not because of any major sale."

"I thought the money came from Mum's art," I say.

"Her art?" Sam's expression changes—he looks cautious, like he's searching for the best words to use in a delicate situation. "No," he says finally. "I can categorically say that the money didn't come from the sale of Laura's art. Even though it seemed that way."

"I can't make sense of how that would be possible," I counter. "Given the publicity Mum had in the nineties with those paintings, and how much of a household name she became. Some of them still hang in the Tate Modern," I say. "Others are part of prestigious private collections."

Sam shrugs. "Laura had two things happen for her at the

same time. Fame and money. But what's the expression? Correlation does not equal causation." He refills his glass and takes a swig of his drink, looking pleased with himself.

That's rather cryptic, and I don't know if I believe him. Crane shoots me a glance that tells me he's skeptical as well. But he doesn't interject, so we're both curious to see how Sam spins this tale.

"So what happened to the money, if you claim this Ponzi-scheme story was just something she told me because it was simpler? How did she lose that money?" I ask.

"The money was never lost," Sam says. "Laura found out what I'd stolen, and she gave the money away to make it right. I never bankrupted her. She bankrupted herself."

I bite the inside of my cheek, trying to balance my disbelief of this with what I know of Mum. Parting with millions of pounds over something like integrity is actually the sort of thing she'd do. I may be critical of her inability to be organized, and I roll my eyes at how reckless and immature she can be at times, but those are small things. Sneaking into a film without paying would square with Mum because she'd see it as stealing from the Man. But Sam stealing something from the house and selling it? I could see her persuaded to part with the money to make it right.

And I'd like to think that, in her place, I'd do the same thing.

"Do you know who she gave it to?" I ask.

Sam shakes his head. "I never found out. By that point our relationship was in the toilet, and there was no way Laura would confide in me."

"I assume that if it was something you found in the house that you sold . . ." I pause here, hoping he might decide to fill me in on what those valuable items were, but he's quiet.

"That it might have been something that belonged to Frances or her late husband, Ford Gravesdown. So logic would suggest that Mum might have given the money to Frances."

Crane sets down his glass after taking a small sip, his plate empty and his share of the starters untouched. "But hadn't Laura been Frances's heir for years? And this was well-known to the family, right? So Laura wouldn't really have been doing much to right a wrong by giving money to Frances, if the items stolen were hers in the first place."

"It would really help if you just told us what you took," I say to Sam, letting my frustration show on my face.

Sam winces like even considering this is painful. "It's a sensitive topic, and telling you about that would be the one thing in this story that might betray Laura."

"That doesn't make sense," I say, "seeing how, in this story, you've made Mum sound like she tried to do what was right. Was that not the case?"

"Let's just say that Laura giving the money away was the best option she could find, in terms of doing the right thing. That's what she told me, in any event," Sam says. "But the exact nature of the theft . . . what it was, and what was done with it . . . if any of that is brought to light, it could do a lot of damage. If I'm being cagey now, it's because I'm trying to protect your mother."

"So, what does this have to do with Felicity Rowe?" I ask.

"Well, it all goes back to Castle Knoll," Sam says. "Fliss was from there, and we all heard rumors about her less-than-upstanding character once she left. Small village and all." He gives Crane an apologetic look. "The gossip does the rounds. Even to me, coming and going like I have over the years, I knew the gist of how Fliss operated." I make a mental note to ask someone later—whether that's Crane, Sam, or my mum—about exactly what Felicity took from the Crane family.

"I know for a fact that after things went sour with Laura and me, Laura swore to keep to herself and not let anyone else anywhere near her life and her home. I think mostly this was to protect you, Annie," Sam continues. "And I know you're probably wary of my timing in popping back into Laura's life—with the inheritance and all, it looks like a convenient and lucrative time to rekindle old flames."

"The thought had crossed my mind," I say evenly. There's no sense in denying it, and I find I want him to know that he hasn't won me over. Not by a mile, no matter how effective his whole "let's share information, I want to help, we need to protect Laura" approach might be. And I must admit it's a decent approach.

"I'd judge you if it didn't," he says. "I'd worry you were just as accepting of people as your mum. But I'm pleased to see you have the good sense to question people's motives. And this is my exact take on Fliss. Because I know, without a shred of doubt, that Laura would still refuse to open up her home and her life to anyone professionally . . . unless someone came to her with information. Information they shouldn't have, that they might have acquired back in Castle Knoll."

"You're saying Fliss wormed her way into Laura's life using *blackmail*?" Crane asks, not hiding his disbelief. "I mean, a decade ago she made some bad choices, but even for her that sounds . . . extreme."

"Well, people change, and sometimes for the worse," Sam says. His expression has darkened, and I sense he's thinking many things at once as he says this.

"And you're saying that an elaborate scheme was set up by

Fliss for the purposes of . . . what? If she had information to blackmail Mum and she needed money, wouldn't she just use normal methods of extortion?" I ask. "Why move in? Why the pretense of an apprenticeship?"

We're all quiet, because it seems none of us has an answer for this.

"How about we leave that as an open question," I venture, "and ask a more immediate one. Such as, what was Mum's relationship with Felicity like recently? Mum seemed to really like her, but Mum can be hard to live with. And the one hard piece of evidence we have at the moment is the fact that Felicity seems to have intentionally put a bunch of Mum's very valuable art into the skip."

Sam leans in again, his eyes sparkling at me from across the table. "Maybe there's more to the story of Fliss and Laura than we know," he says, and one corner of his mouth lifts playfully. "Maybe things started out well but went south. And then Fliss decided to take revenge. Maybe she was out to destroy Laura's career."

The three of us are quiet as this theory hangs in the air. Because if it's true that Felicity was trying to exact some kind of revenge on Mum—to the point where she would destroy her work before her new show is launched—then the person with the strongest motive to kill her is Mum.

CHAPTER 9

October 19, 1968

FORD OFFERED TO BUY ME A DEEP BLUE VELVET COCKtail dress for the party, and I let him. Shoes and a handbag followed. As we walked up the wide marble steps of the address Vera had provided, he stopped just short of the top step and turned to me. "You look beautiful," he said.

I let my eyes narrow to show my cynicism, but my mouth twisted in a wry smile. "I'll remind you now—and I know you won't need reminding a second time—that normally I wouldn't have let you choose what I wear to anything. But I see this dress as armor, something I need to navigate the scene inside."

His smile matched mine, and I could tell he was enjoying this. "So, I'm your weapons master? Fitting you with the appropriate accoutrements for the battle ahead?"

A small snort escaped me as we ascended the final step, and I reached out and pressed the bell. "The next time we go out, remind me to take you to a place where the use of words like 'accoutrements' will get you thrown out."

"So, there will be a next time?" He murmured the question over my shoulder as a butler opened the large black door.

I didn't have time to think of a smart remark as we were ushered into a circular hall that was so big it felt like a ballroom. An opulent staircase swooped from my right, up and across the back of the space in a manner that suggested it wasn't merely there to get people from one floor to another. It was sculpted white marble, like the steps outside, but polished to a gleam and telegraphing wealth and power beyond the scale of either of Ford's fancy houses.

I felt him take my arm, and he leaned in, clearly having read my expression as I took in our surroundings.

"You see, there's money, and there's wealth*. This is the latter," he said. "My family might have a title that came with some land in the country, and a house that everyone in Castle Knoll thinks is a palace, but you've been to my London residence. It's spacious enough and well decorated, but . . ." He trailed off as someone took our coats and champagne was brought to us on a silver tray. Voices floated from the next room, the laughter contained and polite.*

I tightened my arm around Ford's. "Until now, I thought both of your houses were as opulent as they came," I said in a low voice. We followed the butler across the bright marble floor, polished like the staircase, but inlaid with smaller pieces of shiny black stone in a delicate diamond pattern. "I never thought I'd find myself in a world where we might both *be considered country bumpkins."*

Ford grinned at me and leaned in. "Now you get the measure of things. My father might have run in these circles, but he was very much on the periphery."

I thought of Elaine, so nice one minute but the next making a snide comment about whether or not I could find a date who owned a suit. I was suddenly very glad to be walking in with Lord Gravesdown on my arm in a dress I hadn't made myself. Knowing that even he was out of his depth here made me realize just how off-kilter Elaine's judgment really was. Who was she to look down her nose at me, simply because she was back with Max?

We entered a parlor of sorts, more intimate but still grand in scale. It had a high, domed ceiling painted with frescoes and lit from below, making the cherubs and clouds depicted there seem to glow.

There were about forty people mingling and drinking, but the room was large enough that it felt exclusive and not crowded in the slightest. Vera was in a floor-length gown of blood red, something silk and timeless. Her diamond chandelier earrings winked in the light from the sconces on the walls. She spotted me immediately and didn't even bother to make an excuse to the woman she'd been in conversation with. She simply rushed over to me, kissing me on each cheek multiple times, as if we were in France and I were her closest friend.

"Frances, so good of you to come!" she said, and took my arm, pulling me away from Ford so that we were both facing him. "You look lovely in a rather normal way," she said, looking me up and down.

Her expression wasn't snide, but I didn't know what to make of that comment. "Are you disappointed I didn't make a fool of myself in a homemade dress?" I asked.

"Oh no! That wasn't what I meant at all," she said quickly. She pressed her lips together, clearly trying to find a way to explain. "I suppose I thought that if anyone was going to be brave enough to be trendy, it would have been you. Everyone here"—she swept an arm out, gesturing at the couples milling around us—"it's like an exercise on how to fit in. In these circles, no one is talking about new science fiction or cool music. Everyone dresses the same. It's beyond boring."

"Just because I'm dressed for the occasion doesn't mean I can't still talk about Dune *or the Stones," I said, and gave a half shrug. "I once had a long conversation about* On the Road *with my eighty-year-old neighbor, so you can never judge who's read what."*

Vera laughed and looked relieved. "Do you know, I only read Kerouac so I could sound cool at parties in Hampstead."

I gave her a conspiratorial smile. "Well, I think beat writers are fading anyway. That was the scene ten years ago. I'll take you to the Crawdaddy Club sometime. This band called Led Zeppelin are playing there next month."

"You see?" Vera said, elbowing me gently. "I knew you had your finger on the pulse of everything interesting."

"And all it took was getting a job as a waitress," I said, grinning.

"Is that where you met this handsome devil?" Vera said, and she beamed at Ford.

"Oh, how rude of me, sorry!" I said, turning to Ford. He was watching us good-naturedly and didn't seem offended that I'd briefly forgotten him. "Vera Huntington, this is Ford Gravesdown," I said. "He and I know each other from Castle Knoll."

Ford gave Vera one of his most charming smiles and shook the hand she offered. "Gravesdown, I know that name," Vera said. "Yes, I think we've met before, years ago."

"You may be thinking of my late brother," Ford said. "He and my father used to attend parties hosted by your parents, though it's been a very long time."

Vera gave a noncommittal nod, and the conversation faltered a bit, until Elaine's voice floated from behind where Vera and I were standing. "Frances, what a lovely dress," she cooed. "Don't you just look adorable."

I turned and regarded Elaine, startled by her tone. No one wants to feel like a little girl among the grown-ups, and I wondered why she'd suddenly be trying to put me in my place. But then I noticed the tightness around her eyes and the way she gripped the stem of her champagne glass—underneath her condescension, she was uncomfortable. I wondered if she felt just as out of place as I did and if she was hiding it with feigned arrogance. But then why take a swipe at me?

Out of the corner of my eye, I spotted Max holding court in the corner, like he often did at the end of lectures. He was pretending not to watch us, but I could tell by the way he gestured and the careful lilt to his laugh that he'd seen us—and wanted us to see him.

Then Elaine's eyes drifted his way and I watched her jaw set. That small thing was enough to show me that Elaine's attitude wasn't to do with me, not really. Something was going on with Max, and I was simply an easy target for her frustration.

"Thank you, Elaine," I said. I made the introduction to Ford and saw her eyes widen just a fraction when I included his title. The conversation wasn't free-flowing or easy now that Elaine had joined us. We all stood there awkwardly, as if we weren't sure how to behave.

"Vera, darling, there you are," said a stout man with a well-kept salt-and-pepper beard. I was about to ask if this was Vera's father, but he hooked an arm about Vera's waist in a way that was decidedly unfatherly. "I'm glad to see your little friends aren't as low as the last bunch." He gave me and Elaine a cursory once-over, and we must have looked the part, because he looked directly at Ford and said, "I think Vera was playing a silly game at the last party. She brought a couple of girls she'd picked up at one of those Soho haunts I keep forbidding her to visit."

Soho had its fair share of risqué places, but something about this man's demeanor suggested that he was probably envisaging somewhere like Benny's diner.

"I understand you are the current Lord Gravesdown," the man said, and he reached between Elaine and me to extend his hand to Ford. "I'm Dr. Alasdair Huntington. I crossed paths with your father at a few parties. I was sorry to hear of his passing."

"Thank you," Ford said stiffly as he shook the man's hand. "Your name sounds familiar . . . I think I read about you in The Times *the other day. You're revolutionizing heart surgery techniques. Is that right?"*

The doctor smiled broadly. "Indeed," he said. "Any innovation is risky, of course, but a lot of lives will be saved if my newest methods are approved. Until then, there are patients constantly in need of surgery, so that keeps me busy day to day."

I was surprised that this was the man Vera had married. I didn't care how wealthy and powerful her family were; this wasn't a Jane Austen novel. There was no real reason she'd needed to marry a pompous man in his forties who supposedly ignored her most of the time. He leaned closer to Ford, and I could smell his breath—sour, with a tang of cigar smoke.

"Let's look at some art and let the gentlemen chat, shall we?" Vera hooked my arm and pulled me away before I could reply. I let her. I wanted to find out more about this glamorous woman who had married a surgeon twice her age and felt so bored at parties she begged to invite friends she barely knew. "I've a surprise to show you," she murmured.

Vera beckoned to Elaine to follow, and she joined ranks like she was eager to leave the men behind. I wondered again at her constant change in tone—a friend one minute, a rival the next. But it was those tiny hints of discomfort tinged with fear that made me reluctant to dismiss her completely. Something bigger was going on under the surface, and I felt compelled to know what it was. I threw a last look at Ford over my shoulder and noticed that Max had joined him and the doctor in conversation. Ford lifted his glass as he saw me, a show of camaraderie.

I smiled, because if there was one thing I'd never have to worry about with Ford it was whether or not his feelings would be hurt if I wandered off at a party because I was chasing some intrigue. I knew he'd always understand.

Vera led us down a wide hallway lined with classical art. It was empty of people, everyone else sticking to protocol and enjoying champagne and canapés before they were led to whichever room the auction would take place in.

"Vera, forgive me if this is a silly question," I started, "but is this your house?"

Elaine snorted, and I ignored her.

"Lord, no," Vera said, and she reached into a potted plant and pulled out a flask and a packet of Benson & Hedges. I wondered where she might hide a lighter, because she had no handbag, but she grinned at me, reached into her cleavage, and pulled out a rectangular metal lighter with a shamrock on one side. "I keep it wedged in my bra," she said. "I figure if I've got the curves, why not use them for a bit of storage, hmm?"

I laughed, because this woman was like a character in a film, played by Marilyn Monroe. Perhaps that's what she was going for, with her peroxide hair and airy demeanor. Some kind of throwback to Gentlemen Prefer Blondes.

"It's the house of some earl or other," she said airily, as if the information didn't really matter. And perhaps it didn't. "Alasdair knows him. The man funds quite a bit of Alasdair's private medical research. The things the university determined were too risky."

"Your husband . . ." I said, trying to find the polite words to ask about what seemed like a mismatch.

"Frightful bore, isn't he?" Vera said, and she laughed. She placed a cigarette between her lips and lit it, taking a moment to savor the first inhalation before continuing. "And I know you're just dying to know why I married him." Vera offered me a cigarette, and I declined. But Elaine took one, and Vera lit it for her.

"I am, if I'm honest," I admitted.

"Well," Vera said, "let's do a trade, while we walk to see this surprise I want to show you. I'll tell you why I married Alasdair, and you can tell me how on earth the trendy little waitress from Benny's managed to snag Ford Gravesdown."

"Oh," I said, "that's boring, I'm afraid. I already told you I know him from Castle Knoll. It's where his estate is, and I grew up in the village. My parents own the bakery." I don't know why I added that last piece of information. I think it just slipped out because a part of me didn't want to pretend my family and my home didn't exist.

"Better and better!" Elaine exclaimed. "The Gravesdown lord and the village baker. Historically the lords always had their pick of the village girls." She took a long drag on her cigarette and blew the smoke ineffectively over her shoulder. It hung in the air and I tried my best not to cough. "Good to know that country tradition hasn't died out, the peasants lining up for the lords to take them home."

I took a moment to swallow my outrage, reminding myself that Elaine had shown herself to be an extremely inconsistent person. But it smarted—I'd started building a friendship with her, laughing and eating chips on the floor of my flat, only for her to suddenly decide I was beneath her. A deep breath helped steady me, and I remembered that people behave in certain ways for a reason. I wanted to know what was under the surface of Elaine.

And at least I felt confident in my connection with Ford. No matter what Elaine said, she couldn't interfere with that.

Vera was walking ahead of us, leading us farther into the house, but I could see a smirk on her face. I felt a wave of indignation build and worried that I'd already let my guard down with her as well. In her crimson dress with her flask and cigarettes hidden in the potted plant of a house that wasn't even hers . . . had she invited me for the sake of drama and amusement? Flattering me for being the trendy one but secretly hoping I'd do something to embarrass myself because it would be funny? To this high-society crowd, I might as well have been Eliza Doolittle, cockney accent and all.

"Yes, well," I said, trying to feign a casualness I didn't feel, "don't forget the other country traditions. As a peasant, I'm most definitely a witch, and I lured Ford to me with my seduction spells." I smiled at Elaine as we walked.

"Is that what you did to Max, then?" Elaine said, her features suddenly electric in their intensity. My steps faltered. Max being drawn to me in any way beyond academic competition was news to me. But it made sense as a reason for the sudden shift in Elaine's behavior toward me. It was almost boring in its simplicity, and I relaxed. A case of simple jealousy.

I didn't have time to reply, because Vera paused dramatically in front of a large oak door and whispered, "We're here," and swung it inward. The three of us walked in silence into a huge windowless room at the heart of the house, clearly designed to display paintings and keep out any natural light that might damage them. Painting after painting stretched along the walls. The room was long and rectangular and reminded me of the National Gallery.

I recognized the bold colors of a Matisse in the center of one long wall, and the three of us were quiet as we walked down the impressive gallery. The room itself was quite dim, but each can-

vas was lit with its own special light above it, just like in the museums. As a result, there was a hushed atmosphere, while the spotlights on the art amplified colors and textures.

"Here," Vera said finally, stopping in front of a medium-sized canvas. "Here's the surprise."

It was a vivid nude, with bold brushstrokes and colors I couldn't quite pin down. Like Monet's water lilies, the naked woman lounging on the sofa came together better if you stood a few steps back. But it was good. Very good, in fact. The expression on her face was captivating, but she was looking at the painter with something like fear. It was the fear that made the woman so familiar.

I heard a small squeak next to me, and once I looked at Elaine and saw how her face mirrored the painting, I connected the dots.

The naked woman, stretching in that classic pose with one arm behind her head, the other casually at her side, was Elaine. The pose imitated Matisse's Blue Nude, *which I'd seen printed on a postcard somewhere. But it was done in a style all its own, as if the artist was experimenting and was getting close to finding their true form.*

I looked from the painting to Elaine and back to the painting again. Judging by Elaine's face, she'd never seen this before. Perhaps it was done from a photograph or from the artist's memory.

"Do you like it?" Vera asked, her voice carrying a note of breathy appreciation for the piece.

"Vera," Elaine said, her voice almost a whisper. "What have you done?"

"This is your work?" I asked. There was no placard near the painting, no information declaring who had painted it or what its title was.

"Of course. Isn't it exquisite?"

It was then that Elaine threw her champagne glass at the canvas. It bounced almost comically off the nude depiction of herself and shattered on the marble floor. She looked daggers at Vera and then bolted from the room.

CHAPTER 10

"I STILL CAN'T GET MY HEAD AROUND THE FACT THAT Mum apparently bankrupted herself in the name of doing the right thing," I say. Crane and I are walking through Mayfair, and the leather boots I'd put on to go to the restaurant have numbed my toes to the point at which I'm wondering if they ever existed in the first place. I spy a cozy-looking pub and grab his arm. "Come on," I say. "I feel like a pint, to rinse the taste of champagne out of my mouth."

Though the lunch had been delicious, my dad had conveniently had to take a "call" just when the bill arrived. When it was clear that he'd stepped out of the restaurant intending not to return, I shrugged and paid the three-hundred-pound tab. I'd like to say I was surprised, but I'd seen that one coming. And, besides, I'd recently inherited the Gravesdown fortune, so we all knew I could afford it.

Sometimes the heiress aspect of my life still feels like a practical joke. As if at any moment a lawyer will knock on my door and tell me my inheritance was just part of a hidden-camera experiment to see what someone might do with sudden wealth when it comes with a side of murder investigations.

I study Crane as he settles into the booth across from me, two pints of cloudy ale between us. In London, he seems like a piece of Castle Knoll. He has a sort of earthy presence that's hard to explain—or maybe I just think this because of his penchant for wearing natural fibers and forest greens, along with his deep brown eyes and dark beard. But something about him being here is grounding me as I wade through the chaos of unpacking my London upbringing.

"You said something in passing yesterday that I think we need to revisit with regard to what happened to Fliss," Crane says. "I'm not being permitted any inside information. Last night, before I found a hotel room, I contacted the detective in charge of the case to learn what I could"—he sighs and carefully sips his pint—"and was told in no uncertain terms to stay out of it."

"You realize you're playing my song, right?" I say.

Crane attempts to sigh a second time, but he can't keep the laugh from creeping in, so it comes out as a breathy sort of reluctant amusement. "I know you have significant past experience with investigating murders when you've been expressly told to stay out of them," he says.

"Hey, if you recall correctly, the first murder I solved was Aunt Frances's and I was actually invited right on into that one," I counter.

"Fair enough," he says. "But suffice to say, I'm new to the 'let's poke around and solve something without the police knowing what we're up to' thing. Being, you know, a member of the police."

"I try to forget that as often as I can," I say lightly. "Otherwise, I'd feel worse than I do every time I get you to bend the rules for me."

He pinches the bridge of his nose like this has been a long day pounding the pavement and interrogating suspects, rather than conversation over champagne in a Michelin-starred restaurant. "Anyway, the thing that's been bothering me is something you said earlier. About Frances's diary, and your reasons for coming up to London."

"The heart connection," I say slowly. "Peony Lane's fortune for me, along with the heart on Mum's front step and her new obsession with painting the human heart . . . and then Fliss, well."

"Your fortune?" he asks. "You never mentioned that."

I dutifully recite the words to him. I'm beyond feeling silly about Peony Lane's fortunes around Crane. They've featured in every murder we've solved so far, and I trust that he won't raise any eyebrows if my focus on this one seems at all superstitious.

"Huh," he says when I finish. "That's suitably dark and cryptic, everything I'd expect a Peony Lane fortune to be. But what I was talking about was the other thing you said. In Frances's diary, you mentioned there was an old case where a girl was murdered and found missing her heart."

"Oh, yeah, that sounded tragic," I say. "I've got that diary back at the house and I've read it from cover to cover. It's fascinating. But, like I said, that case was open-and-shut. Vera Huntington, wealthy socialite, killed at twenty-one by her husband. It made all kinds of headlines back in 1968 when they arrested him."

"One thing I can do," Crane says, "is get hold of the records of that old case. Did Frances's diary say what happened to the husband?"

I shake my head and sit back in my seat. Laughter booms from the booth next to us, where a couple of businessmen are already three pints in. The clatter of silverware and the yellow light filtering through the vintage glass in the pub windows makes me feel rather cozy, and it reminds me of the front room in Chelsea—the one with the scratched-up wood-paneled walls and chipped marble fireplace. I have great affection for the chip in that fireplace. It happened when I opened up a bowling ball Mum gave me one Christmas and immediately dropped it on the hearth. The ball was fine, but that small section of fireplace will always remind me of the Christmas I was eight.

"In the diary, Frances says Vera's husband was about twenty years older than she was, so if he's still in prison he'd be about ninety-five," I say. "You think somehow there's a nonagenarian serial killer out there reliving past crimes?"

"That's highly unlikely," Crane says, "but like you said the day you found Fliss, copycats are certainly worth considering."

"But why would someone suddenly copy a murder from 1968?" I ask. "I mean, there are some very weird similarities between the two cases, but is a copycat really likely?"

Crane lifts an eyebrow. "Perhaps. What kind of similarities? Is this more intel from Frances's diary?"

"Yes," I say. "And I'll give it to you to read—I think it's in the stack of diaries I brought with me. Given how gripping the first two have been, I've been reading up on her life." I pause, feeling like I need to explain, because I don't want to seem as though I have some kind of Aunt Frances obsession. "It makes me feel more plugged into this whole inheritance situation," I continue. "Like maybe if I know her better, I'll deserve it more."

Crane nods. "I understand," he says. "But I don't think you should worry about what you deserve when it comes to the choices Frances made in her will."

I shrug and push the conversation back in the direction of the investigation. "Anyway, with the diary that starts in October 1968, there's so much about her psychology course at UCL. It's an interesting insight into her mind—it turns out she was academically very bright, on top of the cleverness she showed when looking into town secrets. But there's a bit about her life in London interspersed in there, and this Vera character featured heavily for a while. There aren't many similarities between Felicity and Vera. But they were both artists, and both visited the Chelsea house, but decades apart. The most eerie similarity is the way they both died."

We're quiet for a moment, thinking. Finally, Crane says, "We should verify what your dad said about Laura. Large amounts of money can be tracked, even charitable donations. Do you know which charity might be likely for her to give to, if she gave it to a charity at all? Or should we just try asking and leveling with her that Sam told us the reason for their split?"

"We can try," I say. "If it was charity, she'd probably give to some art students' fund or donate to an organization that helped bring art lessons to underprivileged kids or something. That is, if what Sam said was even true." I tap my nails on the lacquered wood of the table, thinking. "The thing with Mum is she's never been all that socially minded. I mean, she cares about the planet and human rights as much as the rest of us, but she's always had a habit of cutting corners for her own amusement. She's like Holly Golightly in that way."

"Who's Holly Golightly?" Crane asks.

"You've never seen *Breakfast at Tiffany's*? Well, in the movie, Holly meets this young writer, and they run around New York entertaining themselves by being slightly ridiculous. They dare each other to shoplift, and run around with silly masks on, that sort of thing."

Crane nods. He doesn't know Mum well, but she makes that exact kind of impression. "Rather harmless rule breaking," he says, "but that doesn't seem consistent with someone worried about balancing the justice scales. That would be someone more like—"

"Frances," I say. "Exactly. So, if Mum did give away all the money she got from the sale of her paintings so that she could pay for whatever it was my dad stole, I would suspect that at the very least it wasn't her idea. But even more likely, she was pressured into it."

"Frances *would* be the type to disinherit her, if something like that occurred, right?" Crane asks. "And she did pass over Laura for the inheritance, but not until relatively recently. And this whole donation thing happened . . . when? Back in the nineties?"

"Yeah," I say. I pause. "Hey, what if we're getting too caught up in the Frances of it all?"

"What do you mean?" He looks at me, bemused.

"I mean, Frances is a difficult presence to extract from the Chelsea house, but what if this had nothing to do with her? What if whatever Sam found in the house didn't belong to Frances, or was something she didn't know about?"

"You mean something that belonged to the Gravesdown family that Ford left there?" he asks.

"It's the most logical thing," I say. "Sam telling us that he just 'found' something valuable enough to make millions when sold—that can't have been just anything. It would have to have been something like a priceless antique or jewelry. And I suppose the timing of the sale just happened to make it look like Mum was really successful. She did get a lot of press for her art, but I suppose that didn't necessarily mean money."

Crane nods and takes a sip of his pint. "Sam wasn't wrong about Laura's fame and money potentially being two separate things. But the good thing is, that's something we can check. I'll make some calls and see how we might track the history of who bought each painting of hers, and for how much and when. It's something to go on, at least."

"Okay. In the meantime, I'll try to soften Mum up and see if she can tell me more about what exactly Sam got up to, and where all her money really went. Something isn't adding up here, and I think a bit of digging might tell us exactly what that is."

CHAPTER 11

"WERE YOU LOVERS, THEN?" I ASKED VERA. WE WERE still standing in the dimly lit room where the nude painting of Elaine hung proudly.

"No, nothing like that," Vera said, waving a hand to bat away the question.

"Then why paint her like this?" I asked. "Why put it up for auction and invite her to watch it be sold to the highest bidder?"

Vera looked me square in the eye, with a fierceness I suspected she'd brought me there specifically to see. I was being warned. But about what, I couldn't say.

"Why?" she repeated. The clack of a man's shoes sounded at the doorway, and we turned just as Max strode in. He was on his own, no sign of Elaine.

"Stick close to Ford Gravesdown, if you know what's good for you," Vera whispered to me. I opened my mouth to ask why, but she turned away and smiled as her brother approached.

"Well, you had to go and spoil the reveal like that," he said, clearly annoyed with Vera. "Giving her a chance to see it before everyone else. But it's no matter. When this painting is hanging

in the lobby of the Savoy or the office of some banker, I'll be sure to take Elaine to visit it." He held out his hand to Vera, and she put the flask into it without looking at him. "Frances," he said, acknowledging me for the first time that evening. "Isn't my sister talented? I simply can't wait to see which collector snaps up this gem."

Unease trickled down my spine as I started to piece together what was happening. Elaine had broken up with Max. She'd told me so on the first day I met her. And she'd warned me that he was particularly fond of revenge. Even if they'd got back together, it looked like Max was the type of person not to let something go. It was either his punishment for Elaine daring to leave him previously, or his way of keeping her in line now that they were back together. Or both.

"What kind of threat did you use to get Elaine to come back to you?" I asked. "Because it was clear that tonight was the first time she'd seen this painting."

"Oh, I simply reminded her that I could destroy her academic career if I circulated the photo of her in this pose." He waved toward the painting. "I must say it was so much better to make a grand gesture. Vera produced such an accurate likeness from that photo, didn't you, dear?"

Vera looked as if she was made of stone, and I realized she was yet another person whose strings Max was pulling. But she had taken what little power she could in bringing Elaine to see the painting ahead of the auction, so that Elaine could at least avoid being blindsided in front of a room full of London society.

"If you'll excuse me," I said darkly. "I think I've neglected Ford a bit too long." I made my way quickly past the rows of paintings and into the long hallway.

Elaine was leaning against the wall, wiping away tears and breathing heavily. I was surprised to see Ford standing over her, one arm on the wall near her head, speaking quickly and in a low voice. It gave me the tiniest of starts, because to the normal passerby, it would look as if he was attempting to make an unwelcome conquest of her. But I could see how she was nodding and setting her features. Something else was going on.

"There you are," he said as I approached. "I found your friend extremely upset, and she's told me what Max and Vera have done. I've suggested a quick plan to rally her, but I think a boost in confidence might help, too, if you could?"

"Of course," I said, unsure what Ford meant but taking Elaine's arm nonetheless. She might have shown herself to be inconsistent as a friend, but coming together against Max seemed the right thing to do after what I'd just seen. Working out how Vera was entangled in it all could wait until we'd put Max in his place for tonight. "What sort of plan have you formed?"

"Elaine's going to beam proudly at the painting and speak gushingly about how important her work as an artist's model has been to the emerging talent of the artists represented here. It's not uncommon for artists' models to attend the galas celebrating the work that includes them. They're respected and seen as fascinating creatures—muses, if you will. Elaine is simply going to steal the narrative from Max and make the whole thing seem intentional."

I smiled at Ford. Elaine might be able to pull that off, if she could cover up her true feelings. But she was anxious, embarrassed, and afraid—that much was clear.

"That sounds like a perfect plan," I said. Ford handed me my bag, and I opened it to get out a tissue. I dabbed a smudge of mascara from the corner of Elaine's eye, where it had run just a little. There was something in her expression. Behind the emotions she was feeling at what Max had done, she looked conflicted, regretful even. I decided this was in response to my being so willing to help, even after she'd been unkind. "You know," I said

quietly, "that first day in class, Max used my notes to make all his comments. And I found that the best way to unsettle him was to be utterly unrattled by it. It takes the power away, you see."

Elaine sniffed and nodded again. "I do. But he'll know, Frances." She looked at me, her brown eyes wide and watery. "He'll know that's not how I really feel, deep down. So the power will still be with him. He'll just see me playacting in a desperate attempt to save face. He'll know that I'm horrified to see my naked body up there. He knows how insecure I am, that's one of his talents—he takes the things you hate about yourself, and he presses on them. I'm not pretty, I'm not slim. He tells me this all the time. And tonight, doing this to me, he'll still know he's won, in the end."

But Elaine did just as Ford suggested, and she pulled it off quite well. I tried to help wherever I could, keeping the conversation light and sparkling, focused on the other works of art. Vera was on the edge of things, watching us as if she were a misbehaving child who had been banished to the kitchens, sneaking out to watch the adults at their party.

The auction was a silent one, and I could tell Elaine felt nauseated knowing that her likeness had been purchased for thousands of pounds. I wondered who the money would go to, from the sale. Vera, presumably, which made everything seem slightly worse. Max had used Vera to get revenge on Elaine, and she'd be paid handsomely on top of it. Not that she needed the money, of course. I hoped whoever bought the painting had done so because they'd recognized the talent displayed there and because they simply liked it.

As the butler was handing me my coat, a representative of the art broker who had set up the auction approached Ford with some papers. "If you'd sign here, sir," the young man said, "we'll have your painting delivered to you tomorrow afternoon."

"Thank you," he replied. As I gave him a long look, he added,

"What? I dislike Max more than I've disliked anyone in a long time. I had it on good authority that, until I stepped in, the highest bidder for that painting was an executive at the Bank of England. He planned to hang it in his office. And he's a man who, it turns out, supervises a number of accountants in the bank, and among them is Elaine's father."

My jaws clenched at how intricately Max must have set up his plan for that chain of events to nearly occur. He'd have known where Elaine's father worked, sought out his boss and befriended him, and possibly worked for weeks to entice the man to buy that painting. I could just imagine Max going to that office, casually commenting on the bare walls, how they needed fresh art—something classical, like a nude, but done in a softer style so it didn't look lurid. His voice echoed in my imagination, singing the praises of a new artist on the scene and how the bank manager might have a wonderful opportunity to invest in the sole work of a rising star.

The purchase would never have been guaranteed, of course. But the threat of it would have been real enough to Elaine, and from what Ford had just told me, it had nearly come to pass. Elaine would have had to live with the nightmare of her father going in to work, day after day, having to sit right across from a painting that brought her deep shame and self-loathing.

I gave Ford a long look, feeling my cheeks warm with something like pride. Ford was more than a good date to me that night; he was a partner, someone who not only saw the game being played but stepped in and played it with me. "Thank you," I said, "for doing that, and for coming with me."

Ford squeezed my hand as we walked to where his driver was waiting for us. "I'm happy to do it. Because you were absolutely right. You've made a very powerful enemy."

CHAPTER 12

I HEAD BACK TO CHELSEA ALONE, LEAVING CRANE TO follow up on checking whether Sam's story has any truth to it. Just before we part ways, he turns to me. "I'm going to pull that old case file," he says, "just to see what the details were. Looking at it might point us to a copycat, if that's who killed Fliss."

Felicity. She's yet another question mark in the bad punctuation of all this. Who she really was and what she wanted with Mum are things I need to find out if I want to keep Mum safe. There's always the possibility that whoever killed Felicity was only after her, and now that they've eliminated her, there aren't any more targets. But something about the circumstances of her appearance in Mum's life makes the situation feel rather multilayered.

Beware the heart kept in darkness. It will be death's catalyst if brought into the light without its proper name.

The words from my fortune whisper through my mind, but they're barely there—like a soft breath against my thoughts. I'm not a full convert to Peony Lane's fortune-telling abilities, but I won't deny that her words have a kind of gravity about them. The clues of Peony's previous fortunes have always felt like puzzles that are solvable, but this one feels . . . different somehow. Maybe that's just because it's mine.

I unlock the front door and listen for any sounds in the house. As I take off my coat and hang it on the wobbly stand, I call out, "Mum? You home?"

All I can hear are the heavy hands of the grandfather clock at the end of the hall, so I expect she's out. When she's down in her studio there's always loud music playing, but rather than just assume she's not here I decide to check. My mind keeps serving up the image of Felicity's body in the skip, like a jump scare in a horror film. I'm glad Crane is here in London instead of back in Castle Knoll, but I do wish he'd asked to stay at the house with us. We have plenty of room, and it would have been good to have him just down the hall.

I cross the empty kitchen, now remarkably clean and rubbish-free, and open the basement door, which leads down to Mum's studio. The light in the stairway is off, so I know she's not here, but that basement . . . I have to check it, just to see. I think of Mum's art—the small canvas I took from the safe in Aunt Frances's file room splashed with red, resembling a heart. Was this a very early experiment with what is now evolving into her newest series? I've got that little canvas upstairs in my bedroom, along with Frances's diaries and several notebooks containing outlines of the latest murder mysteries I'm trying to plot out. I wonder if she'd like it, maybe want to include it in her upcoming show.

But perhaps that little canvas is the "heart kept in darkness" from my fortune, and putting it into Mum's show would be fulfilling Peony's death-related prophecy.

I pull the chain that makes the bare bulb in the stairway flicker to life, and when I reach the bottom of the stairs I find the switch that turns on the overhead lights in the basement. A huge expanse of whitewashed walls greets me, with canvases of various sizes leaning up against them. A rectangular window at the top of each wall lets in a slant of light. The windows are situated at ground level so that every so often the shoes of someone on the pavement outside shuffle past. Drop cloths full of the color and texture of spilled creativity line the basement floor and are bunched up in corners, like deflated dirty ghosts. Brushes and palettes are scattered around the space, many of them not washed properly so the paint has hardened on them and presumably made them impossible to use. It gives the impression of a child's toys that haven't been tidied away.

I walk from canvas to canvas and kick myself for not asking to see Mum's new series sooner. I suppose a lot has been happening in the two days I've been here, but Mum's rocky career has been something of a theme in both our lives, and it's important for me to be plugged into what she's trying to accomplish.

Her style has always been abstract and typically features urban decay being reclaimed by nature. Frantic brushstrokes evoke the angled architecture of brutalist buildings, with hazy smears of tree roots or bamboo shoots rending them apart.

That series took off in the early nineties, when she was straight out of art school. I realize I'm curious to hear what Crane finds out about how much it sold for and what she was paid for the pieces. Not only because of Sam's claim that the money didn't come from Laura's art, but also because I want to know more about her rise to fame. It was always just a story told one way. Mum became an overnight sensation, then lost all her money. Her next series flopped and she spent two decades trying to relaunch herself. She's been doing better recently—her work is getting good reviews and people are buying more of it.

But the canvases I see around me are both a departure in style and a return to form. Gone are the urban/nature juxtapositions, replaced with renderings of the human heart. There's a moment where being surrounded by hearts feels jarring, almost like the universe is screaming at me that I'm missing something, with all these heart references popping up in my life. But I'm quickly drawn into the art itself. The brushstrokes and color choices are very Laura Adams, and the blue and purple veins branching across deep red curving shapes seem to echo back to her first paintings—they're like tree roots made flesh. The whole series is visceral but full of life at the same time. These paintings aren't what I'd imagined they would be—I'd worried she was going for something violent and disembodied, just for shock and a desperate attempt to say, "Look at me! I'm still here."

But this is . . . fantastic. She's evolved, and she's built on her previous work but is accomplishing new things at the same time. I turn to the far wall, but it's bare—those works must have been packed and moved to the gallery already, or perhaps they were the ones Felicity gathered into bin bags and put into the skip outside. The ones still here are possibly not quite finished.

I decide to head back upstairs and use the empty house as an opportunity to go through Felicity's room. I still have every intention of asking both Mum and Crane more about her, but I want to see what I can learn for myself since neither of them has been especially forthcoming.

I already know which bedroom she was using—there are only two that are suitable for guests. In the others, the beds are so old that springs have popped out of the mattresses or the curtains are moth-eaten. Months ago, I tried to persuade Mum to have some contractors in to renovate—I'd happily pay for it with the inheritance money from Aunt Frances. But Mum was adamant that people in her space doing renovations would be too disruptive to her work.

Of the two usable spare rooms, one is mine, and thankfully Mum had known not to cross the line of giving that to Felicity. The other is the next floor up, directly above mine. I make my way there and turn the handle carefully, feeling like I need to have some modicum of quiet out of respect for the dead.

A simple IKEA double bed is against the far wall, the same one I'd helped Mum assemble about ten years ago when I went through a phase of wanting to be an interior designer when I got older. I'd been about sixteen then, and nothing in this room has changed since she gave me a budget of a hundred pounds to decorate it. The fuzzy neon rug is still the same, as are the small soft furnishings that include a tired beanbag chair—also from IKEA.

Several cardboard boxes I've never seen before slump in one corner. They look ancient, and I know they can't be Felicity's, because the writing on the side says things like *Cycling magazines, Sam 1980–1990* and *Frances chess set collection*. I wonder what they're doing here but decide to focus more on finding out who Felicity was rather than going through my family's old junk.

I flick on the lamp in the corner and notice she must have been living here for some time, as there aren't any suitcases around. She's tidied all her clothes and other things away. I start opening drawers carefully and find the standard sets of things—socks, shirts, jeans. For someone who was supposedly an artist, I don't see any evidence of her work. But then again, not every artist needs to be as untidy as Mum.

I open the large freestanding wardrobe and admire her collection of coats. There's a vintage alligator handbag hanging from a hook just inside, crimson red and in great condition, and I lift it off the hook to examine. Something about it tugs at my memory. It feels like I've seen it before. Was it one of the many things I'd dug out of cupboards in my childhood, something Aunt Frances never cleared out that I used to play dress-up?

The clasp is a simple snap and it pops open easily, but the inside isn't what I expect. I'd thought Felicity might have kept the standard things in here—phone, keys maybe. Or if it was a backup bag, maybe just ChapStick and some mints or something. But it holds sheets and sheets of yellowing paper, all folded in half and tucked neatly away.

I pull them out carefully, expecting a secret novel, or more of Aunt Frances's records that perhaps Felicity had found stashed in the bag. But each sheet is complicated and form-like. It takes me several minutes to make sense of what I'm looking at, but these appear to be medical records. As I flip through, I find that they're for more than one person and are alphabetical. As if someone had opened a file and lifted a section of it straight out. Adam Blaine, Susan Folkestone, Xi Huang Li, Xavier Sandoval, Forrest Tims . . . All in all, there must be medical forms for about twenty people. They date from the mid-1950s to 1968.

I stare into the wardrobe, trying to remember where I've seen this bag before. My mind is turning over memories like loose stones, when I suddenly see a pair of eyes staring back at me from within the wardrobe.

I spring away, holding a scream in the back of my throat, heart pounding. My breath flows out in a shaky stream as I realize the eyes are painted. I step forward gingerly and pull the coats to one side, revealing the huge canvas in the wardrobe. It completely covers the back of it, and I wonder what the hell it's doing here while I try to slow the drumming of my heart. I used this wardrobe as an overflow for my own clothes throughout my childhood, and I've never seen these things here before. I'd have noticed both of them—the bag, because it's cool and I'd have used it. But the painting—it's haunting and rather provocative, and I wouldn't have forgotten seeing something like this. Mum and I would have pulled it out of the wardrobe right away and hung it in the house. Even in the dim light of the wardrobe it's an utterly compelling piece. And there's something familiar about it, even though I know I've never set eyes on it before.

But it's the papers in my other hand that have me shaking. While I don't recognize the names of the patients, I do recognize the name of the surgeon on each form. It's the man from Frances's diary, the one who went to prison for the murder of his wife—Dr. Alasdair Huntington.

CHAPTER 13

MY PHONE BUZZES, AND WHEN I SEE THAT IT'S CRANE, I pick it up immediately.

"Annie, I found some information that's important," he says. "About the sale of your mum's first set of paintings."

"That was quick," I say.

"Well, it wasn't difficult information to track down. Which makes me wonder about Sam Arlington, but I'll get to that in a minute. The important thing is that her work was discovered by a broker who put it directly into a top gallery. It was shown to all the right people straightaway, people looking for something fresh and willing to outbid one another so no one else could swoop in. This was when Damien Hirst was at his peak, putting animals in formaldehyde and displaying them in glass boxes—the modern-art scene was a place where a lot of money was thrown around."

"So, what are you saying, exactly?" I ask.

"I'm saying Laura's first series of paintings sold huge right away. The broker took a commission, but Laura got the rest from the sales," Crane says.

"So Sam lied," I say slowly. "But why? Especially if he knew we'd just check and find out the truth."

"Maybe he thought we wouldn't verify his story," Crane says. "Men who are used to lying often feel invincible, so much so that it doesn't even occur to them to cover their tracks very well."

"That still feels strange, though," I say. "I mean, why tell us that story at all, then? About how he sold something he found in the house, and that Mum never made that kind of money from her art?"

"It could be ego, pure and simple," Crane says. "Sam might want to spread the rumor that Laura's art wasn't worth much until later, making her success seem more like a fluke."

"It's plausible," I say. "And, actually, this fits with an emerging theory of mine." I pause, wondering how to phrase this. "I know you want justice for Fliss," I start carefully. "No matter how things ended with you two, I know you would have wanted to help her. But I just went through her room, and I don't think she was here just for the sake of learning from Mum."

"What makes you say that?" he asks. "I mean, I'm not trying to disagree, this is more just pure curiosity. Because, Annie, I wanted to make this clear earlier . . ." He stops, and the pause feels less like a thinking pause and more like a feeling one. Like he wants to express something about his tangled past with Felicity but not give the wrong impression. "Fliss and I . . . not only was it a long time ago, but there was a lot about that relationship that wasn't ideal for either of us. And even though I was devastated when she left, I . . ." He lets out a stream of air in frustration, and it's clear this isn't a speech he particularly wanted to make to me.

"Hey," I say gently, "I don't want to push for stories you don't want to tell."

"It's not that, not really," he says. "If you feel like Fliss had ulterior motives, you're probably right. Back then, I was in the habit of making excuses for people. But my time with her taught me an important lesson about trusting my gut." He pauses again, as if he might add more, but then he clears his throat and changes the subject. "So, what's this theory of yours? And how do Sam's lies about your mum's art career fit into it?"

I take a beat to let my thoughts reassemble, because Crane talking about Felicity has blown the logic from my mind like seeds off a dandelion head. "Well, there's no solid theory as yet, just several important things that feel connected." I describe the painting I found in the wardrobe, and the red handbag with the medical records. As I'm describing the painting, it hits me that I know what's familiar about it. There are pages in Frances's diary that describe something so similar that it must be the same image. The expression in the woman's eyes, the nude pose on the sofa . . .

"I think I can identify the painting at least," I say. "Ford Gravesdown purchased it in 1968, after attending an art auction at the house in Knightsbridge I told you I was going to go check out."

I fill him in with what details I can remember from the chapters in Frances's diary about the night she went to the auction with Ford. "This painting is the result of Frances's friend Vera helping her brother, Max, try to embarrass Max's girlfriend, to punish her for breaking up with him," I add.

"So, Fliss had these things in her room? Why?" Crane asks.

"I don't know," I say, and pull a hand through my hair. "It's yet another thing I need to ask Mum about. There are some boxes in her room as well. They look like they came out of the attic, possibly."

"What do you mean 'possibly'? Haven't you been up there?"

"No," I say haltingly. "I mean, this house had enough weird nooks and crannies to investigate in my childhood, and there was cool stuff to find in far easier and sunnier places. I didn't need to go up into the attic for that. I still wouldn't. The floorboards are likely rotted through, and the spiders have been roaming unchecked for so long they probably have their own political system."

Crane laughs but stays focused. "So either Fliss was helping Laura with some organizing or she was poking around on her own for reasons unknown. Regardless, I think we can be confident that Fliss was interested in, or at least aware of, Vera Huntington. That makes it feel a lot less likely that they were murdered in the same way coincidentally," Crane says. "But the diary was with you, right? In Castle Knoll? So, she wouldn't have learned about Vera from that."

"I had the diary, yeah. And Mum never read the later volumes Frances wrote. She's only read the first one, and that was because I lent it to her."

"Maybe she didn't know about the painting's history, then," Crane says. "Fliss was an artist and, according to you, that painting is compelling."

"It is—so why hide it in the back of a wardrobe, with a handbag full of medical records signed by Vera's husband?" I ask. "The other attic boxes were out in the open, but the things relating to Vera were hidden away." I bite my lip. "It can't be a coincidence," I say finally. "Felicity dies in the same way as Vera, more than fifty years later, and in her room are some key pieces to Vera's life."

"Hmm, I think you're right. Even if Fliss just found these things and thought they were interesting, the connection is too close to overlook," Crane says. "Can you put that handbag somewhere safe, along with Frances's diaries? We should meet tomorrow to go through them really thoroughly and see if there's anything we're missing."

"Of course," I say. "Let's have breakfast at the Green Market café on King's Road." He agrees, and as we hang up, I'm already walking down the stairs with the medical documents under one arm. Before I left Felicity's room, I snapped several photos of the painting in the wardrobe and put the empty bag back on its hook.

I go into my room and stand on the tattered chaise longue that sits against one far wall and pull out the vent near the ceiling. The central heating was upgraded years ago, so these vents don't do anything but act as a tunnel for mice. I've been using this spot to hide things for years, and while I think Mum probably knows about it, it doesn't feel right just leaving the diaries and medical documents out in the open.

Then I call a taxi and give them the address I found scribbled in the margins of Frances's diary—a large house in Knightsbridge that held art auctions and lavish parties in the sixties. I don't care if it's now a Whole Foods or a drug den; I'm going to trace the steps of this painting backward through time, and this is the place to start.

CHAPTER 14

October 23, 1968

I DIDN'T HAVE THE CHANCE TO TALK TO ELAINE AT THE university the following week. She stayed at home, presumably saying she was ill. That left me taking notes and trying to focus on Professor Dane's lecture, with Max hovering over my shoulder yet again.

He didn't say anything; he didn't have to. His presence alone was unsettling, and I was considering complaining to Professor Dane once the lecture was over. But what would I actually say? Max sits next to me and looks over my shoulder, and he used my notes once to make comments? The painting of Elaine wasn't university related; it wasn't grounds for complaint. Really, all Max had done was behave in an arrogant fashion with a dash of plagiarism.

So, after the lecture finished, I gathered my books and my notes and hurried out of the lecture theater, planning to head straight to Benny's to do a bit of studying if I couldn't catch an extra shift.

The sleek black car was waiting for Max, as it always did. When the back window rolled down and Vera poked her head out, I readied myself to hurry even more—Max had to be right behind me.

But it wasn't Max that Vera shouted for. "Frances!" she yelled, catching my eye. Then, once I was closer, she added more quietly, "Quick, get in before Max sees!" The back door swung open, and Vera slid over on the cream leather seats to make room for me. I hopped inside without thinking and closed the door. The rear window was still down, and I glanced outside to see Max just making it to the curb, a look of surprised fury on his face.

"Is that something he'll make you pay for later?" I asked. "Letting me steal his lift?"

"It will be good for him to get the tube. Or learn to call a taxi," Vera said, lighting a cigarette. She rolled down the other window, which I thought was rather considerate, as she'd worked out by then that I didn't smoke.

"Why do you collect him after class every day?" I asked. "You're married, you have your own life. You're not his mother." That sounded more confrontational than I'd meant it to, but I'd seen how Max pushed Vera around, so I dropped any pretense at politeness. It wasn't that I hated Vera or anything—I suspected she was being manipulated or even threatened by Max, so I could forgive her for choices that weren't fully her own. But I also didn't want to make excuses for her if I was wrong.

Vera sighed. "Every Wednesday, just after Max finishes, we have lunch with our father. It's boring, really, and that's why I felt like breaking with tradition today. Especially as you proved to be such a dark horse at the art auction," she said, and looped an arm through mine while keeping the other near the window with the cigarette. "I thought to myself, now there's a girl worth knowing. And besides, Alasdair had his eye on you, I could tell."

"Your husband?" I didn't try to keep the incredulity out of my voice.

Vera tutted as if I'd said something idiotic. "Not like that, don't worry. He can barely keep up with me, let alone have the stamina for a mistress. No, I mean he's watching you because he thinks you're a social climber. Alasdair detests people who defy what he calls 'the natural pecking order,' and I think he spent most of the party trying to talk Ford Gravesdown out of any association with you. Which I'm afraid is my fault. I wanted to annoy my husband, so I told him how much I was enjoying my new friendship with the baker girl from the countryside who now works at an imitation American diner in Soho."

"Why did you marry him? I mean, you're from this prominent family, presumably you have all kinds of choice in who you marry. And you're young—you must be, what, twenty-five?"

"Twenty-one," Vera said, and took a long drag on her cigarette. "Alasdair has aged me, surely. But your question is valid—I married him at nineteen, when he was nearly forty. As to why, well, if I'm not trying to annoy one man, I'm trying to annoy another. In this case, my father. Alasdair was a great friend of his and I started a steamy love affair with him mostly out of boredom, if I'm honest. There's something about being the most exciting thing in a man's life that just lights my fire, you know? When I realized how much I could anger my father if I married Alasdair, that's exactly what I did."

I looked at Vera, and even with the tiny scraps of psychology I'd gathered so far from my course, I could see a desperate need for attention that would fuel self-destruction. Given what I already knew of Max, this said quite a lot about the toxicity of their family, and I was starting to regret my know-your-enemy approach when it came to them.

"So you're no romantic," I said flatly. "And you seem to mention quite often how easily bored you are—that's why you invited me to the party the other night, I suppose. Or was that part of a

long-drawn-out plan of Max's to get revenge on Elaine for dumping him, and to intimidate me in the process?"

"You're better at psychology than Max," Vera said, pointing the lit end of her cigarette at me and giving me a shrewd look. "I'd love to see you outperform him on all your exams." She turned to the window for a moment. "Honestly, though, it was nothing like that. I was just in need of a friend," she said, her voice quieter.

The car stopped and I realized it had driven to my accommodation without my having to tell the driver where to go. Something in me took pity on Vera, so I said suddenly, "You can come in for a cup of tea if you don't make any snide comments about the state of my flat."

She laughed and put out her cigarette in the ashtray near the door handle. "That sounds lovely. I can tell you all about my art—it's my passion. But we must try to avoid Elaine. I feel terrible about that painting. I think it's a rather good piece—I'm proud of it, actually—but I feel awful about the circumstances of its creation." Then she added, "We should talk about Max too."

I led Vera up the narrow staircase to my little loft bedroom, which was quite airy and bright but rather sparse. I'd started collecting fashion magazines and had taped several interesting designs for dresses and suits around the walls. I'd managed to acquire a secondhand sewing machine that sat on the desk in the corner with a tangle of fabric jammed into the feed dogs. I'd take it apart later, but I pulled the wicker chair away from the desk and offered it to Vera. "I've a hot plate and a kettle, but it takes ages to boil. I hope you don't mind waiting. We'll have to steal some milk from the fridge downstairs."

Vera sat and looked around the room, her face carefully neutral. "To be honest, a chat is better than a cup of tea. I've never been a tea person, really."

"So, your art," I started, "it's really quite remarkable. I mean,

assuming you normally employ your talents outside of revenge plots with your brother?"

"I've been painting as long as I can remember," Vera said. Her face took on a wistful expression, and I could almost see images and ideas forming behind her eyes. "I have some more avant-garde things, darker and more human abstracts, with animalistic themes. But Alasdair often finds them and burns them."

Shock made my mouth fall slightly open, but anger shut it again. "How cruel," I managed.

"He's particular about what his wife should be doing," she said, and shrugged. "He was happy to furnish me with canvases and supplies when I was painting landscapes and things that a woman two hundred years ago would have painted. I think for a while he loved the idea that he might have a wife with twee little hobbies that kept her busy, but at home."

"Burning your work sounds like grounds for divorce," I said. But then I saw Vera's face fall and wondered if it was more complicated than that. "But I've never been married, so what do I know?" I winced at that, because technically that was a lie. I had been married, briefly. I married Archie Foyle last year after a whirlwind romance, but it fell apart quickly, and we annulled it quietly without anyone knowing we'd married in the first place.

"Honestly, for a heart surgeon, he's got some terrible health habits, so I've actually been hoping he might fall victim to natural causes before too long."

"Vera!" I said, shocked.

"Oh, I'm not going to murder him," she said. "The cruelest thing he does to me is just treat me like a doll, or try to control my hobbies or who I'm friends with. He doesn't hit me or anything so vulgar."

"Still . . ."

"And I'm sure he's found out about a few of the affairs I've

had, and he hasn't said a word. I mean, that's a lucky thing, isn't it? To have a husband who lets you screw the gardener, and simply looks the other way and tells you to be at your best for a medical gala later?"

"You're starting to sound like a character on TV," I said. And I was beginning to wonder if half the things she was saying were true. But then I thought of Dr. Huntington, the sneering man with sour breath who ignored me when I was standing right in front of him. "I suppose one has to be rather detached to be a surgeon in the first place," I said slowly. "But presumably he saves a lot of lives with his heart surgeries and things like that?"

"Oh, don't start. I've heard more about the ins and outs of heart surgery than I ever needed to. It's the only thing he seems to discuss at dinner. He even likes to use his steak to demonstrate a particular surgical technique to guests. It's foul. But everyone says he's the best, and whenever we go out with his colleagues or the medical board or university patrons, they all sing his praises. A saint of a man, they say. So, you see my problem—if I try to divorce him, he'll simply ruin my reputation by bringing my affairs to light while his lawyers prove without a doubt that he's a pillar of the community. It's not worth the hassle."

"I suppose you have an interesting life, even if it's something of a mess," I said.

Vera laughed weakly. "That's my only consolation—the strange path I've walked is nothing to the odd vibrancy of my own mind." She tapped one side of her head. "The colors I see, Frances! Sometimes at night, when Alasdair is out, I make my room pitch-dark and talk to the colors in my head like they're my friends. They're living things, sometimes. Pieces of me that no one else can see, that I can choose to show to the world if I want, with just a brush, some paint, and my own hand."

I felt in that moment that Vera was walking a tightrope of sanity over dangerous waters. It was clear that she had the kind of creative mind that could either fuel an energetic life or eat her alive. Stifled as she was, I worried it might one day be the latter.

"Don't look so alarmed, Frances!" she said. "Sometimes I talk about things in abstractions because it makes me feel more connected to deeper things. Surely the students who sit in Benny's writing poetry talk in the same way sometimes." She took out her lighter and fiddled with it, leaning back in the wicker chair so that it creaked slightly. "Anyway, I'm not in a terrible position with regard to the men in my life. Max, my father, my husband . . . they may be bullies, but I'll give you some advice for free, Frances." She leaned forward and looked at me intently. "When you're surrounded by calculating and powerful men who think of you as a piece of furniture, you're in the best *position to collect information."*

"What, like secrets?" I asked.

"Secrets, lies, misdeeds . . ." Vera said. "Information is power, Frances. And I've started collecting a whole lot of it. It makes me feel so much more secure, knowing I have things I can threaten these men with. Information I can sell to the newspapers if I have to, secrets I can expose. I highly recommend starting a collection of your own. Ford seems upstanding, but anyone can have a dark side."

Vera was speaking about habits I'd already started forming in trying to outrun my fortune, seeing if I might root out who my eventual murderer could be before they struck. It was uncanny. I felt seen, appreciated even. As if she was something of a kindred spirit, and she and I could be a strange sort of club where it wasn't unusual to watch your own back and try to keep an eye on who might be the next to betray you. Besides, what she said made sense. Knowing secrets could mean power.

"Come dancing with me tonight," Vera said, changing the

subject abruptly. "I'll go home and get dressed and I'll pick you up from here in a few hours. Leave Ford Gravesdown behind. There's a new club called Hatchetts Playground in Piccadilly. We'll drink Moscow mules and get blisters on our feet from dancing until the sun rises."

I looked at Vera and hesitated a moment. I was there for university; I didn't want to waste the chance I had at an education because I spent too much time out having fun. "I don't think so," I said finally. "I need to study. If I'm not prepared properly for my next class, it just gives Max more chances to undermine me in front of Professor Dane."

Vera looked me in the eye, pleading. "Then let's do both. We can go out for the night and strategize at the same time. I want Max off my back, and I think he's getting a bit too interested in competing with you. We both need a way to take him down several notches, so let's hatch a plan but have fun while we do it."

"You aren't seriously suggesting we can formulate some kind of Max upheaval while on the dance floor in Hatchetts?" I ask. But secretly I wanted a reason to go there. It was the nightclub everyone was at, a kind of see-and-be-seen sort of place. I'd tried to get in before but had been turned away. I was sure Vera wouldn't even have to queue.

"All right, but I'll meet you there. I've some things to do first," I said.

CHAPTER 15

MY SEARCH RESULTS FOR THE ADDRESS IN KNIGHTSbridge from Frances's diary—the place where she and Ford went to that art auction—reveal that the place is now an art gallery. I'm pleasantly surprised, but I suppose it stands to reason that it could have turned into one if the previous owners amassed a huge art collection and no longer wanted to use the property as a residence. A lot of wealthy old families in England had multiple homes—a house in town and another in the country, like Aunt Frances did—but many struggled with the cost and upkeep as time went by. Quite a few large country houses are now owned by the National Trust and are tourist attractions.

As the taxi pulls up in front of an enormous white stone mansion on a tree-lined street, I look at the gleaming marble steps at the front and feel transported to Frances's evening spent drinking champagne with Vera and trying to outsmart Max as he sought to humiliate Elaine.

The entrance hall is just as she described it, from the diamond patterns inlaid in the floor to the sweeping carved marble staircase. I have to pay to enter, as it's a private collection, so I pause and buy a ticket from a young man behind a small desk. He gives me a map, and I spend another tenner on a brochure that has information on the gallery and the artists included in it. I do a quick flip through to see if anything of Mum's is here, but don't see her name.

The place is relatively empty, but full of fascinating art. It reminds me of one of the smaller Guggenheim collections I've visited—the one in Venice, where Peggy Guggenheim had a sculpture garden that includes headstones for her many dead dogs. The map tells me this place also has a sculpture garden, as well as a wing for modern art, a classical sculpture room, and something called "the aqua experience," which seems a bit try-hard and apparently involves immersive water sounds from the bottom of the English Channel broadcast live into a coffin-sized box you lie in. The idea is terrifying to me, so I head to the portrait gallery instead.

Rows of faces stare out at me, many of them ancestors of the former owners of this house and collection, the brochure informs me. It's not a family name Frances ever mentioned in her diary, so I don't think there are any leads to follow here. I'm most curious to find out if Vera Huntington ever painted anything else, and what connected her to Felicity.

I walk past stoic men posed against burgundy backgrounds, wearing military medals or sitting with hunting dogs, and start to feel like I've wasted a trip. But then, near the end of the hall, I spy the same evocative style as the portrait in the cupboard—sad but energetic eyes, vigorous brushstrokes, and a different approach from the typical portrait colors. It's a young man leaning against a window. He's wearing a simple jumper and trousers, but his golden hair is brushed back and slightly long, and his chin is sharp and distinctive.

Based on Vera's painting of Elaine, and the image I've formed of Max Torrence from Frances's descriptions in her diary, I have an instinct that this was painted by Vera Huntington. I'm not an art expert by any means, but I've learned enough to see the similarities between the painting of Elaine, which I've just seen, and the colors and style of this painting. I'd have to make some comparisons to be sure, so I take out my phone and snap a photo of it. Out of nowhere, a sharp voice makes me jump.

"There's no photography in the gallery," a woman says. She has a white pixie haircut and is probably in her mid-seventies. She's tall but unremarkable, and she hunches as she walks, but I get the impression that it's not from injury or arthritis. I suspect she's one of those women who always felt too tall and developed a lifetime habit of trying to make herself smaller.

"I'm sorry," I say, tucking my phone away.

"You'll have to delete that picture," the woman says. She gestures toward my pocket. "Come on, take it out. I want to see you delete it."

I feel a bit cornered, which makes me defensive. I understand the rules of art galleries, but this woman doesn't understand the rules of murder investigations. Still, I grudgingly pull my phone out of my pocket and open my camera. I pull up the photo and show it to her, then press delete, planning to recover it later and hoping she doesn't know that modern phones have that feature.

"There," I say. "Apologies. I just really found this painting interesting . . ." I look at the woman's name tag. ". . . Marie."

"Well, if you want details on it, Mr. Ego himself usually takes over at the front desk about now," Marie says.

"The artist?" I ask. I'd been rather certain this was one of Vera's paintings; it's such a match in style to the one I found in the wardrobe in Fliss's room.

"The subject," she replies curtly. "His name is Max, and he's the gallery's own personal ghost. Can't seem to get rid of him."

I feel that now-familiar jolt in my chest, the spark of a connection when I'm chasing down answers and am rewarded by something turning up. Max Torrence is still alive, and not only that, he's the connection to this gallery I didn't know I was looking for. I feel one step closer to bridging the gap between Felicity and Vera.

I turn and scan the hallway I just came through. "Thank you for that. It's really helpful information," I say to Marie. I want to get her on my side, because I suspect I might be coming back here, if Max Torrence is a constant fixture at this gallery, both on the wall and in the flesh. "My name is Annie, and I'm doing a sort of . . . project on art in the 1960s."

"Like an article?" She seems to soften, but only slightly. "The gallery could use the publicity. Which paper do you write for?" Marie looks at me intensely. I can see she's razor-sharp and trying to catch me in a lie.

I think quickly. "It's a book I'm writing actually, still in the research stage, but I've got interested publishers." This isn't entirely a lie. It's just that the book I'm writing is a murder mystery and doesn't involve art. At least, not yet. Perhaps it should. Maybe that might help the "interested publishers" to be a bit more interested. At the moment, lukewarm is the best I can describe their level of interest. Maybe I should be writing a fictionalized version of the murder of Vera Huntington.

"Ah, you're one of those." Marie looks more relaxed, like she's met enough writers in her time to know how many of us start projects and don't finish them.

I shrug off her judgment, because I have a job to do. "I'll see if I can find Max, then," I say cheerfully. "Thanks again, Marie." I walk back the way I came, my winter boots squeaking a little on the shiny floor as I go. When I look back just before I turn the corner into the main hall, I see that Marie is still there. She's looking at the portrait of Max with an intensity I can't quite pin down. Affection? Loathing? Whatever it is, it's either an office romance or an office rivalry, and I'm rather amused to find that even in one's seventies, there's still room for some drama.

As I make my way back toward the museum entrance, something catches my eye in another room to my left. It's the modern-art room, and I take a quick detour inside in case I overlooked something in the brochure, and perhaps some of Mum's older works are here.

I don't see any of her stuff, but there are pillars in the center with sculptures on them—things made of twisted metal fibers, bent together to form dancing figures. It's not the most original work I've ever seen, but it's not bad. My eyes drift down to the name of the artist on the plaque next to each figure, and I stop short. "*Electric Dancers* by Felicity Rowe, temporary collection." That must be why her name didn't pop out in the brochure—not that I was looking for it, but I'd have noticed if it was there. Either this is a new addition to the gallery or one that wasn't deemed important enough to stay. But Felicity's work being here has added a layer of intrigue to my thoughts. It cements the gallery as the crossroads for all the meandering threads of her murder case. This is where Vera's history and Felicity's recent movements collided. I just can't see yet how that might have led to her murder.

I wander around the different pieces of her art, thinking. It looks like she was doing well enough to have work displayed in this gallery, but what brought her here of all places? There are lots of art galleries around London. Why this one?

I exit the room, make my way to the entrance, and find Marie was right—the small desk where I bought my ticket is now occupied by an older man with his back to me. Max still has hair to his shoulders, thick and well-kept. He clearly goes to a salon and has blond highlights put in to balance the gray.

"Excuse me, would you be Max Torrence?" I ask. I include the surname because I want to be sure about that painting, and about this man.

He turns abruptly, sees me, and smiles. "Who's asking?" There's a casual sort of twinkle about him, as if he's used to charming people immediately. From the accounts in Frances's diary, I'd add that he's used to charming people right up until he stabs them in the back. Because finding out that Max Torrence is not only still around but still on the periphery of the London art scene? This makes me wish I'd called Crane.

Frances's diary was never kind to Max, but more than that.

Frances met Max and Vera in September 1968, and Vera was brutally murdered in November. By December, the police had investigated and Dr. Alasdair Huntington was sent to prison for killing his wife. And all the while Frances was convinced that they had the wrong man.

She was certain that Vera was killed by her brother, Max Torrence. She was just never able to prove it.

CHAPTER 16

October 26, 1968

VERA WAS AS GOOD AS HER WORD. SHE GOT US INTO Hatchetts Playground, and we danced until dawn. But very few plans were made with regard to Max. It was as if he didn't exist while we were there. I tried a few times to ask about his relationship with Elaine, and what else he had done in the past to get his way, but Vera consistently dodged my questions.

I soon gave up, because it was loud but fun in the club, and the kind of place where people were loose and a little wild but in a way that felt free rather than intimidating. I'd been to a jazz club the previous week that had made me feel the same way, though the music was better there. I thought of Ford several times as we drank and danced, and decided that as soon as I'd been home and slept for a bit, I'd go and see him.

Vera and I parted ways in the early hours, and as we said good-bye, she asked me something strange.

"I need a favor, Frances, if you don't mind? I just wondered if I could store some things at yours. A bag, maybe a trunk full of some stuff that Alasdair won't like me having."

"Nothing illegal, I hope," I said, giving her an assessing look.

"No! Nothing like that!" Vera said, and she laughed a little nervously. "It's silly, really, but part of me wants to protect my interests. Keep some things safe that I worry Alasdair might destroy. A couple of family heirlooms that mean a lot to me, that I know he'd go after if he wanted to break my spirit. And some new things of mine that I don't want to see go up in flames."

"You mentioned he burned your art in the past when he didn't like it," I say, "but does he make a habit of destroying your things too? Because, Vera, that's really not okay."

Vera just shrugged. "He's cut up dresses of mine if he doesn't like them, and smashed jewelry boxes. I just . . . I don't know, maybe it's my way of justifying keeping part of me away from him, if I leave some things at yours. It's the chance to escape, should things turn really bad. Please, can you just keep some things for me?" She was starting to look over her shoulder, as if Alasdair might materialize at any moment.

"Of course," I said. "But please, Vera, think about maybe filing a report with the police, if he's destroying your things. Just to start a record of his behavior."

"I will," she said. "There's a young constable I met while I was out in Soho last week. I've got his phone number. I'll ring him and get his advice. And thank you, Frances. I'll send someone I trust round to yours with some of my things, if that's all right."

"Certainly," I said. I gave her a hug and whispered, "Please be careful, you've suddenly got me very worried."

She nodded weakly, but smiled. "Let's go dancing again soon. That was the most fun I've had in ages. I forgot who I was for a moment there."

Ford answered the door the next afternoon when I rang the bell, and though I'd made an extra effort to appear well rested, he said, "You look like you could use some coffee."

His smile was good-natured as I told him about my evening, while we drank coffee in the sitting room with the record player on low. But I saw his smile falter around the edges a few times when I mentioned Vera and the things she'd said over the course of the evening.

"What do you know about her family?" Ford asked finally.

"The Torrences? Next to nothing, save what you've told me about your father being friends with them," I said.

Ford's brow furrowed. He poured a little cream into his coffee and stirred it thoughtfully. "I'm not inclined to trust anything they say, but during the party the other night, Vera's husband, Alasdair, told me she's been given a curious diagnosis by her father."

"Isn't her father a famous psychologist? Elaine mentioned he was the head of the psychology department at the university," I said. "Wouldn't a father giving his own daughter a diagnosis be rather unethical? Family bias and all that?"

"You'd know about the ethics of psychology better than me," Ford said. "But in that family, I don't think they're so concerned with those things. But Alasdair told me Vera's been treated for years as a pathological liar. There were other psychoses mentioned, but the one thing Alasdair seemed to want to warn me about in particular was that she's prone to quite a bit of fabrication."

I felt my spine straighten as if someone had pulled a secret cord within it. A pulse of anger followed, because while Vera might be outlandish and even a little strange, she was also troubled and trying to stay afloat, despite being surrounded by men who all wanted to control her. Alasdair, Max, her father—they all forced her to be whatever specific thing suited them.

"Are you sure this isn't a case of a woman being a bit too independent, and therefore being discredited before she even has a chance to find her voice?" I asked.

Ford paused, but just as he finally drew breath to speak, the doorbell rang. We sat in silence for a moment, listening to the voice of the housekeeper speaking to whoever had come calling. A man, by the sound of it.

"My lord, there's a Constable Folkestone here to see you and Miss Adams," the housekeeper said when she entered the room. "Shall I tell him to come in, or take his card?"

Ford looked at me quizzically, and I shrugged. I had no idea why a constable would be asking for either of us.

"Show him in," Ford said.

A moment later, a young man with short black hair entered the sitting room. His expression was rather worried, and for a moment I expected some terrible news. Could something have happened to my family back in Castle Knoll? Or was there an issue with Ford's nephew, Saxon, who was away at boarding school?

"Thank you for seeing me, my lord, miss." He nodded to each of us in turn. "I'm sorry to interrupt, but I'm looking for Vera Huntington, on behalf of her family. I understand from her brother that you're friendly with her, Miss Adams?"

"I am," I said slowly. "And we were out dancing together until the early hours this morning, but we parted ways to go home. Did she not return?" Worry started to prickle along my skin. Vera had gone from suggesting we make a plan to put Max in his place, to dancing and pretending he didn't exist, to asking me to store some things so her husband didn't destroy them. Was her inconsistency due to the exaggeration of a threat, or was the threat genuine? Had something happened to her?

"She walked straight to the police station to find me at around six A.M.," he said. "She and I had met last week, and she came to me anxious about her safety. We had a chat, and I sent her home, promising to look into her concerns. She mentioned you, Miss

Adams, as a confidante, and also Lord Gravesdown, as a person she trusted. So when I paid a call to her home this afternoon and her husband told me she'd come home briefly but disappeared again soon after, I thought I might come to talk to you."

I looked at Ford, wondering what to make of this. His expression was pensive and watchful. I don't think he had the measure of what was going on either.

"Are you here on behalf of Vera, or because her husband wants her found?" I asked. "I'll add that she's not here, by the way."

"Neither, actually. It was her brother, Max, who called me, but really, I'm here because I'm worried about her, given our conversation. Her husband seemed unconcerned that she had gone out again. But her brother was also there, looking through her things. Specifically, he was asking about her red handbag. He said there was something of his in it that she'd stolen. So I'm now caught between checking up on a potential missing person and investigating a possible theft."

"Did Max tell you what she'd stolen?" I asked. My heart had dropped into my stomach. Vera had just asked permission to store some things at my flat, saying she wanted to keep them safe from Alasdair. But if she'd taken something from Max, she was using me as both a hiding place and possibly a patsy. If she'd stolen something of value and wanted to get away with it, putting it in my flat was a great way to shift blame if anyone came looking.

"He wasn't specific, so I can't file any official report. Unless he tells me what the item is, and its value, I can't arrest anyone for the theft. It's a bit of a gray area, you see."

I nodded. "Well, all of this is news to me," I said, trying to add a breezy tone to my voice. "But I appreciate your instinct to look into it, as the stories seem to contradict each other. I'm afraid I can't help you with anything."

The constable nodded resignedly. "Not to worry, it was

necessary to follow up, in any case. Do ring me if she turns up, or if you learn about the whereabouts of this red handbag." He left a card with his telephone number written on it.

"We certainly will," Ford said, joining the conversation just as it was over. "I'll show you out," he said, and gave a polite gesture of dismissal to the housekeeper, who was hovering nearby.

When Ford returned, he gave me a serious look. "I've made sure he's well and truly gone, because you look terrified, Frances."

"I need to go back to my flat to see if Vera delivered anything there," I said, my voice shaking. "I told her she could store some things with me to keep them safe. And I think I've been played for a fool."

CHAPTER 17

SEVERAL ITEMS HAD BEEN PLACED NEATLY ON THE floor just inside my flat. Before I'd left, I'd given the landlady permission to unlock the door, telling her someone was coming to deliver some things. The presence of the large trunk, the leather suitcase, and the hatbox indicated that the delivery had certainly been made.

But it was the red handbag that stood out, like a drop of blood on snow, that had my pulse racing.

"That can't be good," Ford said, eyeing the handbag and closing the door behind him. He looked around the little room, at the magazine pictures I'd taped to the walls and the psychology books neatly stacked on the bedside table. "Though I must admit I'm enjoying the chance of a small glimpse into your world. You're so often in mine that this is a rare treat."

"I'm often in your library, not your bedroom," I quipped, then blushed furiously when I realized what I'd accidentally implied. "I mean . . ." I started, scrambling to find the words to say that romance was the last thing on my mind. But my eyes fell on Vera's handbag, which was staring at me like a living thing.

"Don't worry, Frances," Ford said, sounding relaxed. "I realize we're in the midst of some strangeness with your new friend, and I'm genuinely here to help."

I nodded absently as I reached for the handbag. My fingers shook as I undid the clasp, and I reached in and pulled out a folded stack of papers.

"What is it?" Ford asked.

I flipped through them. Some looked like financial records that I could make no sense of. Others were handwritten pages on notepaper.

"These are . . . essays. Research. There are some notes addressed to Max. Here." I pointed, showing Ford. "Whoever wrote this was giving advice to Max in the margins." Ford and I silently read for a moment, and I stopped at one missive that said, Max, be sure to change the spelling of "definitely" when you type this. You always spell it wrong. It will add authenticity to it if you write your usual "definately." *Another read,* The case study you're using for this is the Asch experiments, because my research uses the Milgram device and otherwise these papers will be too similar. I know you wanted to use Milgram, but if you want me to keep doing this for you, you'll have to let me choose the material.

"They're all signed E," I said. "Elaine. She's been writing his essays and doing his research. Her final project for this term is on the Milgram device, she told me."

"So, Vera has evidence that Max is cheating on his degree. The son of the department head isn't doing any of his own work," Ford said. "He'll probably get away with it too."

"Even if Vera exposes him?" I asked.

"It depends on how much evidence she's collected," Ford said. "Let's see if anything else is hidden in here."

We opened the suitcase and searched through the piles of clothing. I didn't feel bad going through Vera's things—they were in my possession because I was doing her a favor. But I suppose there was mistrust beneath my actions. I wanted to believe I was helping her keep valuable things safe from her husband, rather than being used to hide stolen items, but the documents we'd found were already unraveling my belief that Vera's motives were exactly as she'd said.

We pulled out several beaded gowns from the suitcase, a tiara that looked like a family heirloom and was possibly made with real diamonds, and another handbag (one of the Gucci ones that President Kennedy's wife favored) with more papers.

Vera's voice echoed in my memory. Information is power, Frances. And I've started collecting a whole lot of it.

And she had. There were even more documents in the bottom of the suitcase. Handfuls of medical records, people it looked like her husband had treated, but neither Ford nor I could think why those might be part of her collection. There were copies of letters, pleading ones from her father to the board of trustees at the university asking them to overlook his sexual indiscretions with a student. I shuddered as I flipped through page after page of evidence of the Torrence and Huntington families' misdeeds.

"What should we do about this?" Ford asked.

I gathered the papers into a small stack and folded them along the middle. Then I added them to the red handbag, forcing the clasp to shut around the now-thick stack inside. "We find Vera and give her these papers back," I said. "I'm not going to be a depository for her collection of secrets. The rest of the things can stay until she's ready to find somewhere new to keep them."

"Are you sure about that, Frances?" Ford asked. He was holding the diamond tiara up to the light, examining it. "I think this

might be worth quite a lot of money. It could be that this is what Max was searching for, if it's a family heirloom. The essays can be discredited. Max would only have to say that Elaine fabricated them as some sort of revenge. Or it could be that Max is really just his father's errand boy, and he's doing a family cleanup for him. That would mean he was actually after that letter from his father, the one that exposes his relationship with the student."

"Either way, I don't want to be in the middle of any of this," I said.

"I think that's wise," Ford agreed. "But consider getting rid of all of these things, please, Frances? Or at least let me store them in Chelsea. That way, even Vera won't be sure where they are, in case she's framing you so that Max can take his petty revenge on you for undermining him in class."

"That would be quite extreme of Max," I said. "Using Vera to plant valuable items in my flat, then calling the police and having me go to prison for the theft? He's not planning that, Ford. Think about it." I started pacing around the large trunk, which we had yet to open. I prayed to God there wasn't a body inside it, but it was just like me to wonder if there might be. "If Max wanted me to go down for stealing these things, he'd need to have told the police what had been stolen in the first place, when he mentioned to the constable that Vera had something of his in her red handbag."

"All right, but at least let me get these things out of here, while you try to return that handbag to Vera," Ford said.

I sighed, the ache of dancing all night still echoing through my feet. "Let's at least see what's in the trunk first."

Ford unlatched its brass buckles and we lifted the lid together. I smelled turpentine and the aroma of oil paints as I peered at a colorful collection of canvases and art supplies. "It's just some of her paintings," I said. "Actually, look." I pointed to the wardrobe, where one door was slightly ajar. I swung it open and saw many additional canvases stacked inside. "She's included more here. This large one, it's Max, see?"

Ford pulled it out and examined it. "It is. Well, let's get these things into the car."

CHAPTER 18

"MY NAME IS ANNIE," I SAY TO MAX AS HE SITS BEHIND the desk in the gallery, like the conductor at the front of a train. I'm careful not to use my surname, even though it's a common one. If Aunt Frances even half suspected that Max had killed Vera, perhaps something had happened that made Felicity a target as well, after all these years. And that then leads back to our Chelsea house. Max could make the connection to Frances, no matter how much time has passed.

But there's so much more I need to investigate, because I still haven't uncovered any reason someone would want Felicity dead. I thought Crane was giving me information about her when we were talking earlier, but thinking back . . . I still don't know who she really was. Who were her friends? Did she have enemies? Perhaps Crane doesn't know either. He did say it had been ten years since they'd spoken.

"Max Torrence." He holds out his hand for me to shake. "What can I help you with? Private tour? Or looking to buy some of the pieces we have that are up for sale?"

I give him what I hope is a friendly smile but can't help feeling that there's a bit of my apprehension leaking through. "I was told by your colleague Marie that the portrait at the end of the hallway is of you. I wondered if you could tell me more about it, and about the artist," I say.

He beams. He's clearly proud of that painting, and there's no trace of grief for his murdered sister on his face, which I find telling, even if it has been decades since she died. "Yes, that's me. You've got great taste. It's a real one of a kind."

It's more like part of a set, I think to myself. Mentally, I picture the nude of Elaine side by side with the portrait of Max, and it does feel like the two paintings belong together.

"Did you know the artist?" I ask.

"Not very well," he says. "A chap from the art school needed someone to sit for him and I obliged. Don't think his career went anywhere unfortunately, but it was fun standing there like a model and then getting to see such a flattering likeness." He smiles again, a wistful look passing over his face.

He's lying, I'm fairly certain. I have a good enough eye from growing up with Mum to be able to see that the artist's style matches the painting of Elaine. There's a slim chance someone imitated Vera's style while painting Max, but I've thankfully got the photo on my phone to examine more closely later.

"How did the painting come to be here, then?" I ask.

"Oh, I asked my family to buy it. It hung in our home in Regent's Park for years—it was a nice way to support a struggling artist. Then when I came to work here, I donated it. Thought it would be a good sort of joke." He winks at me, and I fix my smile in place, like it's plaster setting in the sun. "You know, me being a volunteer and wandering the halls where my own likeness hangs."

"I don't know if the joke's landing with Marie," I say, stirring the pot to see if anything floats to the surface.

He waves his hand as if to brush away the entire idea of Marie. "Mr. Ego, she calls me. I quite like that, so she's not doing me any damage with her name-calling. I'm protected by my ego, of course. I'm quite untouchable." When he says that last, he looks at me more intently than before.

He wags a finger at me, silently searching my face as if trying to place me. "You look familiar . . . Have we met before?"

"No," I say, taking a small step backward and trying my best to look anonymous. "I'm certain we haven't."

"A relative, then?" he continues. "Are you one of those girls who's the spitting image of her mother?" His eyes have lost their humor now, and unease prickles at the back of my neck. I take a second step back, and then a third, but he leans forward across the desk.

The thing is, I *do* look remarkably like Mum. I'm told this constantly. I'm likely being paranoid, and he's just remembering a random blond girlfriend he had decades ago, or he's just trying to make more conversation, albeit in a creepy way.

But come to think of it, if Felicity came and went from this gallery because of her sculpture displays, it's extremely possible Mum has been here too. I swallow hard and realize I need to ask Max about Felicity or I might lose my chance to get more answers.

I snap my smile back into place. "Maybe you're thinking of my friend Fliss. Those are her sculptures in your modern-art display. Even though we have different-colored hair, people always say we could be sisters," I add. It's a terrible lie, but it's the only natural way I can think of to bring Felicity into the conversation.

Max's eyes flash angrily, then narrow. "Laura." He lets Mum's name hang between us, like it's the diagnosis to a bad set of symptoms.

"Excuse me?"

He stands, his features set. "I can see it now. You've got to be Laura's daughter. We don't allow her in here, so if she sent you—"

"I don't know what you're talking about," I say. "I just came to see Fliss's work, and I—"

He cuts me off. "I think you should leave."

My phone buzzes, and I'm relieved to see that it's Crane. I give Max a pointed look and step outside to take the call.

"Annie, where are you?" he asks.

"I went to that address I mentioned in Knightsbridge," I say. "But I've finished here now, and I've got a lot of things to catch you up on."

"Good. I'm nearby so I'll pick you up. I found out something rather interesting about that address."

"Is it that Max Torrence, brother of the murdered Vera Huntington, volunteers here? Or that Felicity has a sculpture series on display here?" I offer. My heart is beating quickly, and I scan the road for signs of his car, telling myself that Mum probably just made Max angry by being overly involved in Felicity's work whenever they delivered it to that gallery. She couldn't have done anything to make herself a target. She's Mum—she's mouthy sometimes, but she's not running around making serious enemies.

Besides, Max couldn't have killed Felicity. I mean, not without help. He looked to be in average shape for someone in their seventies, and I can't see him overpowering a woman in her twenties, then lifting her body into a skip. Still, I don't like that he not only knows Mum but has banned her from that gallery.

"Neither of those things," Crane says. "But they're worrying connections. This is all painting a very dark picture, no pun intended," he adds. His car pulls up at the bottom of the steps, and I hop inside. The heat is on full blast and it's a relief even after only a minute in the cold.

"So, what did you find out about that place?" I ask. "Because this is a lot of secrets for one address."

"That's precisely why I think this is a break in the case," Crane says. He turns away from the warm glow of the imposing houses on that street and onto a busier road. We immediately get stuck in traffic, and he turns to me. "I found out where your mum donated all her money."

"Where?" I ask.

"Laura Adams made a whopping seven-point-two-million-pound donation to the newly formed Knightsbridge Nymph Art Gallery in 1992. The very same place you've just visited. Can you think why she'd do that? Completely drain her bank accounts to fund an art gallery?"

"I'm not sure. To bolster her public image maybe? I mean, at the time it probably turned a couple of heads, but I imagine it looked like she was just being generous," I say slowly. Internally, though, I wonder, Then why would Max have such a dislike for her? Why would she be banned from that gallery?

"The donation was made anonymously. I had to dig through a mountain of tax records to trace it back to her," Crane says. "So this wasn't for her public image."

"And if it were anonymous, maybe even most people from the gallery wouldn't know who made the donation," I say.

"Why would the gallery employees' opinions matter?" he asks.

I explain about the weird conversation I've just had with Max.

Crane is silent for a moment, thinking. "So what connects Laura to that gallery, other than Fliss?" he asks finally.

"I think . . ." I start, then close my eyes as pages of Aunt Frances's diary float through my memory. ". . . I think it's less about what connects Mum to the gallery, and more what connects Mum to Max Torrence. And I think Aunt Frances's diary is the key to that."

"How so?"

"The tiara," I say quietly.

"The what?" Crane asks as the traffic creeps forward again.

"I'm developing a theory, so bear with me. My dad—I mean Sam," I correct myself, still not wanting to think of that increasingly slimy man as my father. "Sam said he found something in the Chelsea house, something valuable, that he sold for a lot of money. He told us that was where Mum's fortune came from, but what if he kept the money after all?"

"I did confirm that Laura's money came from the sale of her paintings, so what Sam told us in that respect was a lie," Crane says.

"And the reason he'd lie about that is to keep us from knowing that he's had money from the sale of a stolen object all this time. In Great Aunt Frances's diary, Vera Huntington went to Frances with trunks full of valuable items she was worried her husband might get angry and ruin. Among those items was a diamond heirloom tiara, and Ford mentioned to her that he thought the diamonds were extremely valuable. Vera wanted Frances to keep these items safe, but Ford ended up taking them to his house in Chelsea. The same house that Frances continued to own for decades, and that she let me and Mum—and now we know my dad—live in after she had permanently settled in Castle Knoll."

"So, your theory is that Sam found the tiara and sold it on the black market, but somehow Max Torrence found out about it and threatened them," Crane says slowly.

I nod. "And Sam told Mum he didn't have the money anymore, for whatever reason, but that his neck was on the line over this. So Mum bailed him out."

"Then the donation to the gallery makes a lot of sense," Crane says. "Because otherwise it's difficult to hide the transfer of that large an amount of money."

"And it all went quiet," I say. "Until Felicity. She's got work on display there, and something must have happened to get Max agitated again. My guess is that she dug into the past of that house, learned about Vera, and found something that proved Max was Vera's real killer."

"So he killed Fliss," Crane says, finishing my thought. I smile slightly, because being so in step with each other while thinking through theories is incredibly satisfying. "But then," he continues, "why do it in the same way he killed Vera? That kind of similarity just puts a spotlight on the old case. Not to mention the logistics of a man in his seventies being able to lift a body into a skip."

I pause, thinking. "I suppose he could have had help," I say. "But as for why he'd do it in the same way . . . I don't know. Perhaps ego, alongside a decent dose of psychopathy?" I offer. "Vera's husband went down for that crime decades ago, so Max probably thought he was untouchable." His words from earlier echo through my mind. "He'd killed before in that manner, and from what Frances's diary says of

Max and his personality, I think he's got some rather unhinged tendencies lurking beneath the surface."

"Serial killers are very rare, Annie," Crane says, "but I see your point. He's aging now, and the temptation to relive pieces of one's past as the years narrow down can be strong."

"Like elderly people wanting to go back to the place they met their partners, or re-create first dates. Only with murder."

"I wouldn't put it like that, but . . ." He takes his eyes off the road briefly, and I can tell he's not admonishing me for the comparison but is amused at my need to make light of dark moments.

"But I'm quite possibly right," I say.

"You're quite possibly right. I'd bring in Sam for questioning, but this isn't my case. We can't compel him to talk to us, but we do need to ask him a few more questions. Laura too."

"I know," I say. "Let's go to the house. I want to show you those medical records as well. If that was the information Felicity had, and she ended up dead . . . there's a missing piece that could be quite important. Did you happen to get hold of the original file on Vera's murder?"

"I did," Crane says. "For the sake of ethics, though, I did tell the detective in charge of Fliss's case that she should really be looking into the file herself. She half listened, then skimmed it, decided this was an unrelated incident, and let me take it."

"What's that other file, then?" I ask, noticing two files in the back seat, one looking quite new.

"Oh, the detective did ask for my help on something, given that I'm law enforcement in Castle Knoll. Those are Fliss's phone records. She wanted my help in tracking down a few old numbers that may trace back to the area," he says.

"Boring stuff. I suspect it's just a box-ticking exercise, but I'm happy to help."

"Okay. Well, let's pick apart Vera's file together," I say, "because if Frances was convinced that Max was the guilty party, and now we've got a connection between Felicity and Max by way of that art gallery . . ." I trail off. "Something went wrong in the investigation of that murder back in 1968, and I think if we find out what it was, we might be able to put Max away for good. And we need to work quickly, because I didn't like the way he looked when he mentioned Mum."

CHAPTER 19

October 31, 1968

THE BEST I COULD DO WAS GET THE HANDBAG TO Elaine, because Vera was nowhere to be found. Elaine knew that after the support we gave her at the art auction—helping her hold her head high, and Ford's purchase of the painting to keep it out of the public eye—it was the least she could do. But after Ford left with his car full of Vera's other things, Elaine emerged from her room, looking like the ghost of herself.

"Vera has evidence that Max is using you to pass his course," I said. Elaine just nodded, looking lost. "She's got evidence of a lot of other things, too," I continued, "but I can't be the custodian of it. I need to find her to give this back to her." I held the red handbag up between us.

"I think I know where she is," Elaine said quietly. "I can take it to her. I want Max brought down as badly as she does. Maybe even more. But obviously I've got to protect myself too."

"Can I trust you? If you're lying, Elaine, and you and Max are still together and you're under his thumb . . ."

"I promise, Frances." She looked me in the eyes then, and I saw anger, hurt, fear, but also a quiet determination that I'd

previously never seen in her before. "Let me take care of this. I've been passive for so long, I'd like to help."

"Okay," I said, and handed her the bag. "If you can't find her, and you don't want to be the person who has this amount of inflammatory evidence, come and talk to me. Ford will know what to do with it."

Elaine nodded and looped the bag over her shoulder. "Thank you," she whispered, and quietly disappeared back into her room.

After that I felt idle, sort of untethered. Days went by this way, until I had a shift at Benny's. It passed with me barely registering who came and went, and the sun set without me realizing it had started sinking in the first place. Just as my shift was ending, I looked to the door of the diner, and Ford was there. He was wearing a tan trench coat that instantly brought to mind Humphrey Bogart as Philip Marlowe. As suave and cultured as I'd always thought Ford was, neither of us really fitted into the world around us. He was old-fashioned for a young man, in a way that his peers probably thought rather strange.

I smiled at him, and he walked toward me with his hands in his coat pockets.

"It's Thursday night," he said. "Ronnie Scott's, remember?"

"Ah, sorry, I'd forgotten," I said.

"We don't have to go. I know you've only recently been dancing, and maybe a loud evening of jazz is the last thing on your mind."

"No, I'd welcome the distraction," I said. I gave him a genuine smile. He was starting to feel familiar, like a piece of home. Not like in Castle Knoll last year, when we seemed to always be tiptoeing around each other, wondering about motivations and following some unwritten social plan that in fact suited neither of us.

"Perfect," he said. "We'll have to hurry, though, and we'll

probably end up standing at the back, but it'll be a chance to let the music wrap around us and push all the other thoughts out of our minds." He smiled and looked more relaxed than I'd ever seen him.

"That sounds wonderful," I said. I waved to Benny and hung my apron on the peg in the kitchen. The night-shift girl would wear it now.

An hour into the set, when the sax was playing a melancholy tune so soulful that it bled into the cracks between the floorboards, the blond bouffant of Vera Huntington broke through the crowd at the bar.

"Vera?" I said, happy but confused to see her there. Then I took in her expression, which was wild-eyed and strange. She was out of breath, and her eyes were darting around the club, as if at any moment someone would emerge from the crowd and come for her. "What's wrong? Has something happened?" I took her by the arm and led her a little away from where Ford was standing.

"I got in over my head, Frances," Vera said. She was crying, and I'd never seen her cry.

"What do you mean?" I asked. I thought of all the documents in that handbag she'd tried to get me to keep for her. My eyes darted to her hands, which were empty, and back to her face. It occurred to me then that she must have more information, secrets that weren't written down, and that the papers in that handbag were just the tip of the iceberg.

"I shouldn't tell you any more," Vera said. "This is very much a curiosity-killing-the-cat kind of situation, Frances."

I watched Vera, my mind racing. I'd tried to reject my role as her secret keeper, but what if my unwillingness led to her getting hurt? I didn't want anything to happen to her, but I was also starting to fear for my own safety, my own involvement in this. I took a deep breath. Frances Adams might be the kind of person who is worried about a fortune predicting her own murder, but she's not a coward. A person can be watchful, clever, and cautious without being a bystander. "I can help you, but only if you tell me everything. I can't fix something I don't have all the pieces to."

Vera swallowed hard. "I'm sorry, Frances, I can't risk it."

That rang alarm bells in my mind. It spoke of larger problems than the essays in Elaine's handwriting. Now I was positive there were other secrets somewhere. Ones I hadn't found.

She talked nervously about needing friends in low places, someone else to help her so that she could keep me out of danger. But it all sounded like scared ramblings to me. If she had a secret about someone powerful, the most important thing she could do to protect herself was to let it out in the most significant way possible. Go to the papers, or someone high up in the police.

"Vera, tell me honestly—is someone threatening you? Is it your brother?"

"He'll kill me," she whispered.

There was a long pause. The solo finished and the delighted audience erupted, but I hadn't even realized the band was still playing. I was using a heartbeat's gap of time to come to a decision about myself. I truly was afraid of the terrible things in the world, the killers and abusers and people who made life on earth just that much worse for everyone else. But I wasn't too afraid to wage a battle against them.

The audience was quiet as sheet music was shuffled onstage, the musicians picking up their instruments again and filling their lungs, ready to set the mood with another number. The upright bass plucked an experimental string.

I turned to Vera and watched her expression change when she saw the determination in my face. "What if you got to him first?" I asked.

The music filled the club, and Vera stared at the stage, transfixed. "I could . . . You're right. What if I got to him first?"

I sensed that her mind was racing—she was miles away. I had the sudden worry that I'd set off a spark that had struck a powder keg within her. "Vera?" I prodded her gently. She started nodding as if I'd just said something significant, still watching the stage.

"I think . . . yes. Thank you, Frances. I forgot who I was for a moment there," she said. It was the second time I'd heard her say that, and something about it unsettled me. But we were quiet for the rest of the set, me watching Vera from the corner of my eye, and Vera transfixed by the musicians but clearly not seeing them at all.

She was quiet as we left the club, and Ford and I exchanged worried glances. He had been a discreet distance away while we talked, and it was loud in there. He could tell something wasn't right. The three of us walked through Soho toward where he had parked his car. He offered to give Vera a lift somewhere, even if it wasn't home, but she looked over at the nearest pub and shook her head. There were a few men outside it drinking and smoking, swaying slightly but in good spirits.

"No, there's someone I need to see," she said. And without saying good-bye, she walked over to the pub and caught the arm of a man I recognized.

"Ford, is that . . . ?"

"It is," he said, instantly knowing what connection I'd made. "That's the man who came to my house looking for Vera. Constable Folkestone, I think he was called."

"I'm surprised Vera trusts him, but then . . . she said she'd met him before. I mean, even before she went and talked to him at the police station, the morning after we went dancing. I wonder if she's known him for longer than she implied." Ford and I watched the two of them as Vera leaned toward the constable and talked urgently in his ear.

I quickly whispered the extent of what Vera had said to me.

"Well," he said when I'd finished, "if she's going to the police, that's probably a move in a positive direction. This may be the time to bow out, Frances."

I nodded slowly. Ford was making sense, of course, but something still didn't feel right.

"Let's get you home," Ford said, and gently pulled my arm.

I looked up at him and took a step closer, tucking myself against the shelter of his tall frame as we walked. "Can I stay with you?" I asked.

He smiled and turned to kiss my forehead. "Of course."

CHAPTER 20

I CALL MUM AS WE DRIVE, NEEDING TO MAKE SURE she's okay. I want her to know that Felicity was most likely targeted by Max, and that I know she gave all her money to the gallery in Knightsbridge. But I have so many questions crowding my mind that I almost can't remember why I'm calling. I take a breath and try to settle my thoughts, pushing down the emotions that come with discovering all these things and not having talked to her about any of them yet. She just needs to know that we're getting closer to finding out who killed Felicity and why, and that none of us are safe until we do.

"Annie?" She picks up straightaway, which makes the tightness in my chest loosen just a touch. "I can't talk right now, I'm with Sam," she says.

"Are you okay?" I ask. She doesn't sound like she's in trouble, but she doesn't sound completely herself either. Maybe she's still a bit angry from the other day, and I have to admit I've not tried to smooth things over. I've just gone into full murder-solving mode and chosen the company of Crane above everyone else because he's in the same mindset.

"I'm fine, I just— Meet me at the house in an hour, okay?" she says. "Sam and I are just on our way back. We'll talk then."

"Okay, Mum, but I've got some—" I hear the line go silent and know she's hung up. "Well, that's unhelpful," I say.

Crane and I reach the Chelsea house, and as we go through the front door, I feel the echoey silence of Mum's absence. It's funny, when she's home, she looms large in the house. The smell of paint, the shuffling of her feet as she paces while working, her music and the aroma of takeaway wafting through the rooms in equal measure . . . So when the house is empty, it's unsettling. The creaks and moans of the old building suddenly remind me that this house has a history, which Mum's personality drowns out most of the time.

"Let's go to my room. We can look at the file and I'll get out those papers I mentioned, along with the diary," I say as I walk upstairs. Crane follows me, but I see him casually looking into each room we pass, not out of nosiness but with that wary make-sure-everything's-clear police instinct he has. It gives me a reassuring warmth, with a touch of something else I can't really name. He's got the files from the back seat of his car—the old police file for Vera Huntington's murder, and the thin one that contains Felicity's phone records.

"Can I ask you something?" I say as we get to my room. I walk through the door and head straight to the vent where I've hidden the documents from the red handbag, but he leans against the doorframe with his hands in his pockets. I can tell he's still on high alert—his dark eyes are watchful, taking in the details of the room as well as tracking my progress unscrewing the vent while I balance on the chaise longue.

"Technically you just did," he says, and a corner of his mouth twitches upward.

"Cute," I say, my voice deadpan but my half smile mirroring his. I pull the papers and the diary carefully from the vent, then screw the cover back into place. "You can come in, you know," I say as I step down and wander over to the bed, perching on the edge.

"Wanting to get me at ease before you interrogate me? You learn fast," he says. But he pushes off the doorframe lightly and makes his way over to me.

"Can I get you some coffee or some water, sir? We're all friends here. This is just an informal chat," I say, repeating lines from just about every police procedural I've ever seen.

"No need for my lawyer, then?" he replies in kind, sitting next to me.

I raise an eyebrow and let my smile grow another fraction. "That depends. Do you have something to hide?"

He laughs lightly, but then his eyes dart to the file in his hands—the one at the top, with the phone records. He shuffles it behind Vera's file, which he opens to a faded newspaper clipping that reads, SOCIALITE AND HEIRESS VERA HUNTINGTON FOUND BRUTALLY MURDERED—HUSBAND ARRESTED. There's a picture of Vera wearing a fur coat and large diamond earrings, walking with her husband up the stairs to some gala or party, and the glamour of that photo under such a grisly headline just serves to make it an even more salacious news item.

"There's no mention of her being an artist," I murmur. "But, then, I suppose not a lot of people knew. I mean, other than her family and a small group of friends." This makes me think of Felicity and her career change from lawyer to artist. I've not even asked if there was a story about her in the papers. Or if she has family back in Castle Knoll, people who will be grieving for her.

"What did you want to ask me?"

"Oh, um . . ." Thinking of Felicity has made me feel strange, and a realization is dawning on me that has been growing for a long time. I've got this vague jealousy toward her, which doesn't suit me and I know it. I'm jealous that she might have had Crane's heart, even if she didn't keep it forever. And although I have his friendship, I see now in a flash of terrible clarity that it's not enough.

But the middle of a murder investigation is terrible timing to broach this topic. Especially when he might be grieving someone he once loved or, for all I know, still holds dear.

Following footsteps can lead to bad places—tread lightly, or not at all. Those words from my fortune start to buzz at the edges of my thoughts. Do they mean following in Felicity's footsteps? I suppose acting on any feelings I have for Crane might not be treading lightly. But am I the sort of person who can feel like this about someone and tread not at all?

Out of the corner of my eye I notice he's been watching me as I think through all this. I should face him and ask him more about how he feels investigating the murder of someone he once loved. Ask him if he's okay. But my eyes are fixed across from us, where the small canvas of Mum's that I pulled from the locked file drawer in Castle Knoll is sitting on the floor, resting lightly against the wall.

I lose myself in it for a moment. The red splashes of paint that form the curve of a disembodied heart practically shout at me. The brushstrokes are curious and familiar, but there's something new calling out to me. I've looked at countless reproductions of Mum's art, on posters and postcards at the Tate Modern gift shop, in originals in galleries and online. Mum's style is imprinted on my brain, but . . . something's off. Something in this painting is tugging at my memory, unpicking stitches that have been years in the making. The art I was looking at only hours before in the gallery, and in Felicity's wardrobe. The similarity suddenly strikes me, lightning quick. I have to be imagining this. I pray that I'm imagining it.

"Annie?" Crane is watching me stare at the painting. I've moved slightly forward without realizing it, and his hand reaches out gingerly to circle my wrist. In any other moment, I'd be thinking about how there's some significance in the way my heart is beating as I feel his fingers grip me in a gentle but firm way that is distinctively Rowan Crane. But my heart beats for conflicted reasons, as my eyes drift to the familiar hurried dashes of Mum's signature—her initials, *LFA*, Laura Frances Adams.

I turn to Crane. "I need to check something," I say, my voice shaking. "I really hope I'm wrong, but please can you just . . . not judge me if I am? Or, I don't know, if I'm right and I—" I'm babbling as I fumble for my phone, and Crane can sense that I've connected some dots that are emotional as well as case related. He nods, removes his fingers from my wrist, and hands me my phone from where it's lying on the bed.

I open the photos, flip to the portrait of Max Torrence, and zoom in on the bottom right corner. It's there, the same dimensions and shape I was expecting, just in a muted color so it didn't stand out when I was at the gallery. The artist's signature, three initials—*VFH*.

I can see it immediately now, how little it took to shift the *V* to an *L* and connect the top of the *H* to make it an *A*.

I still don't quite trust what my gut is telling me, but the facts are starting to stack up terribly. How, after her first explosive art show, Mum's future paintings never landed quite the same. How she's always been secretive about her process, never doing interviews, rarely talking about her inspiration for that first series, always focusing on what she wants to do next.

I look away from my phone and back at Crane, swallowing hard. "I know what Sam found in the house, what he took and sold. And it wasn't a diamond tiara."

CHAPTER 21

November 6, 1968

MY CONCERN FOR VERA STARTED TO EBB AS SHE RE-sumed her normal routine of shouting for Max out of the window of the sleek black car on Wednesdays. Whatever the constable had said to her after that night at Ronnie Scott's, she seemed confident again, and it was as if none of those fears had ever existed.

The change in her was so sudden that it had me wondering about what Ford had been told by Dr. Huntington at the party—that Vera was a pathological liar. I still didn't want to believe it could be true. Surely people weren't diagnosed with that sort of thing now. These weren't Victorian times, when an angry husband could tuck his wife into an asylum with a case of "hysteria."

After lectures I decided to call in at Professor Dane's office and ask him more about what signs might give away someone's loose relationship with the truth.

"Come in." The professor's voice sounded from the other side of the door after I knocked. "Frances"—his face brightened when he saw me—"how nice of you to drop in. Settling in okay? I've been impressed with the comments you've been making in class

lately, and I don't think it's breaking the rules if I tell you that your first essay went very well." He indicated a stack of papers near his elbow, recently marked.

"Thank you. That's a relief," I said. "I'm finding my feet, I think." He gestured to the chair across from his desk, and I took it. "In fact, I seem to be developing several side interests in psychology, and I wondered if I might ask you about one of them."

"Of course," he said. "If it's not my area of expertise, I can point you in the direction of another member of the academic staff who might help. Thinking of final projects already?"

"Something like that. I was wondering about personality disorders. Specifically, compulsive lying. Do you know much about the signs of it? Why someone might do it, and how to tell when they do?"

"Well, I know a bit. Personality disorders are relevant to my own research into why people kill. 'Compulsive liar' isn't in itself a diagnosis, but it's a symptom of a larger personality disorder. It could be a symptom of psychotic depressive reaction or psychosis. Actually, Max Torrence is doing a deep study of it. I see you sit together every day so I'm surprised he hasn't mentioned it. He did his case-study paper on the evolution of the polygraph and its uses in psychological experiments."

"He did?" I sat a bit forward in my chair. "I thought his paper was on the Asch experiments." My mind was racing through the handwritten notes I'd seen, with Elaine's words in the margin. She'd instructed Max that his essay would be on the Asch experiments, because she wanted to write on the Milgram device.

"You must be confusing him with your friend Elaine. She wrote a very thorough essay on the Asch case. Max has done some first-rate work looking at how polygraphs might be used to detect habitual liars."

"Interesting," I said. Maybe Max had changed his mind about

handing in someone else's work when he knew Vera was on to him. "Can you give me some practical examples of how pathological liars can be spotted?"

"Well, they are often inconsistent in their stories but never back down if confronted with the inconsistencies. They embellish with a lot of detail, so sometimes it's easier to spot a compulsive liar when they're supplying details that really aren't needed, given the subject matter. They'll often go to great extremes to protect their lies as well."

I was taking in each of these things, but while I was trying to compare them to Vera's behavior, it was Elaine who kept floating to the surface of my mind.

What if Max was doing his own work all along? I still didn't think his hands were clean—he had orchestrated Elaine's humiliation on a grand scale, but . . .

No. I was just turning over every stone looking for nefarious motives, and I'd run out of people to suspect, so now I'd come round to Elaine. She had, after all, given Vera the red handbag for me, just like she'd said she would.

After some more conversation and thoughtful questions from Professor Dane, I said good-bye and made my way back to my rented room. I spent the weekend going between shifts at Benny's and my room, and each time I came or went I knocked on Elaine's door. She never answered.

She'd missed lectures all the previous week, and I'd hoped that now things seemed to be settling down, she'd be back. We had only one lecture together, and that was Professor Dane's, which met twice a week—a lecture on Wednesdays and the seminar on Fridays. So on Monday when I left for Intro to Psychology and she didn't answer yet again, I spent that lecture feeling increasingly worried.

It was possible I was now growing a bit too paranoid, inventing danger when there wasn't any. But still, at the end of Monday I decided to see Ford.

He greeted me warmly when I arrived unannounced, yet I found myself on edge as I settled into a seat by the fire. The other night after Ronnie Scott's, when I'd asked to stay, there was a moment of tension as to what that might have truly meant. But I was rattled after talking to Vera, and so tired. I explained to Ford that I just wanted to be somewhere I felt safe. He said he understood, and he offered me the guest room.

As we sat next to each other on the sofa, he was close enough for me to feel the electricity between us, but with enough distance that I didn't feel like he was trying to cultivate a romantic moment. "You seem preoccupied," he said. When he noticed my hands were simply rotating the stem of the glass he'd given me, rather than sipping from it, he gently took it from me and set it on the end table. He put his hands over mine, and his expression took on a twinge of concern. "Frances?"

The doorbell sounded, and I jumped. Ford stayed where he was, giving my hands a gentle squeeze. "Mrs. Blanchard will answer. I'll tell her to dismiss whoever it is."

I nodded, grateful. I couldn't understand why I was so jumpy, but I felt as if I was on the edge of something bad, and that I didn't know nearly enough about the people around me to stay out of its way. The carefree London life I'd been enjoying so far was starting to wear thin around the edges, and the old Frances who worried about fortunes and murder was coming back to the forefront of my personality. I suppose I should have suspected this would happen. After all, I'd had this thought when I met Professor Dane on my first day and he'd mentioned he taught about the minds of killers. Even then, I'd thought to myself that no matter where I went, I couldn't outrun myself.

"It's Constable Folkestone again, my lord," the housekeeper

said, interrupting my thoughts. "Shall I tell him to come back later? He was asking for Miss Adams."

Ford looked at me, and I drew a deep breath, straightening my shoulders. "Let's speak to him," I said. "I'm curious about what he might want."

A moment later the constable entered, and my heart fell to my stomach when I saw he was holding Vera's red handbag.

"I have a message for you from Vera," the constable said. He held out the handbag, and I took it gingerly. "This is for you. She wants you to have it. She says don't try to give it to Elaine again."

"I . . . Very well," I said, confused. "She didn't say anything else? Is she all right?"

The constable merely shrugged and said, "I'll show myself out."

CHAPTER 22

*"I THINK I KNOW WHAT MIGHT HELP YOU FEEL A BIT more at ease," Ford said. I had taken up my wineglass again, and was drinking from it in such small sips and with such agitation that I felt like a confused hummingbird. Constable Folkestone's visit had unsettled me. And his message—*Don't try to give it to Elaine again. *Was that Vera threatening me? If I didn't keep her secrets, would there be trouble?*

"What do you think would help?" I asked Ford. "I'm willing to try anything. My nerves feel like a bundle of live wires."

He crossed the room and opened the rolltop desk in the corner. When he came back to sit next to me, he was holding a couple of notebooks and pens. He reached for the decanter that sat on the coffee table and filled his glass. "I think a proper investigation is what's needed," he said. "This is all a jumble right now, and when I feel like this in my life, I find that being organized and trying to make sense of things helps me feel more in control."

I looked into my glass and smiled. I knew then that Ford would never judge me for the way my mind worked, for the way I worried about things or let fear drive me sometimes. He saw the rational side of me, but he also saw the side that pushed ideas further than most people tended to let them go. He accepted all these things as strengths, as part of me, and not just eccentricities.

When I looked back at him, he was opening the notebooks and writing down key pieces of information, his brow lightly creased in concentration. After a moment, he noticed I was simply sitting there in the orange light of the fire watching him write. He straightened his shoulders and turned to me. "What?" he asked, and his face held an innocence I'd never seen in it before. As if, at last, his guard was completely down. His brown eyes were wide and soft, and the thick lashes that framed them added even more depth to the look he was giving me.

I set down my wineglass and leaned toward him, pausing as my nose brushed his. My smile broadened as I said, "Seeing you write everything down like that, diving headfirst into a quest to make sense of the problems I'm stuck in, all to help me feel more at ease . . . I think I can finally admit that I've fallen in love with you."

He dropped his pen as I kissed him. It wasn't the soft brief kisses we'd shared before, but a deeper kiss that asked for everything else he could give me. He carried me up the stairs to the bedroom, as if I was his bride in an old film, and we shut the door on the problems of the outside world and pretended we were the only two people who mattered.

It was the furious knocking on the bedroom door that woke me, tangled in Ford's sheets, with his breath gentle against my neck as he slept through the noise.

"Ford," I whispered, nudging him. Dim light struggled through the crack in the curtains—it had to be early morning.

The knocking sounded louder, and he blinked himself awake.

His first expression was one of satisfied happiness. But then the knocking sounded again, and he moved to get the dressing gown that was pooled on the floor next to the bed. He slipped it on as he padded to the door and opened it a crack.

His housekeeper was on the other side, looking nervous. "I'm so sorry to wake you, my lord. It's just—the morning news. There's been a bulletin I thought you'd want to know about right away. It's a terrible business." She whispered something to him that I couldn't hear, and he turned back to me.

"Frances, we should see this," he said, his voice serious. "Something was reported on the 8:10 bulletin that will play again at 8:55, which is in two minutes. Hurry, the television downstairs is already on."

I found my clothes as quickly as I could, though they were scattered about the room. We hurried downstairs and stood in front of the television, which was in a different sitting room in the house, one I'd yet to visit because it wasn't populated with books and picture windows. We stood rather solemnly waiting for the bulletin to play, with the smell of coffee being brewed in the background.

"It's the plague of vagrants in the city," a man was on the screen ranting, being led by the elbow toward a white stone building. "There's an epidemic of layabouts and criminals that haunt the Soho streets, sleeping rough and going after wealthy innocent women," he shouted into a microphone that was angled toward him. "You mark my words, they did this! I've worked my entire life to contribute to making a better society, cleaning up the streets, funding art, making sure our educated ideas aren't erased by the burden of people who waste their lives not appreciating them!" He dissolved into an inaudible jumble, and I finally recognized him.

"That's Vera's husband, Dr. Huntington," I said. "What's going on?"

The reporter finally flashed onto the screen, stone-faced and focused.

"If you're just joining us, that was a statement from Dr. Alasdair Huntington, husband of the murdered socialite Vera Huntington. Her body was tragically found in an alleyway in Soho yesterday evening, with her heart surgically removed. Her husband has willingly come in for questioning, but the body was discovered by local police and formally identified by the victim's brother, Max Torrence. The family are understandably devastated by their loss. Mrs. Huntington was described as being full of life and a joy to all those who knew her. The investigation is ongoing, and we will broadcast updates as they come in."

I sank onto the sofa, not quite believing what I'd just heard. I looked at Ford, feeling lost. He sat next to me, pulling me close to him, placing a kiss in my hair.

"Murdered, they said." I repeated the word from the news bulletin, fractured and half-remembered. "Missing her heart?" Tears constricted my throat, mixed with the rekindling of an old fear I thought I'd grown beyond—murder had lately become just a thing I studied in psychology books. But now Vera . . .

I choked back a sob, feeling selfish for how afraid I suddenly was. Vera was this magnetic, complicated, sometimes calculating but always interesting person. She was so many things, but would now be reduced to the facts we all examined in wondering who killed her.

I sat there and cried quietly, flipping through my memories of Vera like treasured photographs. Then I squared my shoulders and vowed to keep hold of all the bright and unique things Vera was, while fighting to find out what had happened to her. If everyone else was going to catalog her life to solve her death, like a puzzle, I would solve it using the genuine appreciation of our short time together, alongside my determination to find justice for her.

"That constable . . ." I said slowly. "He brought Vera's handbag back with the message that I wasn't to try to give it to Elaine again. What could it mean?" My hands were shaking and sweating at the same time. I wiped them on my crumpled trousers, my outfit from yesterday. It was all I'd had to throw on that morning. "She wanted me to hold on to those secrets, and I couldn't. I tried to give them back, and now this?"

"I'm so sorry, Frances," Ford said. "I know this is a terrible shock, but please don't blame yourself."

I shook my head, trying to recall what I might have missed about Vera's final night out. "The last person I saw her talking to was Constable Folkestone. But she implied the secrets she had were big ones." I turned to Ford while wiping my eyes. "What if the police aren't on her side? What if whatever Vera knew . . . if it was a secret about someone powerful, that person could have paid off the police."

Ford rubbed my shoulder gently, thinking. I appreciated yet again how united we were. He wasn't trying to convince me that I was overthinking this; he was considering my theory.

"It's worth talking to the constable again and asking him for more details about how that handbag came to be in his possession," he said.

"Do you think he could have killed her?" I asked.

Ford's face took on a look of concentration while he stared at the television, not taking in what was playing on it. "I think it's very possible," he said eventually. "That's the thing about powerful men—they get others to do their dirty work for them. And a member of the police is a good candidate for that. Find someone young who wants to advance in their career and make promises in exchange for their help in getting problems to disappear."

I nodded. "Do you think they'll even let us talk to him?"

Ford reached for my hand and squeezed it. "It's not only likely they will, but rather inevitable. And I want you to stick with me through this, Frances. I've got my lawyer on retainer."

"What do you mean, inevitable?" I asked.

"Because Constable Folkestone knows that you and Vera were not only close, but that Vera tried to let you in on what she knew. I think it's only a matter of time before they bring you in for questioning."

Something hardened in my stomach, like a stone. Dread or concentrated fear. Vera was worried that the secrets she'd found out would lead to someone silencing her, and they did. But not before she'd come to me.

So now I was just another problematic woman who could talk. I was a loose end, needing to be clipped.

CHAPTER 23

"WHAT DO YOU MEAN?" CRANE IS LOOKING AT ME INtently. We're still sitting on the bed in my room, and I've got Max's portrait open on my phone—the one painted by Vera Huntington.

I stand up and cross to where that small canvas of Mum's is still leaning, staring at us like judge and jury. I bring it back to the bed, where Crane takes it carefully.

"Look at Mum's signature—*LFA*." I point to the bottom corner. "With the right tools, an art restorer or skilled valuer could verify what I'm about to say, but . . . I'm almost positive that this signature was originally Vera's. Vera Huntington painted all the work that was in Mum's first collection." I swallow, feeling ill.

"Your mum . . . Are you telling me she's a fraud?" Crane asks, his voice dropping lower, reflecting the seriousness of the accusation.

I nod, my throat constricting as I put more pieces together. "I think that's why this one canvas was locked in Frances's files, along with other secrets." I swallow hard, trying to push down the burning sensation of tears creeping up my throat. I remember my fortune yet again. *Beware the heart kept in darkness. It will be death's catalyst if brought into the light without its proper name.* Had I done that? In taking this painting out of the depths of Frances's file cabinets, had I started a chain of deaths? Or was this all on Mum? These paintings were put into the world without Vera's name on them. Mum had done that, so was it Mum who death was coming for?

I breathe in deeply through my nose and out through my mouth, something I learned from a wellness video to stave off panic. "Frances's diary mentioned that among the things Vera left with her, there were countless canvases," I continue. My voice is still shaking with anger and shock, but I grit my teeth and focus on the facts. "Vera's husband, Alasdair Huntington, was controlling and possibly abusive. She worried he would destroy her things to break her spirit—he'd burned art of hers before."

"But why would Laura steal old art and say it was her own?" Crane asks. It's a testament to just how shocked I am that I'm only just realizing he's rubbing my back in slow circles, trying to calm me down. A flicker of heat spreads through me, and I feel more grounded. He continues, "Laura *can* paint; she's talented. Her later work proves that. The rest of her art wasn't plagiarized as well, was it?"

"No," I say. "The rest is genuine, but it makes sense now why those shows have always had mixed reviews. The most recent one did better because it was referred to as a revival of her old style." I let out a long sigh, but I feel a pinch in my chest that won't go away. "She only started really gaining traction in the art world again when she painted in a way that imitated those early works. A critic even said it in almost those exact words: 'This newest Laura Adams series is a throwback, proving that Adams only does well when it seems she's embodying a caricature of her old self.'"

I'm silently crying now, in that slow, grieving way where hot tears flow continuously while you try to push through and function in the moment. Crane is sitting close but isn't touching me now, and I have a flash of insecurity. Suddenly I feel extremely young next to him. In reality, I'm only five years younger, but this whole messy family drama, as well as his history with Felicity, is making me feel small. I mentally gather myself up as I realize I've been thinking only of me.

"Hey," I say gently, turning to him. "I never checked to see how you're doing . . . I mean, with everything that happened to Felicity. I know things were sort of history with you both, but you cared about her once, and I just . . ." I trail off as his features close down slightly.

"You don't have to worry about me," he says.

"I know I don't have to, but I'm choosing to," I reply quietly. "I mean, if you want to take some time, go back to Castle Knoll and talk to people there . . . Does she have any family? Or maybe, I don't know, this is the kind of thing people take some time out for, right? You don't have to push yourself to solve this. There are people on the case."

"You want me to go?" he asks, blinking at me with surprise.

"No! That wasn't what I was saying at all," I say, running a hand down my face in frustration. "I'm coming at this all wrong. I just, I don't want to be the biggest ego in the room. My problems aren't the only ones here and I'm just trying to say that I get it, if you need to sort through some feelings when it comes to Felicity."

He lets out a sigh as he looks down at the papers in his

lap. "I need to solve this case, Annie. There are things I should maybe explain about Fliss . . ." He sweeps his fingers through his hair, tugging at it in that frustrated way he does. "But I also don't want you to think I'm just this guy who does nothing but obsess over unsolved murders."

I flush. It's the first time he's ever suggested that he cares what I think of him.

He's looking straight ahead again, and I grab his chin and turn his face toward mine. His beard is soft under my fingers, and the intimacy of touching it feels overwhelming enough for me to drop my hand. "We aren't machines stuck in a loop of puzzles and clues. If I've learned one thing from Frances through her journals, it's that we doggedly pursue answers to these injustices because we care deeply about the people around us. Even the criminals—there are broken, twisted people out there who do unconscionable things, and finding who they are and why they've done what they've done provides a sense of order and closure that is extremely rare in this world." I blink at him and notice that he's looking at me with something akin to wonder.

"You don't . . . you don't think it's unhealthy that I have zero other hobbies?" he asks.

"I mean, it's probably unhealthy that it never occurred to me to ask if you have hobbies," I say, and he laughs weakly. "And I think it's maybe a bit strange on both our parts that we've gone from solving murders, straight to thinking we'd judge each other for obsessively solving murders."

"We don't really have an in-between, do we?" he asks.

"Do you have any hobbies?" I raise my eyebrows as I look at him, hoping he can tell that I'm trying to see the humor in this moment. "Painting small figurines in your downtime? Or are you secretly really into karaoke?"

He smiles and fidgets with the corners of the papers in his lap. "I'm actually very good at poker," he says. "And, um, I do a lot of long-distance running? But you knew that—you've seen me out running along the ridge."

I roll my eyes in a good-natured way. "Yes, the whole village is well aware that you've got the fitness of a gazelle. A very chiseled gazelle."

"Hey, now." He taps me lightly with the stack of papers. "There's nothing wrong with caring about your health . . ." He trails off, his eyes on the medical records next to me. "Actually"—he reaches for the pages and flips through them—"have you looked at these closely?"

"I've tried, but I can't make any sense of them," I say. "Google was no help either. If I search those medical terms, it just brings up even more medical terms I don't understand."

"I have a cardiologist friend I can call for some expert advice," he says, his eyes scanning the documents. "Can I take these?"

"Of course," I say. "Just let me make a note of the names of the patients in case it's important. Can you read them out to me? I'll write them in my phone."

"Adam Blaine, Xi Huang Li, Xavier Sandoval, Forrest Tims, Susan Folkestone . . ." He's flipping through the pages.

"Did you say Folkestone?" I pause as I tap it into my phone. "That name sounds familiar. I think . . ." I grab Frances's diary and leaf through it. "I think that name is in here . . . There." I point to an open page. "That's the same surname as the constable who visited Frances and Ford in Chelsea. The one Vera went to when she was afraid her husband would hurt her. Could that be a connection?"

Crane looks at the pages intently. "It's worth checking up

on," he says slowly. "Because, Annie, all of these people were patients of Dr. Huntington. But more significantly"—he points to a line in the paperwork that I'd overlooked in the complexity of all the medical terms, a line that says *cause of death*—"all of them died on his operating table."

CHAPTER 24

THE SOUND OF THE FRONT DOOR SLAMMING ECHOES through the house, and I jump. Crane is on his feet so fast I don't see him move, and he's standing at the crack of the open bedroom door in a way that looks like police training is kicking in. He's got his shoulder angled to the gap, so his chest is still facing the inside of the bedroom, but he's looking down the hall, scanning the space for threats. If this were an American police drama, he'd have a pistol in his hands held down near his waist, ready to aim at the first sign of an intruder.

"Annie?" Mum's voice comes from downstairs, but Crane doesn't relax his stance. Her voice sounds panicked, shrill.

"Mum?" I call out. I move from the bed and approach the door. I have to nudge Crane to one side with a look that says, *It's my mum, calm down*. Finally he relents, but he's barely a breath behind me as I head down the hallway and to the stairs. I've instinctively grabbed everything off the bed and am clutching the files Crane brought—as well as the papers from Vera's handbag and Frances's diary—as if someone is already trying to pry them out of my hands.

I see Mum just inside the hall, her face ashen. "Oh, good," she says when she sees Crane. "I'm glad you're here."

"Are you okay? Has something happened?" Crane asks. He edges around me and descends the stairs toward Mum, leaving me to take up the rear.

"There's another animal part on the steps," she says, her voice decidedly less breezy than before. "I don't think the neighbor's cat is doing this. This is . . ." Mum trails off and moves away from the door so Crane can open it.

I look at her, partly because I'm concerned, partly because I have so many questions to ask her, and also because it means I don't have to see the bloody mass laid before the front door. Crane crouches, and I can tell he's examining the thing closely but not touching it. He takes out his phone and makes a call, then starts snapping photos.

"It must have been put here in the last hour or so," I say. "Crane and I haven't been back that long. Is . . . uh . . . is Sam with you?" I ask.

"He had somewhere to be, so he dropped me off," she says.

"Where, exactly?" I ask.

"Don't start this again, Annie," Mum says, exasperation replacing the fear in her voice.

My hand finds the sore spot at the back of my neck, and I take a deep breath. She's right. This isn't what I need to be focusing on. There are bigger conversations that Mum and I need to have, about her art, her past, her choices. Crane finishes photographing the bloody front steps and comes inside, closing the door and locking it.

"There's not a lot we can do about that animal part," Crane says, "but I'll put a call into the station to log repeated threatening behavior."

I nod, but I'm looking at Mum, trying to find a way into the horrible conversation of whether or not she faked her entire art career. "Can we go into the kitchen?" I ask. "There's something more important I need to ask you. About your early paintings," I add. "About where they really came from."

And it's like a hammer falls between us. Mum's face crumples and she closes her eyes, breathing deeply. A few seconds pass, then a few more, and Mum doesn't open her eyes. She knows exactly what I'm talking about. And I know now that I'm not grasping at nothing. There's truth to be uncovered here, and I'm not going to like it.

Finally she opens her eyes, and they're watery and tired. "Let's get a drink. And I'll answer any questions you have," she says weakly. "Perhaps letting it all out will free up something that's been knotted inside me for decades." She exhales, her shoulders falling.

We walk into the kitchen, where Mum reaches into a cupboard. She pulls out three mismatched glasses and a half-empty bottle of single malt. She pours two fingers into each of the glasses, then hands one to me and one to Crane. The glass she's given me was once a Nutella jar, and Mum's drinking from a pint glass she stole from the pub up the road. She's given Crane the only proper Scotch glass in the house, and for a moment I imagine Ford Gravesdown sipping from it in front of his fireplace fifty years ago.

The three of us sit around the table, and Mum takes a long drink, draining her glass. She fills it again and takes a smaller sip.

"Go ahead," she says finally. "Ask." Her voice is rough

from the Scotch but holds a hint of bitterness. She doesn't want to talk to me about these things, but I sense she needs to, now that I've hinted that I know.

I clear my throat after taking a sip from my own glass. The burn of the alcohol feels unwelcome, but the discomfort is somehow fitting—harsh flavors for a harsh moment.

"I found things in Felicity's room that relate to a woman who was murdered in the sixties named Vera Huntington," I say evenly. "Through some digging, and comparing her signature and art style to yours, Mum . . ." I swallow, unable to finish my sentence. Once I say the words, there will be no taking them back. But I have to know. "Did you pretend that Vera's art was your own, back in the nineties? Was all of your early work done by someone else?"

Mum looks down at her glass for a long time. When she looks back up at me, the moisture in her eyes has become tears, and they've traveled in streaks down her face. She wipes at them absently with the back of her hand.

"The first thing you need to know," she says, "is that I never condoned the sale of those paintings under my name. Sam found them when you were about a year old, Annie, up in the attic along with some other random things. Lots of it was junk, but there were some cool vintage items—a Chanel beaded gown, a handbag, things I thought Frances wore in the sixties when she and Ford were first married. Most of those things went back into the attic, because I expected Frances might want them eventually."

"Was there a diamond tiara?" I ask. I don't want to get her off the subject, but I need to know if she or Sam ever found it.

Mum shakes her head. "No, nothing like that. No jewelry at all, but quite a lot of canvases. Really arresting art. I was struck by the talent of the artist. Sam brought all the canvases down to the living room, and we lined them up like a museum exhibition. We talked about contacting Frances, finding out who the artist was, and maybe seeing if we could show them and bring some attention to whoever it was."

I sip my drink slowly, and by now the potent flavor of the whisky is warming as it hits my tongue, rather than abrasive. Crane hasn't touched his, and I notice he's sitting where he can see the door to the kitchen and is listening, but also watching our surroundings carefully. He's still locked in police mode, and I feel the hair on my arms prickle. Crane has good instincts, and if he's on alert, we should all be worried. I set my glass down.

"Sam took the canvases to a broker the next morning, before I was even out of bed. I came down and they were gone, but I wasn't worried. He told me he'd tracked down the artist and that they were really excited to hear that those paintings hadn't been lost. Sam had this very intricate story—just full of detail on who he was, his life, why he never made it as an artist. I just, I believed it all. It took weeks for it to come out that he'd changed the signatures and sold them as my work. But he pleaded with me, saying it was money for our life together, and for you, Annie, so that we wouldn't always have to live like squatters in Aunt Frances's house."

"Why was he so sure that the real artist wasn't going to see the paintings and sue you both?" Crane asks. His eyes are briefly on Mum, then back on the door.

Mum sighs. "Sam has always been bold like that. He acts as though he's untouchable, and then it's like a self-fulfilling prophecy—the rest of the world doesn't touch him. Sam said that if anyone tried to accuse us of stealing the art, there was nothing they could do to prove I hadn't painted it. No paper trails, no history attached to it. Sure, some expert could probably have proved they were a few decades old, but who was going to do that? Who had any reason to doubt they were mine? We argued and argued, but those paintings became a sensation almost overnight. The amount of press and money . . . I wanted to come clean about them, I really did." She gives me a pleading look, willing me to understand. I'm not sure how I'd feel if I were in her place. A lie, once out in the world, just gets bigger with each telling. There had to be a point where she felt she was in too deep to go back.

"What did Frances say? She had to have known. She'd have recognized those paintings," I say, my voice neutral but my emotions bubbling just under the surface. I'm starting to feel betrayed, too—those images, the abstract renderings of urban spaces being reclaimed by nature, I'd always associated those with Mum. I'd felt like they were a part of her. I'd grown up seeing them all the time—they were printed on postcards in train stations; reproductions were often framed in office buildings. I think there was even one on the wall in the dentist's office I went to. The thought that they were never hers, always Vera's . . . I felt I was losing part of the Mum I knew. The woman sitting across from me was being replaced with some stranger.

Mum takes another sip and nods. "Things between me and Sam disintegrated rapidly, I filed for divorce and custody of you, and Frances supported me. She told me about Vera. We were going to go to the press together and confess everything, and tell Vera's story to put everything right."

"But you didn't," I say, and my voice grows sharper, surprising even me. My whole body feels like a shattered window, like I was flimsy and transparent before, and someone has come along and exploited my fragility by throwing a big rock. "Why?"

"Because I started getting phone calls, horrible ones. Someone would call and they'd threaten me. They'd disguised their voice with one of those modulators and they'd threaten to come and cut my heart out." Her hands are shaking terribly now, and one of them hovers over her eyes as a tear falls onto the table. "Even worse, they threatened you, too, Annie. You were only a year old, so they had to have been watching us. I was terrified. When they said that if I gave up all the money from the sale of the paintings, they'd stop threatening me and wouldn't expose me, I agreed. They sent an emissary, a man for me to deal with to get everything in place. He was the only person I ever saw or spoke to in person, and he arranged for me to transfer the funds to an art gallery under the ruse of a donation. He told me that if I ever tried to sell Vera's art as mine again, the threats I'd had over the phone would be made real. So I never did. Everything else I've ever tried to sell has been my own work, I swear."

"Were there other canvases left in the house?" Crane asks.

Mum nods. "Only a few. They didn't fit with the other series. The portrait you found in Fliss's room, and a few smaller canvases that were the more visceral reds, the ones that look like hearts. The other series, the one Sam sold as mine, had more canvases and continuity, so I think that's why he took those and left the reds behind."

"The ones Felicity's body was found lying on in the skip," I say.

Mum simply nods again.

"But you're imitating that series now, aren't you?" I ask. "The reds and human-heart motif, isn't that derivative? Flying a bit too close to the sun, given the threats you've had in the past?"

Mum sniffs, but she straightens her shoulders and looks

at me. "If you look at my work, really *look* at it—you'll see it's very different from Vera's. The heart theme is something I need to paint to cleanse my conscience, to make something my own while paying homage to someone whose shoulders I've stood on unfairly. The new series I'm painting is a soul-searching project for me, Annie, and I won't have you accusing me of being derivative."

There's a weighty silence in which I decide it'll take time for me to truly understand and come to terms with what Mum has been telling me. Then I remember the bloody thing on the porch and feel a sting of horror. Time might not be something we have, if Crane and I don't figure out who killed Felicity and why.

"This emissary you talked to," I say slowly. "Was his name Max Torrence?"

Mum blinks, then gets a faraway look on her face, trying to remember. "No . . . no, I don't think he was called Max. I think his first name was Brian or something, but he mostly used his surname. It was the name of a town, I think, like Ferndown or Farnham or something."

"Folkestone," Crane says suddenly, and he meets my eyes.

"Yes, that's it. That was his name," Mum says. "Brian Folkestone."

CHAPTER 25

"SO WHERE DO WE GO FROM HERE?" I ASKED FORD. I'D got out the red handbag and checked its contents—only to find that the earlier documents pertaining to the Torrence family had been removed. All that remained were the medical records, and I couldn't make head or tail of those.

"I think we should talk to Elaine," Ford said. "The return of that handbag missing those papers . . . The message the constable gave has to be significant in some way. He mentioned Elaine, and there's no reason he'd know her . . . unless Vera really did tell him about her."

I nodded. "That's right. Elaine said some things to me the other day that aren't adding up, about the work she did for Max. And those notes are missing now. I'd thought she wrote Max's essay, and she corroborated that version of events. But when I talked to Professor Dane last week, he said Max had submitted a different paper. I don't think Elaine really was doing his work for him, but she wanted it to look as if she was."

"You think she was trying to set him up? Some kind of revenge

for the stunt he pulled with that nude painting of her?" Ford asked.

"Potentially," I said. "But, if so, she was pretty clumsy about it."

Ford gave me a conspiratorial smile. "Not everyone has intricate minds like ours—people may plot revenge and try to get away with murder, but not everyone will succeed."

I smiled back at him, embracing the dark undertone of the conversation and enjoying the fact that Ford would see the gallows humor developing within it. "Then let's hope that the two of us never feel the need to commit murder. If we decided to work together, no one could stand in our way."

"And we'd absolutely get away with it," Ford added. He laughed, and I rolled my eyes good-naturedly.

"Just imagine if I had that line in my fortune completely backward. The fortune-teller said, All signs point to your murder. *I honestly can't see myself killing anyone, but what if that was really my fate? I was destined to murder someone, instead of be murdered myself."*

Ford and I walked toward the hall, and he helped me into my coat. "I think the trouble with fortunes," he said, "is that the interpretation can change with every new piece of information."

"Do you think I'm working too hard to unravel the meaning of mine?" I asked.

"No, on the contrary—you turn those words around from every angle, which makes you see more than most people. You look round the edges of things, Frances, and that's one of the many reasons I love you." He let those words hang in the air, and his cheeks flushed. I smiled back at him, because now it felt as if the two of us had really clicked into place. I'd told him yesterday evening that I was falling in love with him, not expecting him to say it back but hoping nonetheless.

He reached for his hat, almost shy now. "And the ancient Greeks would approve of your thinking as well," he continued. "The greatest fortune-teller in history was the Oracle of Delphi. And do you know what was inscribed on a column at her temple?"

"'Know thyself,'" I said.

"That's the most famous, but there were two more. The one that applies best to you is 'Surety brings ruin.' I'd like to think it means that the more inquiry you apply to your life and those around you, the safer you are from your own downfall."

Ford swung open the front door. Outside was a woman in a neatly pressed police uniform, with her hand raised as if she was seconds away from knocking. For a fraction of a moment we all stared at one another in awkward silence, but then she spoke. "Frances Adams? I need you to accompany me to the police station, please, for questioning in the murder of Vera Huntington."

Ford and I exchanged a look. He'd been right—it was only a matter of time until they called for me.

"Very well," I said. "But I'd like Lord Gravesdown to accompany me."

"And Miss Adams will have her lawyer present," Ford added.

"There's no need for that," the woman said. "This is just routine, to get information about Vera from her friends and the people who saw her last."

"Then it shouldn't matter if we bring a lawyer," Ford said, and smiled. "We'll be at the station once we've made that call. There's no need for a police escort."

The woman looked taken aback, which told me that Ford had made the right choice in telling her we'd bring a lawyer. If this really was a voluntary questioning, they'd have set up an appointment time and simply asked me to be there. This woman had been sent to the house to collect me, whether I wanted to go or not. She was simply reluctant to use those words.

Vera's husband would have been questioned at the station for some time now. Given his power and influence, games were likely being played that Ford and I couldn't see. If Constable Folkestone really was in the pocket of either Vera's husband or her father, it was entirely possible that scapegoats were being found, if they hadn't been already.

"I'm afraid that won't be possible," the woman said. "You're to drive with me to the station. Miss Adams is a person of interest in the murder of Vera Huntington."

She'd finally said it—I was the person being thrown under the bus for this. My heart started to pound, but Ford took my hand and held it firmly. The worrying pulse dimmed to background noise.

"You'll kindly wait here, then, while I phone Miss Adams's lawyer. Then we'll both travel with you," Ford said tersely.

"Miss Adams will come with me, and you are welcome to make your calls and follow, but my orders were clear. Collect her, and her only."

Ford squared his shoulders and took a calm step toward the woman. "I'm sorry, but it seems you're trying to get away with not following proper procedure. If Frances is a person of interest, her giving information is voluntary. Unless she's arrested—and you'd need to have evidence linking her to Vera's murder in order to do so, which I'm certain you don't," Ford's voice was rising, his words more sharply articulated with each sentence.

"Are you refusing to comply, Miss Adams?" The police officer turned to me, and there was a challenge in her eyes.

I looked at Ford, but he hadn't taken his eyes off the constable.

"I am," I said after a pause. "It's as Lord Gravesdown said. You can't arrest me unless you have evidence, right?"

"We need reasonable suspicion," the woman said smugly.

"Which you've just given me. Frances Adams, I am arresting you on suspicion of the murder of Vera Huntington. You do not have to say anything . . ."

I looked at her in horror, unable to believe what was happening. I'd accepted this was a possibility; that possibility felt like telling myself a story from a film or a novel. And now someone really was pointing the finger at me to save themselves. They might have even planned ahead and already laid a trail of breadcrumbs that led right to my door.

The woman was still speaking, but I barely registered her words. She had a hand on my arm and was leading me down the steps toward a waiting police car. ". . . but it may harm your defense if you do not mention when questioned something which you later rely on in court. Anything you do say may be given in evidence."

Ford was behind me, and he met my eyes before I was nudged into the back seat. "I'll be right behind you, and I'll have a team of lawyers in tow."

I gritted my teeth and tried to muster my best brave face. "Thank you," I said.

As the police car drove off, I tried in vain to hold in the emotions threatening to bubble over, but out they came. I found myself crying horribly—out of fear, grief, and anger at the whole messy situation. Vera had been my friend. She might have been a conflicted woman, but she didn't deserve the horrible fate she had been handed. A fate that I was supposedly due to share eventually.

I shuddered as I sobbed in the back of the police car, feeling so alone and afraid. Perhaps this was how it all started. Perhaps this was the start of my "slow demise." I thought of the line from my fortune: Your slow demise begins right when you hold the queen in the palm of your hand. *My mind flashed to when I had held the diamond tiara Vera had included among the things she'd wanted me to keep for her. Was that the moment? Or had it been earlier, holding a different type of queen? Ford's chess piece, or a queen from a deck of cards? Would I ever know?*

Ford had said I was clever because I never settled into one interpretation of my fortune. It felt less like a compliment now. Thinking too much around the edges of things, as he put it, was just another way of getting oneself into trouble. Vera's words from the night she died suddenly sliced through me like a knife.

This is very much a curiosity-killing-the-cat type of situation.

CHAPTER 26

"I NEED TO LIE DOWN," MUM SAYS, CLOSING HER EYES.

If I'm honest, I don't want to talk much more with her either, but there's something I can't understand. "Fine, but I need you to answer one more question," I say.

She doesn't open her eyes but groans. "Sam," she says.

"Exactly. Why the hell would you ever let that man back into your life?" I ask, my voice a mixture of incredulity and outrage.

"I know you probably won't understand, but I'd been sinking under the weight of those lies for so many years," she says. She opens her eyes, and they're bloodshot and tired. "I'd forced Sam out of my life when everything to do with the paintings was finally settled, the money was gone, and I knew we'd be safe. I never told Frances about the threats. I think she saw my gallery donation as me paying penance, and she approved of it. I felt there was no need to tell her anything else, and she let us stay in her house because I think she felt that I'd balanced the scales. And she had believed that this was Sam's doing, not mine."

She draws in a shaky breath, and her features pinch with the thoughts going through her mind. "But I felt so isolated for so long, Annie. Every time I tried to date or have any kind of a life, I couldn't fully let go and let anyone in. I lived in constant fear of being exposed. It's been my own personal purgatory. Sam got in contact when he saw your name in the papers, when you solved Frances's murder and inherited. He admitted it was bad timing for him to get back in touch, that he understood if I thought he was just trying to get close to me again because of all this money coming our way. But he insisted he had so many regrets, he was tired of trying to stay away, and he missed me. He missed you, too—not knowing you has really eaten him up, Annie. I suppose it did help that Frances never liked him, and now she was gone."

I clamp my jaws shut, deciding not to add any commentary to that. My dad wasn't barred from seeing me for all these years—as far as I know there wasn't any kind of restraining order or legal document prohibiting him from contact. He could have sent me a card on my birthday, or asked to visit at Christmas, or *anything*. I've been here all this time. I'm not hard to find.

But then I think about Mum and decide to let her make excuses for Sam if she wants to. She's in danger, whether she understands the extent of it or not, and is crumbling under the weight of a huge confession right now. Her gray curls are coming loose from the scarf she's tied them up in—today's is a friendly blue. The lines on her face deepen, like cracks in a sunbaked desert, as she cries quietly. Interrogating her about my dad isn't going to build a bridge right now. It'll push her further away.

I place my hand over hers. "I'm sorry you've been feeling

so alone," I say. "I wish I'd known, so you didn't have to deal with this on your own all these years."

She breathes deeply. She gives me a weak smile and squeezes my hand in return. "Thank you, Annie," she says. "I appreciate that." She braces her hands on the kitchen table and pushes herself up, swaying slightly. "I'm going to lie on the sofa for a bit, but if you need anything, wake me."

She shuffles out of the room, and I feel a pang as I notice that she looks years older. Sharing her secrets hasn't made her feel any lighter. I think she's sunk under the weight of my disappointment. I make a promise to myself to look at her new series in the basement again soon, to really look at the paintings this time, in light of what I know about Vera and the other art I've seen.

Crane moves his chair closer to mine, leaning in so he can speak quietly. "You gave your mum some grace there," he says.

I look at the whisky that remains in my glass and decide to leave it. "Yep," I say, aware that my response sounds clipped and childish.

"I can see why you did. But, Annie, your dad . . ."

"I know," I say. I look at the empty doorway Mum just shuffled through. "There's a nest of lies we've yet to uncover about Sam. Or am I being paranoid?" I give Crane a genuinely questioning look, because I'm starting to doubt myself. I'm biased when it comes to Sam. I thought I wasn't angry about not growing up with a dad, and I think that's still true. But what I *am* angry about is how expertly he's manipulated Mum.

"I don't think you're being paranoid," Crane says. "Sam never made contact with you. Was there a legal reason?"

"No, and you read my mind. He could have sent a card or

phoned, if he didn't want to run into Mum. But it was like he didn't exist."

"So I don't buy that he's been eaten up with grief at not seeing you all these years," Crane says. "If he didn't contact you, there might have been a reason he's hiding."

"Other than the classic one of not giving a shit about being a dad?" I retort.

Crane gives me a small nod of understanding, indicating I'm justified if I want to be snarky. "Other than that one, yeah," he says. "He could have been in hiding."

"Hiding from what? Like he pulled a large con and had to go underground? This isn't *Ocean's Eleven*, and you've met the man. He's not *that* clever," I say. But then something from Frances's diary comes back to me. It was gnawing at me while Mum was speaking, and it's finally floated to the forefront of my mind.

"Something's just occurred to you," Crane says, interested.

I laugh lightly. "I do love that you can read my face so well. But yes. Frances was studying psychology, and she specifically looked into pathological liars. She went to her professor and asked how you might spot them. She took a lot of notes in that diary, and two things Mum said about Sam stood out to me. One was that he lied blatantly to her, saying he'd found the creator of the paintings and that they were dead. He used lots of detail, embellished the backstory considerably. This was something Frances learned that compulsive liars do. But then I thought of the other things Frances was learning, about why people kill. The sense of being untouchable, of being owed something by the world, of wanting to get revenge on people who have wronged them . . ."

Crane's eyes are scanning the room, and I know he's

thinking quickly, putting together pieces of a puzzle in his mind.

"Sam came back into your mum's life and was shortly followed by Fliss. What if . . ." Crane rubs his wrist where his watch strap sits, frustrated. "What if Fliss found out Laura's secret and was planning to expose her? That would explain those paintings in the skip. If she was heading out with them to prove to the world that Laura Adams was a fraud, and Sam killed her to protect Laura's secret, he might have had to flee the scene before he could do anything with those paintings. They just ended up in the skip so he could get away quickly."

Crane has just introduced the idea of my father as a killer, but all I feel toward Sam is anger and mistrust, so I honestly think it's a plausible theory.

"Felicity's last words to you were 'I've made a terrible mistake,'" I say. "Maybe she initially thought about exposing Mum, then changed her mind and tried to get rid of any of Vera's remaining canvases. But then . . . why is someone still leaving threats? Those animal parts . . ." I shudder.

Crane rubs his forehead, frustrated. "You're right, it doesn't quite fit. I feel like we're missing something. All those connections to the gallery in Knightsbridge, and Fliss having her only sculptures displayed there . . ."

"Maybe we should look into the Folkestone connection," I say. "If he was the middleman who brought Mum's money to the Knightsbridge gallery, it proves that the gallery is the key to all this. It's where everyone's paths seem to converge."

"Let's go, then," Crane says. "But wait just a minute while I clear the bloody thing off the front step so you don't have to see it."

"Thanks," I say.

I pick up the files that Crane had set on the table, ready to bring them along. Absently, I open the newer folder—the one with Felicity's phone records in it. Lists of numbers with durations of calls and dates are in one long spreadsheet, most of it just washing over me as my eyes scan. A lot of them say *unknown caller*, or names I don't recognize.

I stop short when I see *Rowan Crane*. And it's not only on the day she died, like he said. That call is there, too, of course, but it's the other times his name comes up that have my heart pounding. They spoke a week before she died for just over half an hour. And then again a few days before, another lengthy call. All in all they spoke nine times over the last six weeks. Something I didn't think possible happens: My trust in Rowan Crane cracks.

I hear him call my name from the front door, and I swallow hard. "It's all clear now. Are you coming, Annie?"

I close the file and take a deep breath. "On my way," I say.

I try hard to neutralize my expression as I join him in the foyer. I don't know if I'm convincing, but I've got to try to keep calm, at least until I work out what I've just seen.

Because I can't fathom why Rowan Crane, the most steadfast person I know and who I trust more than anyone, would lie to me.

CHAPTER 27

JUST BEFORE WE LEAVE, WE MAKE MUM PROMISE NOT to answer the door to anyone except me or Crane.

"But my broker is coming to pick up the art for the new show," she says. "He'll be in and out. He's harmless, I promise. I've worked with him for my whole career."

"His name isn't Max Torrence, is it?" Crane asks, raising an eyebrow. I try not to look at him, because I can still see his name all over Fliss's phone records.

"No," Mum says, her voice weary. "Annie knows him. His name is Bob, and she's met him several times."

"That's true," I say. "Bob's all right. I dated his son briefly, back when I was a teenager." I don't know why I added that detail—it just sort of slipped out.

Crane gives me a look I can't decipher.

"What? I didn't exactly sit at home on my own throughout my teens, especially not when Mum had endless invites to all the cool art shows. In 2012 I had an embarrassing thing for hipsters."

"I'll bet you did," Crane mutters, but his voice is good-natured. Even ten minutes ago I'd have said something coy right back, but now I just bite my lip and look to the door. "All right," he adds, "Bob the broker can collect the canvases, but don't answer the door to anyone else."

"I won't," Mum says, and returns to her napping pose on the sofa. Looking at her, I realize I'm possibly using Crane's lies about Felicity to distract me from the bigger issue I'm facing—the fact that my mum lied in a far more monumental way, for years, to the entire world as well as to me. I sigh inwardly. So what if Crane didn't tell me he was talking to Felicity? He's entitled to his own romantic entanglements. What do I care?

I care a lot, it turns out. But I need to care more about Mum and what she's facing now, because I don't think that whoever killed Felicity is planning on leaving her alone.

Crane calls his cardiologist friend while we drive. I catch only small pieces of his side of the conversation, as my thoughts spin around one another and threaten to fire up emotions I've left dormant for years in a gold medal–winning bout of repression.

"Perfect, thanks for making that call," Crane says, and hangs up. It's then that I see we aren't heading toward the gallery but are battling the traffic on Euston Road.

"Are we not . . . ?"

"Detour," he says. "My cardiologist friend came through. There's an expert in the pathology department at University College Hospital who is happy to consult on the cold case of Vera Huntington." Crane gives me a quick look before turning his eyes back to the road, and I catch a small spark of excitement there.

"You think there's something in those medical records that can give us some answers?" I ask. I admit, it's nice to be back on the trail of something that doesn't entirely have to do with the duplicity of my family members.

Crane pulls off Euston Road and into the basement car park of UCH. We get out, and he extends his hand for the files I'm clutching. I quickly shuffle Vera's file over Felicity's, in a rather obvious embodiment of burying a problem I don't want to think about. *HUNTINGTON, VERA* is printed in bold letters at the top, and the folder is thick, with dog-eared pages. I've also stuffed the diary and the contents from the red handbag into a canvas tote I grabbed from the coat stand in Mum's foyer as we left.

"The medical records from the handbag might hold some answers," Crane says, "but I also want a modern expert's eyes on the autopsy of Vera Huntington. I don't have Felicity's to compare it with, but I've read through this file, and some things about the case don't feel quite right to me."

"Then by all means lead the way," I say, and we head to the hospital lifts.

Eventually we're sitting in a large, brightly lit laboratory. One wall is lined with microscopes, another with computers, and the middle section holds several long metal gurneys that are thankfully unoccupied. I might be upping my frequency of seeing dead bodies, but that doesn't mean I want to invite myself to autopsies.

"Well, I have to say we've come a long way with autopsy procedures in the past few decades," the pathologist says, scanning the file. His name is Kabir, and he's surprisingly young and attractive for a pathologist. I don't know what I expected, but it wasn't a man fresh out of medical school with the physique of a mountain climber and cheekbones that could cut glass.

Crane shifts in the office chair he's been given, making its wheels squeak. Kabir has decided to speak primarily to me, and I don't have the heart to explain that I am not, in fact, a law enforcement officer. Mercifully, Crane hasn't mentioned this either, and I'm enjoying being treated as someone who has actual qualifications in this field. It makes me more confident in my line of questioning.

"Is there anything that stands out to you in this autopsy?" I ask. "Anything that nowadays would have been investigated further, or work that might be done differently?"

Kabir takes a moment to flip through the pages from the file, and pauses when he's near the end. "Is there another page to this? There's a physical sign noted here that should have warranted taking tissue samples from the remaining organs."

"What physical sign?" I ask.

"Her teeth and gums show signs of heavy metal poisoning." He points to a sentence that hangs on its own in the document, like it's been added as an afterthought by the coroner. "A blue line is visible on the gums when there's been prolonged exposure to lead, or possibly mercury. Unless her husband was intentionally poisoning her while planning to remove her heart . . . But he was a surgeon. He'd know better than to use something so easy to spot."

"Dr. Huntington was convicted on the strength of the medical evidence," Crane says. "The manner in which her heart was removed matches surgical techniques that he pioneered. The doctor was also particular about the type of nylon thread he used to make sutures. He was the only surgeon in the area who used it. The thread and the style of the stitches used to close Vera's chest matched Dr. Huntington's methods."

Kabir flips back through the earlier pages, to the police reports and investigation. "It says chloroform was found near the body, with gauze soaked in it, but no one tested her liver or kidneys to see if there were still traces of it in her system. That wasn't always common practice back then, those tests were expensive to run, but in a high-profile case such as this . . ." His brow furrows. "I suppose they felt they wouldn't find any, as chloroform leaves the body quite quickly." He pauses. "Cause of death is listed as removal of her heart, but because of the signs of poisoning, I think we can question whether the victim was dead before her heart was removed."

"You think she could have already been dead when he removed her heart?" I ask.

Kabir nods slowly. "It's very possible."

"Which would throw doubt on the doctor's case, even if he did remove her heart after she died," Crane says.

"He still could have poisoned her," I say.

"But a trial was held," Crane says. "And a conviction made on this cause of death could be overturned in light of new evidence." He looks at Kabir. "If I get an order of exhumation for the remains of Vera Huntington, would it be possible to run tests to see if lead poisoning was a significant factor in her death?"

"Yes, I'd say that's possible. It would be present in her bones," Kabir says. "Her teeth might show signs of it, too, though the dental records in this file don't indicate any such evidence. Which is another thing that doesn't quite add up. These dental records could do with some double-checking."

Crane takes the file as Kabir holds it out to him. "I'll see if I can make that happen. I think I can get a hasty court order of exhumation on the strength of your expert analysis.

Would you mind typing this up so we can start the process ASAP?"

"Of course. I look forward to helping you find some answers," Kabir says. "Plus, I like a good mystery. It's not often I get to use my skills on cold cases. This kind of thing doesn't come up every day."

"We appreciate it," I say. "Next, can you tell us about these medical records?" I ask, handing him the pages from Vera's red handbag.

He flips through them carefully but seems less sure of what he's looking at. "These are harder to decipher," he says. "Nowadays there would have been an inquest for each of these deaths. But back then, they used to take the word of the surgical team if the lead surgeon simply said they'd tried their best. I can show these to a colleague and get back to you, though, if you like?"

"If I could snap some photos of them first, that would be great," I say, taking the pages from him.

"Anything in particular you think I should look for?" Kabir asks.

"Any signs of medical negligence," I say, "particularly in the case of Susan Folkestone, but the others as well. And anything in these records that might connect all those patients."

"I'll let you know," Kabir says.

I lay the pages on one of the metal gurneys so that I can take clear photos of them. As I put the pages side by side and start photographing, it occurs to me that there's something simple in these documents that's been staring us right in the face all along.

"Crane," I say, my voice sharp with the revelation I've just made. “Look at this.” I point to a section of the form—an ordinary little box that we’d overlooked completely. “I’ve found out what connects them all.”

In the address space, for every single patient, are the words *of no fixed abode.*

“Every one of these patients was living on the streets.”

CHAPTER 28

I MANAGED TO RECLAIM SOME OF MY COMPOSURE BY the time I was escorted into the station, but my eyes were still puffy and my nose was rather blocked. I was grateful I'd washed off my mascara the previous night, but that was because I'd been with Ford and it had already smeared. I didn't regret staying the night, but there is something about being led by the elbow into a police station after being arrested for murder, all while wearing yesterday's clothes and smelling vaguely of sweat and men's cologne, that truly humbles a person.

I was led to an open office full of desks, with people milling around holding files, answering phones, and typing. There was a row of plastic chairs against one wall, and I was shocked to see Elaine sitting on one. She was staring straight ahead and didn't turn to acknowledge me.

"You need to wait here until you're called," the arresting constable said.

Dutifully, I sat. I purposely chose the chair directly next to Elaine, even though several others were free.

A minute passed, then another. Elaine was frozen solid, staring ahead. Finally, I couldn't deal with her silence any longer, and I turned to her.

"I don't think you have much to be nervous about," I said, choosing my words carefully. Elaine could have killed Vera, for all I knew. I didn't want to believe that she had, but Vera's murder had rekindled the sense of intense self-preservation that I'd felt so often in Castle Knoll, and I wasn't about to let myself be duped by anyone. "I'm the one they arrested for Vera's murder."

"I'm sorry to hear that," Elaine said stiffly, still not looking at me.

"You may be sorry," I said, turning my head sideways and watching her carefully, "but you're not surprised."

Finally, she turned my way. "No," she said quietly. "I'm not surprised." She resumed looking at the wall. She seemed deflated, like someone who'd been ill for a long time and still wasn't quite right, or someone under the shadow of a burdensome secret.

"And why would that be?" I asked. "I have an alibi, not to mention a complete lack of the surgical skills required to kill Vera, if what they're saying about how she died is true."

"Any skill can be learned," she said, her voice monotone, "if the person doing the learning is determined or desperate enough." She looked at a fixed point on the ceiling, as if she was considering something. She was unnervingly calm—she had the kind of emotional detachment of a person who had used up their ability to care about things, or who never cared to begin with and had finally let that mask slip. "Someone was practicing their surgical skills," she said, "someone who looks at people as if they're pieces of meat."

I shuddered but did my best to hide it. Every scrap of information from Professor Dane's lectures was flooding my mind. Maybe if I flipped through what I'd learned about the psychology of mur-

derers, I'd be able to see the answers clearly. But there were too many things at play, and my first concern was getting out of my current situation.

"How very cryptic of you," I said, my eyes narrowing at Elaine. "But you don't believe I killed Vera."

Elaine drew in a weary breath and let it out again, like even the act of inhaling was strenuous. "No. I don't believe you killed her."

I let that sentence hang in the air for a beat. "Is that because you know who did?"

Elaine looked at me again. This time there was more light in her eyes. "We're both in over our heads, Frances. But there's a real difference between you and me. Any moment your rich boyfriend is going to parade in here with his expensive lawyers and his smooth talk, and whatever charges they'll try to file against you hopefully won't stick. But me? I'm alone. If they come for me, there's very little I can do about it."

"Come for you how?" I grabbed her arm before she could turn away from me again. "Elaine, do you know something about why I've been brought in here? Are people telling lies, or planting evidence to get powerful men off the hook for killing Vera? Because of what she knew?"

"What do you know about Vera's secrets?" Elaine asked sharply. "Frances, whatever it is . . . whatever she told you, they'll kill you over it."

"She didn't tell me anything!" I said. "I only had those papers I showed you! I couldn't make sense of half of it, and the other half was about things I have no doubt the Torrence family could sweep under the carpet if they had to. Nothing that would ruin a career or bring down a family. The only thing that made any sense was the essay with your notes on it. But it wasn't even evidence that Max was cheating, was it?"

Elaine sighed. "That was a paper I'd written that I intended to submit in his name. I added notes in the margins on a day I was particularly angry with Max. I typed it up and handed it in, then planted the draft in the back seat of Vera's car when we were in it together one day. But I'm no mastermind. Of course, when Max submitted his actual work, Professor Dane asked him why he'd written two essays."

"You've really never played much chess, have you?" I murmured, thinking of my games with Ford. "If you had, you'd have learned to think as many moves ahead of your opponent as possible. And that inevitability would have occurred to you."

"Yes, well, hindsight and all that." Elaine's eyes went back to the ceiling, as if a map of better life choices might have been drawn there. "Max would have realized when he talked to Professor Dane. He'd have guessed what I'd tried to do, how flimsy my attempt to get to him was. Nothing ever came of that. I didn't even realize he'd found me out until that painting. It's how we fight, really. Dramatic gestures to undermine each other."

"How very theatrical of you," I said, my voice deadpan. "I'll think of you the next time I read Wuthering Heights.*"*

"I never said we were perfect people," Elaine fired back, "so you can come down off your high horse. For someone who's so in awe of Vera—a textbook case of antisocial personality disorder—you've got a really sanctimonious air about you."

"I thought Vera's father gave her some flimsy diagnosis, just to discredit the information she was threatening to leak," I said.

"Oh, Frances, she really did take you in, didn't she?" Elaine said. Her tone was condescending but confident now. "I thought you were cleverer than that, truly."

I was tempted to tell her that I was. I was clever enough to agitate Elaine so that she'd share what she knew. Or what she thought she knew. Either way, it was information. But I asked what she wanted me to ask. "You think she really had a personality disorder?"

"She was one step away from being sent to a psychiatric hospital," Elaine said. "Those 'lunches' every Wednesday, where Max would join her and they supposedly met with their father and had steak tartare? That was Max making sure Vera went to her electroshock sessions. She was suicidal—she once took sleeping pills and tried to block herself inside a hole in the wall of her cellar."

I blinked, trying to sift through my memories of Vera, of everything she'd ever said to me. She might not have had a mental disorder. And her words to me on the last night I saw her, about how she had a secret about a powerful man she couldn't unlearn . . . The facts were that someone murdered her. If Vera was simply a liar, or had psychiatric problems, why go to those lengths to kill her?

But there was something about Elaine, sitting there looking so indifferent, only coming alive when she had a chance to get one up on me, to try to seem in control. My instincts were firing warnings to me, but I was having a hard time pinning them down.

"Frances Adams," a man said as he emerged from a closed door across the hall from us. "You may come in now."

I looked back to the police station entrance and felt the knots in my stomach unclench just a bit when I saw Ford there with a smartly dressed man of middling years. He nodded to me, and they started walking my way.

As I stood, I took one last look at Elaine and nearly tripped over the satchel she had set on the floor near our feet. Several textbooks spilled out, and I knelt to help collect them. The Diagnostic and Statistical Manual of Mental Disorders *was among them, as was a book called* Antisocial Behaviors. *But it was the copy of* The Bell Jar *that stopped me short.*

I handed it to Elaine, keeping my face blank. But several things about the details of Vera's "condition" as Elaine told it were suddenly thrown into sharp relief.

I'd read The Bell Jar *only last month. In it, a woman receives electroshock therapy for her depression, after she attempts suicide by taking sleeping pills and trying to block herself into a hole in her cellar.*

Perhaps Vera was imitating Sylvia Plath, but I doubted it. It was far more likely that Elaine, lacking the creativity to form proper lies, had simply embellished her stories of Vera by using the easiest source she had to hand. And I felt certain that if I encountered lies about me in the interrogation room, they would be lies Elaine had put there.

CHAPTER 29

"OKAY, YEAH, THANKS," CRANE SAYS INTO HIS PHONE as we walk down the hospital corridor. He hangs up as we get into the lift to head to the car. "I've just had confirmation that Susan Folkestone was the sister of Brian Folkestone. Brian quit the police in 1968, shortly after Vera was murdered. He then set up his own private security company, but he retired about ten years ago."

"Do you know where we might find him?" I ask.

The lift arrives in the basement car park, and we wander toward his car. "If Brian is a person of interest in *either* of these cases . . ."

"Which he should be," I murmur.

". . . which he *is*," Crane corrects me, "then we'll need to be careful when we question him. And there's one other person I've tracked down who I don't think is a threat or a suspect but might be worth talking to." He presses the unlock button on his car, and we get in. Even though it's cold, he's got his shirtsleeves rolled up almost to his elbows, so that his forearms are bare. I never noticed before, but he wears a watch with a faded leather strap and a retro square face.

"Who is it?" I ask.

"A woman named Elaine. She married Max Torrence in 1970, and they had a very public and acrimonious split in 1990, when she alleged a whole lot of misdeeds on Max's part," Crane says. "I have her address. I thought you might want to question her with me."

I straighten up a little in my seat as we drive out of the car park and into the traffic of Tottenham Court Road. "Max and Elaine got married? Yikes," I say. "Frances's diary has a lot to say on that relationship. Elaine would be a fascinating person to talk to. Count me in."

"Good," he says.

"Now, tell me, what is your theory on Brian as the killer?" I ask.

"I think Brian murdered Vera in order to cause maximum suffering to her husband, Alasdair Huntington," Crane says.

"In revenge for Alasdair Huntington causing the death of Brian's sister, Susan Folkestone," I say. "It's elaborate, though I suppose I can see that. But then, how does a constable imitate the work of one of London's most celebrated heart surgeons?"

"I wonder if he had help," Crane says. "Maybe someone who knew Alasdair well and potentially had access to his medical supplies, and might have known about his surgical techniques."

"I could buy that . . . Frances's diary did say that Vera talked about how much her husband used to go on about his surgeries. She even said Alasdair liked to demonstrate his skills on pieces of meat at dinner parties. But it's a far cry from putting a scalpel into an overcooked steak to removing someone's heart," I say.

Crane sighs. "You're right, it is a bit far-fetched."

We're both quiet for a moment, thinking. Crane takes a breath to say something, then changes his mind. I break the silence, and the first thing out of my mouth is the biggest thing on my mind. "About Felicity," I say. There's a slight catch in my voice that gives away the fact that I'm not wondering about her murder.

Crane's jaw tightens, but he doesn't look angry. More like he's bracing himself. "You opened that file with the phone records," he says.

"I did," I say. "You had to know I would." When he doesn't reply, I continue. "Why didn't you tell me? You and Felicity . . . were you back together or something?" Even phrasing the question like that makes me feel so young. Like a kid asking about emotions that are over my head.

I bite my lip and look out the window, waiting for his answer. It's not like our friendship has ever crossed any lines into romantic territory, despite the tension between us. But now I'm wondering if that tension is all in my imagination. He's a grown man; he's entitled to have pieces of his life he doesn't broadcast to me. Why did I even ask him about this?

Finally, he says, "I'm sorry I didn't tell you I'd been talking to Fliss." I turn away from the window and study his expression. He's watching the road intently even though we're still stuck in traffic. But then he takes one hand off the wheel and rubs the back of his neck, like the weight of the conversation has turned physical. "It wasn't romantic," he says, and he turns that intense expression directly onto me. "Since you're asking."

That last sentence hangs between us, and it's a subtle acknowledgment of the fact that I've accidentally let my interest in him show. You don't ask someone about their relationship status unless you're also wondering if there's a chance you might find your way into it.

"I didn't tell you because I was trying to sort through some things on my own, just to put some old demons to rest. Fliss may have been an old flame, but she was also the last connection to something that happened to me years ago and that still haunts me to this day," he says quietly.

I think back to the conversation we had last summer, just after the dust was settling on the end of Aunt Frances's murder case. Crane had told me about an incident in his childhood, a case that was never solved.

"So Felicity knew all the people involved in that case, back then?" I ask carefully.

Crane nods but doesn't say anything. He swallows hard, and then it's like he shakes the moment off and shifts into a different set of thoughts. "I wasn't ready to bring all that into the conversation, when the most pressing thing was who killed Fliss." He blinks at the road as the traffic starts to move, and we inch forward. "I didn't lie. She did call me the day she died, and the message she left—*I've made a terrible mistake*—that's all true. I just left out the part where we'd been in contact before then."

I reach out and lightly touch his forearm. "It's okay, I get it," I say gently. He nods again, still looking at the road, and I see that he's blinking hard. He's putting a lot of effort into holding it together, and I feel a pang as I realize just how torn up he must be about Felicity. I don't know if it's guilt from not being there when she called for his help, or the years of shared history between them, or some residue of his first love that might never go away, but I want to fix this for him. "We're going to find out who killed her," I say, with a confidence I don't fully feel.

"I know," he says, and he looks my way for a beat. "And thanks, Annie. For understanding."

"Of course," I say. Even though I don't understand, not entirely. We drive in silence for a while, and it's the thick kind that's awkward rather than companionable. I don't know what's shifted in the energy between me and Crane, but I hope we can get back to where we were. Maybe things will only return to normal when there's closure for him and we find out who killed Felicity.

I'm staring at the data screen in the car dashboard, where his phone is linked up, when a call comes through from an unknown number. There's a flashing accept/decline option. Crane reaches over and pushes accept.

"Detective Crane?" The voice is crisp but also sounds rather brittle. "This is Angela Owens, admin assistant with Kensington Police. This is regarding the Felicity Rowe case. You flagged a cold case as potentially related, a Vera Huntington. Our system says that the Huntington file is checked out to you."

"Yes, that's correct," Crane says.

"Well, I'm afraid we need that file back," the woman says.

"And why would that be?" Crane asks. He doesn't mention that we left the file with Kabir, the pathologist at University College Hospital. "Presumably you checked with the lead detective on that case, who approved the release of the file to me."

"Of course, but he said that new evidence has come to light and he needs to examine the file, just to cross-check a name. Then you can have it back," she says.

Crane and I exchange a look. The lead detective on Felicity's case is female. I was questioned by her extensively because I had found the body. Whoever is at the other end of the line has no idea what they're talking about. But they do know that we have (or had) Vera's file. And they want it badly enough to impersonate a police employee.

"Shall I drop it at the station, then?" Crane asks. He sounds casual, just happy to help. I'm wondering how this woman thinks she's going to fool us into handing over Vera's file. I'm also wondering who she is.

There must be something in that file we missed, something that points to who really killed Vera, and who potentially killed Felicity.

"Oh, I'm just finishing my lunch," the woman says. "If you're nearby, perhaps you can bring the file to me. I'm in the King's Head across from Earl's Court station."

"I know the place," Crane replies. "I'm about ten minutes away. I'll see you shortly."

"Wonderful," she replies. "The pub is empty, you won't miss me." The chirp is gone from her voice, and it's almost as if she knows Crane has seen through her ruse, but that wasn't the point. The point was to get Crane's attention, and she's succeeded.

It's raining in a slow drizzle now, and traffic is moving better. "So who do you think we're really going to meet?" I ask when he's hung up.

"I think the more important question is who could possibly know we have Vera's cold-case file," Crane says.

"The only person other than the police themselves," I say slowly, "is my mum. She saw it in my hands before we left."

"So who could Laura have told?"

We park the car and head through the pub doors. The

only person sitting there is a tall man in his seventies. He has silvery hair and the build of someone who can probably bench-press a considerable amount, age notwithstanding. "Detective Crane," he says, and his voice isn't as deep as I expected it to be, but it's still got force behind it. "My name is Brian Folkestone, and you'll want to hear what I've got to say."

CHAPTER 30

"THE FIRST THING YOU NEED TO KNOW IS THAT I didn't kill Vera," Brian says. His hands are steady, but he's keeping them flat on the table between us, like this is a formal interrogation. I suppose since he was once a police officer he knows better than to hide his hands in front of Crane.

"Do you know who did?" Crane asks.

"I didn't kill Vera," he repeats, "but my hands aren't entirely clean," he says, ignoring the question. "All this business about that new girl being murdered, it's got me wanting to share a bit of what I know. And what I know is connected to what I did. Have you got the file?"

The bartender is watching us, and every moment that goes by when none of us gets up to order drinks is souring his expression. When he sees me looking at him, he says curtly, "No table service, love."

"I think that's bartender-speak for 'Order or get out,'" I mutter. "What'll it be, then?" I look to Brian, my eyebrows raised. I suppose he's an informant, in this scenario, so we might want to make a nice gesture to keep him talking.

I've never been able to tag along with Crane this deep into an investigation before. Previously we've danced around each other and sometimes shared information. But for the most part, he's taken the tone of "Stay out of it, Annie, for your own protection. Let me handle this." I admit I like this new dynamic, where he lets me in a bit more. Of course, that means I see firsthand the pangs of his past failures, and just how haunted he is by tragedies he can't make sense of.

The two men have been quiet a bit too long, still sizing each other up. I wonder if my presence will soften things a little, not quite in a good cop, bad cop way, but more in a good cop, friendly writer approach.

"Beer? Whisky?" I ask Brian. "I've got this image of retired police officers enjoying things like whisky."

"I was private security after I left the police. And I learned never to drink whisky while I was doing that. It's too easy to poison because the flavor's so strong," Folkestone says.

"Just a beer for me, thanks, Annie," Crane adds. Folkestone holds up two fingers in the universal gesture for *Make that two.*

"Private security for who? MI5?" I mutter, heading to the bar. "What the hell has he done in his life to worry that someone's going to poison his whisky?"

I return with three pints of a random beer I pointed to on tap, not keen to waste time away from hearing whatever clearly bananas story Brian Folkestone has cooked up for us. In the minutes we've been here, I've decided that the man reminds me of overzealous mall security in American teen movies. I just can't seem to take him seriously with his cloak-and-dagger bullshit. All this *Have you got the file?* and *Whisky's too easy to poison.*

"The file is police property," Crane says as he takes a sip

from his pint. "I'm sure you know I'd have to account for it, and I never had any intention of handing it over."

"Who was that on the phone, by the way?" I ask. "And how did you know Crane had Vera's file?"

"Oh, that was just my wife," Folkestone says. "I suppose it was old-fashioned of me, but I thought a woman's voice would make you more likely to come. But I knew you had the file because I have a friend who can hack into the police database."

I scoff. "No, you don't."

"Excuse me?" Folkestone looks at me, and I will admit that his glare is rather formidable. But Crane is looking at him with the same incredulity I'm feeling, though he's hiding it a bit better.

"No one says things like 'hack into the database.' It's like you're reading from a bad script. A bad script from twenty years ago," I say.

"All right, fine," Folkestone says, spreading his fingers in front of him, like he's letting go of a card after a magic trick. "I have a file on *her*," he says, looking at Crane but pointing at me, "containing information I've shared with extremely important and dangerous people at the Knightsbridge Nymph Gallery."

"You have that file because you threatened my mum," I say, my voice rising. I don't care if he seems like kind of a clown; this is still the man who terrified Mum out of all of her money.

"Yes," he says. "And I know you have the file because I called the station and asked about it. They know me there—I've consulted for them from time to time. I said I was looking into the cold case for a friend, and they automatically assumed I was working with the detective here, so they let me know he already had the file. Anyway, I need you to give it to me."

Crane says, "No," at the same time that I say, "Why?"

We look at each other, then back to Folkestone. "Felicity Rowe was murdered," I say slowly. "That seems to have bothered you. You said it's made you want to share what you know, so I'm assuming you didn't kill her, but you know something that might help us find out who did."

Folkestone is quiet, staring at his hands.

"Or how about we start with your sister, Susan," Crane says softly. "Annie and I found a collection of old medical records, and we've discovered that each name on those records belonged to someone who died on the operating table of Alasdair Huntington."

"And all of those patients had no fixed address," I add. "Can you tell us about Susan? About what happened?"

Brian Folkestone swallows, then nods. "Susan was a beautiful soul, but she got involved with a bad sort when she was in her teens. Pretty soon she was hooked on some hard drugs. Everything spiraled from there—drugs, then prostitution, then homelessness. I joined the police . . ." He hesitates. ". . . I joined because I wanted to keep an eye on her, and I wanted to help people, but of course my job wasn't to do that. I'd arrest her, almost to keep her safe overnight, and she'd be back on the streets the next day." He rubs one temple and closes his eyes briefly. "I loved my sister, she deserved a way out, and she was finally getting some help. The Centrepoint charity had just started, and they took her in. She was getting clean, but detoxing was hard and she took a turn. She had a heart attack. She was malnourished, drugs had ravaged her body, but she was clean when she went into that hospital. Her heart was beating. I was with the paramedics when they took her in."

"She needed surgery?" I ask.

"To this day I'm not sure. I'm no doctor, but there were some things I remember from the hospital that day, which mattered later. They checked her in as a Jane Doe, even though I gave them her name, filled in the forms. It was me who wrote 'of no fixed abode' on the form. That's what they told me to write when I said she didn't have a home. I think they thought I was just the bobby who brought her in off the street, not her brother. But I saw the surgeon come out just before they wheeled her into the operating theater. He spoke to the nurse, and she said, 'Got another one for you.'" At this point Brian takes a long drink of his pint and coughs.

"What do you think she meant by that?" Crane asks.

"I didn't register it at the time. It wasn't until later—when I met Vera—that things started to come together. But when the nurse said that, the doctor looked at Susan's chart and said, 'I don't know why those paramedics keep reviving these whores.'"

"That's horrendous," I say, my hand tightening around my pint glass.

Brian's expression is dark, as if he's back in that hospital. "I nearly saw red then, but worry for Susan took over. Part of me thought he might have been talking about someone else. Susan had been getting clean. She'd been staying with the Centrepoint people and hadn't been on the streets in a while. I just wanted someone to help her, and he was the one with *doctor* in front of his name. He was all she had.

"Later, he came out and handed the chart back to the nurse, not even looking for a family member waiting there.

He just said, 'The body's been sent down to the morgue, if anyone cares to collect it.' That was when I jumped up and started shouting, but the doctor was already walking along the corridor, and his nurse was holding me back. She was saying all the usual stuff, like they'd done all they could, Susan's heart was just too frail after a life on the streets. I'll never forget that awful woman. Marie, she was called."

"The nurse," I say, thinking quickly. "Do you remember her surname? Did she work very closely with Dr. Huntington?"

Crane picks up my train of thought immediately. "Could she have been familiar with his medical techniques, for example? Enough to be able to imitate his surgical style? His sutures?"

Brian blinks at us as if waking from a dream. "I . . . I suppose so. Cavanaugh, that was her surname. Marie Cavanaugh. Do you think she's the one who killed that girl recently?"

"If she was in some kind of relationship with Dr. Huntington, and he left her or rejected her, she could have killed Vera and framed him to punish him," Crane says. "I don't know how Fliss would connect to this, but it's something to go on."

"I just wanted justice for Susan," Brian says. "I went down to see her, where they told me to go, the morgue in the basement of the hospital. Body after body just in bags. It was horrible. There's a place where they put people they expect no one will collect. The man working down there told me about it. The bodies stayed there for months sometimes, until they'd run out of room and had to bury them in common graves. Often just a number, all those John and Jane Does. That's why I did what I did. I wanted justice."

"What did you do?" I ask. "Please, you could help bring

justice to Felicity Rowe. And the same person might be after my mum now too. I really need to stop them before they hurt anyone else."

"Vera was clever. She'd already worked out what her husband was doing when she came to find me."

"And what, exactly, was he doing?" Crane asks. "We know a lot of his patients died, and we know the thing they had in common was that they were sleeping rough. Can you give us more than that?"

Brian takes a long drink of his beer and then nods slowly. "He was playing God, really. He had these ideas about innovations to heart surgery, but every time he sought approval to try them out, he was denied. And rightly so—the refining of these techniques was so risky that the mortality rate was terrible. So when he had someone on his table he knew wouldn't be missed—someone he judged to be disposable because they had no home, no family, made no contribution to society as he defined it—he used them to test his techniques on, and then threw them away like trash." His face colors as a flush of anger creeps up his neck, and I feel my own palms start to sweat.

"That's horrible," I say, my voice thick with the revulsion that's sitting in my throat. And it's a terrible understatement. It's more than horrible. It's inhumane. Unconscionable.

Brian nods, his expression resolute. "Vera looked up relatives to see if anyone could help her, and found out that Susan had a brother in the police. That was how she found me. Together we were going to try to expose him, stop him. But we had disagreements on how to do this. To be honest, I just wanted to kill the bastard. But then Vera . . . and the doctor getting arrested . . . I couldn't get to him after that. So when someone called me, after the doctor was in prison, and they offered me money to get rid of him, I took it," he says. "I signed in on the visitors log, had a chat with him about Vera, and I killed him."

I blink at him, unsure I've heard correctly, while Crane sits forward in his seat, his posture suddenly rigid. "You . . . killed Alasdair Huntington?" I ask, needing to hear him say it again so that I know I'm not imagining things. It's such a casual admission. I find myself suddenly reassessing all my opinions about Brian Folkestone. Perhaps he's cleverer than I thought, hiding behind a caricature of himself. I'd never expected him to admit to walking into a prison and killing one of the inmates.

And being cavalier enough to admit it to a police officer? Maybe Brian was confident that Crane couldn't do anything about it at this point, but it was a bold move.

"How exactly did you do this?" Crane asks.

"Macallan, eighteen-year double cask, one of those tiny bottles. I laced it with arsenic. I smuggled it in my waistband—they didn't search me that thoroughly because I was police. I told Alasdair it was a treat for him, from a friend," he said.

"And he drank it?" Crane asks. "Just like that?"

"Well, he trusted the name of the friend," Folkestone says. "I was instructed to say that it was from Max Torrence, with a message. A message I was only to give him once he'd drunk it."

"Care to share that message?" I ask, pushing my pint glass away. I'm suddenly not thirsty.

Folkestone nods. "'This is for Vera.'"

CHAPTER 31

SOMEONE WAS PRACTICING THEIR SURGICAL SKILLS, Elaine had said. Someone who looks at people as if they're pieces of meat.

Her words hammered in my mind as I entered the interrogation room, where several photos lay in the center of a rectangular table.

"Please, Miss Adams, have a seat," one of the detectives said. He had short curly hair and a Scottish accent, and I would have found him quite handsome if circumstances were different. Right now, I just thought of him as an adversary. He and another male detective, who was decidedly less handsome and looked as if he already had a foot in retirement, took the chairs on one side of the table. I sat with Ford's lawyer on the other.

My eyes fell to the photos and I physically recoiled. At first I thought they'd put close-up photos of Vera's chest there to shock me. The photos weren't in color, but I could see the texture of what looked like raw flesh, and I was very nearly sick. I sat, closed my eyes, and took a deep breath through my nose, exhaling through my mouth.

If I was going to defend myself in this interrogation, I had to keep my head.

When I opened my eyes again, my brain made better sense of what I was looking at. It actually helped that Elaine's comment was still in my thoughts—what she'd said about pieces of meat suddenly seemed like either a warning or a boast. I noticed a plate, and neat dark lines in the flesh, like pen marks.

"You're quite the seamstress, aren't you, Frances?" the older detective said.

"I don't understand the question," I said. The lawyer looked at me and gave me the barest of nods, as if he approved of my confusion. But inwardly I was tallying up things Elaine had said to me. She wasn't particularly creative, that was certain. What I couldn't work out was, why me? Was she behind this, or did she simply know who was and was trying to warn me?

"We searched your flat after we questioned some of Vera's friends," the Scottish detective said.

I looked at him, certain that my outrage was plain in my eyes, but it didn't feel like something I needed to hide. "You mean after you talked to Elaine," I said.

The lawyer put a hand on my arm. "Is there a direction to this line of questioning?" he asked. "And we'd also like to see a copy of the warrant you used to search the premises."

"The flat was unlocked, the door ajar. That gave us right of entry," the older detective replied.

"I was simply commenting on Miss Adams's sewing materials in her flat—quite a lot of dressmaking going on in there. As well as scraps of fabric, very neat sewing," the Scottish detective said.

Stitches. Those were stitches in that photo, on a prime cut of steak. It was almost laughable, once I realized the absurdity of it all. But I swallowed hard, remembering that they'd be comparing those stitches to Vera's chest, looking for her husband's handiwork, or anything to prove it was his hands that had cut out her heart. Whether it was some extreme psychopathy or some twisted statement he was making, if he did kill her, he'd treated her as just another body on his operating table.

"Do you mind getting to the point?" I asked.

The Scottish detective slid one of the steak photos across the desk to me. "These were found in your flat," he said. "Several pieces of meat, with sutures all over them. Practice, imitating the work of a skilled surgeon."

"That's absurd!" I said. "As you said, my door was ajar. Someone obviously had easy access to my room and put them there!" Elaine must have done it, or Max had, and Elaine knew about it. Either way, someone wanted to shift blame in my direction.

The detectives exchanged a glance but didn't speak. One started shuffling the photos from back to front, and finally a close-up of the real Vera's chest came into view.

I breathed in sharply, unable to look away. The sutures were very particular—I didn't know much about how people might close someone's chest after an operation but imagined it would look much like straight, even stitches. People weren't scarves. I would expect that there would be no need to use extra time or lengths of thread trying to reinforce each stitch.

But this technique did—it looked elaborate, like someone showing off. It looped back on itself and then up again, like an overlock machine would do for a strong hem. I had the impression of someone signing their name in bold calligraphy, and my stomach roiled all over again. If this was Dr. Huntington's regular way of closing a chest, he was an arrogant bastard, and the hospital let him have the run of the place.

"You see our problem, Frances?" the Scottish detective said finally. "This isn't something that just anyone can imitate."

I looked at the detective, my expression calm this time. "I'm going to move past the fact that this is so overly elaborate as to be ridiculous, and simply point out to you that those are extremely expensive cuts of meat. In fact, they're probably expensive enough that the butcher who sold them would remember who bought them. They're fresh, and I have no refrigerator." I leaned in slightly, toward the detective. "Have you thought to check the butcher nearest Max Torrence's residence, and ask who might have bought these cuts of meat recently?"

"Mr. Torrence is not part of this conversation," the older detective said wearily.

"Well, perhaps he should be. His girlfriend, Elaine, was just out in the hall, indicating to me that she already knew why I'd been arrested. My guess is that it was Elaine who told you to search my flat, that there was something that tied me to Vera's death in there. Do you not see how flimsy this is? Where would I get the money to buy such expensive cuts of meat, and how would I know how Dr. Huntington does all this?" I gestured to the photos of the stitches.

"The doctor was famous for demonstrating his skills at dinner parties, on prime cuts of meat," the older detective said.

"Dinner parties I never would have been invited to, given my humble status as the daughter of bakers in rural Dorset," I said. "But Max Torrence would have been. I imagine he was at his sister's house often."

The lawyer coughed, and I paused to look at him. "Miss Adams makes a valid point," he said. "Given that this evidence was found in her residence while access to it was completely open, you have no cause to hold her. If anyone could come and go, it could easily have been planted. Add to that the fact that this evidence does not seem to have been followed up properly—Miss Adams's point about asking the butchers nearest the Huntington and Torrence residences is rudimentary detective work before making an arrest. You'll be lucky if we don't file a complaint," he added.

The Scottish detective gave me a long look but eventually nodded.

"Besides, why would I kill Vera?" I asked.

The lawyer placed a hand on my arm again. "I think it's time to stop talking now, Miss Adams," he said.

"Your friend Elaine gave us a laundry list of reasons," the older detective said.

"The same 'friend' who happens to live across the hall from my flat? Who told you to look there for something incriminating?" I asked.

The detectives exchanged a glance. "It would be too foolish of her to plant that in there," one said. "She'd know it would point back to her, unless she was genuinely telling the truth."

"Which was? What was her story about how she knew it was there?" I asked.

"That you gave her a key and asked her to bring some books for you to the university," the Scottish detective said. "She claims she couldn't find the books so had to search around and eventually found this covered plate in a corner."

"Don't you think it's far more likely that Max Torrence killed his sister, and his girlfriend, Elaine, is helping him cover his tracks?" I asked. "This whole setup has Elaine all over it," I added. "Because if there's one thing I've learned about her recently, it's that she's not that clever."

"That may be true," the older detective said, "and while your lawyer is right and we'll need to release you without charge, I assure you, Miss Adams, you aren't out of the woods yet."

The lawyer stood, and I immediately rose to my feet as well, keen to get out of there. But I couldn't resist trying to prize a little more information from the police while I had the chance.

"I don't understand how Dr. Huntington can't just look at this and give you some concrete reason why he wasn't the one to

do it. You could even pull old medical files and compare side by side," I said.

"Trying to tell us how to do our jobs . . . again?" the Scottish detective replied, raising an eyebrow.

The older detective answered my question, as if his counterpart hadn't spoken. "You see, that's the problem. The doctor admits that the stitches on Vera's chest are such an exact imitation that he couldn't tell them from his own handiwork. The steaks, well, those are a different story. Someone learning the moves. But on Vera's body? It's uncanny."

"And he said that from the photos?" I asked. "Or when he identified her body?"

The older detective gave me a long look, and I could almost see admiration somewhere in it. And a connecting of some previously unconnected dots that I'd only just illuminated for him by asking the right questions. "The doctor didn't identify her body. He never saw her. He was immediately brought in for questioning and has been held for the past twenty-four hours for assaulting a police officer."

"If he didn't identify her, then who . . ." I stopped, realizing why the detective had given me such a long look.

The detective nodded. "Max Torrence did the formal identification of his sister's body." He coughed and looked a bit uneasy. "It was a difficult identification to make; her face was badly damaged. The body has been released and the family insisted on a quick, private burial."

Now I was the one to start connecting dots. If Max killed Vera, then of course he'd be pushing for no one else to see her body and for her to be buried quickly along with whatever story her body might tell about who had really killed her.

"Then I implore you to make sure that whoever performed her autopsy was thorough," I said.

CHAPTER 32

"SO, MAX HAD DR. HUNTINGTON KILLED AND PAID Brian Folkestone to do it," I say as Crane and I walk back to the car. Brian had gotten up to use the toilet while we were midway through our drinks, and Crane had let him, knowing he was likely just going to run off. Which he did. Crane confirmed exactly what I'd been thinking—that even though Brian had confessed, making an arrest based on Brian's story from decades ago, alongside no other evidence, wasn't a good idea.

"If that's true, Max Torrence looks less likely as a suspect for the person who killed Vera and the person who killed Fliss," Crane says. "If he orchestrated a revenge killing after the doctor was behind bars, he must have believed Dr. Huntington killed Vera."

"Or that there was something the doctor might have been able to work out about Vera's death, and use that evidence to appeal. He might have been getting closer to uncovering who killed his wife. If anyone had reasons to examine every scrap of evidence relating to Vera's murder, it was her husband," Crane says.

He picks up his phone and dials as we walk. After a moment I hear him say, "Hi, it's Rowan," and he laughs. "No, I'm not avoiding you, even if I can still smell that sandwich from here." He laughs again. "Well, no egg salad is an unwritten workplace rule. But I don't have time to discuss sandwiches, Amy. I wondered if you could look up a name for me, and give me all the addresses and employment records you can on it? . . . Marie Cavanaugh . . . That's right. I'm specifically looking for someone who was a nurse at the Westminster Hospital in the cardiology department around 1968. Yes, that means we can eliminate anyone born after about 1948. Make it 1950 just to be sure. She'd be in her mid-seventies now . . . Of course, I'll wait."

He leans up against a lamppost while he's on hold, still projecting the image of a Rowan Crane I haven't met yet. The Crane who laughs easily and makes jokes about sandwiches. Or maybe this is the Crane who is trying hard to put a patch over the darker things he's had to grapple with. For instance, investigating the murder of someone he cared about. I give him a quizzical look, and when he glances at me, the ease slips just a bit. I don't like the feeling it leaves me with, like I'm notes in the margin of his narrative, instead of sentences woven within it.

"Oh, you're a star," he says to the woman on the phone. "I knew you'd come through. Perfect, heading there now." He hangs up and we start walking again, reaching his car.

"Heading where?" I ask. "Your colleague found a likely match to Marie Cavanaugh?"

"She did," Crane says. "And it's an all-roads-lead-to-Rome situation." He gives me a pointed look.

"You're kidding," I breathe. "The gallery?" Immediately the image of the woman with the white pixie cut comes into my mind, the one who referred to Max as Mr. Ego. I can see her name tag in white with bold blue letters across it. "*That* Marie? The one who told me off for taking pictures?" I say. "That is absolutely not a coincidence."

"No," Crane says, and his voice has a dark edge to it. "It really isn't. There have been too many threads crossing at that gallery, and I think it's high time we looked at the whole tapestry."

"Wow! Who died and made you Raymond Chandler?" I say.

"Oh, cut it out," he says, and I sense a small bounce hidden underneath his stoicism.

"'That dame had legs for days . . .'" I say in a terrible Bogart impression. I wince.

"Don't quit your day job. You'd make a terrible comedian," he counters.

"My day job as an heiress? Or my day job of following you around, being instrumental in solving murders?"

"Oh." His brow furrows, all hint of lightness gone. "About that. I did say *I'm* driving to interview Marie Cavanaugh."

"I happen to also be present in this car."

"Yes, but she and Max Torrence very likely killed Fliss, and may be behind the threats against Laura too. And given what you told me about Max's reaction to you when he learned you're Laura's daughter . . . I don't want you in the line of fire, okay? I'm dropping you off with your mum. It's about time someone checked in on her anyway."

"Absolutely not. You need me there," I say. "And Marie and Max aren't going to try anything with the police present. They won't be that stupid."

He sighs and opens his mouth to speak, then thinks better of it and closes it again.

I take this as an opportunity to add more persuasive arguments. "You know I'll have an angle on this that might never have occurred to you."

"I can't possibly fathom what you mean," he says wearily, but there's a smile behind his words.

"Have *you* read Frances's diary? The one concerning the events of the winter of '68?"

He shakes his head. We both know he hasn't had time to read that diary yet. I'm the only one of us who knows all the information Frances included there. "This is just for your own—"

I cut him off. "Don't say 'for your own safety.' Being protective was cute for the first couple of murders, but I've more than proven myself by now."

His fingers drum the steering wheel as he thinks. We wait at traffic lights, staring up the road at the turning toward the gallery. It's on the way to Chelsea—he'd have to actually pass the place to drive me home, then loop back again.

"The fact that you've just said 'for the first couple of murders' should be a flashing sign for how sideways your life has gone while spending time with me," he says.

"Oh, believe me, I'd have gotten just as tangled up in these murder investigations without you, thank you very much. You're the Indiana Jones plot hole in this scenario," I say.

"I'm the what?"

"You know, it was a joke on TV for a while. The Indiana Jones plot hole?" He looks at me blankly, then turns back to the road. "In *Raiders of the Lost Ark*, Indiana Jones's presence in the movie doesn't change the story, because in the end the

Nazis get the ark, open it, and get their faces melted off. That would have happened if he was there or not."

"Actually, you could argue that he managed to kill a whole army of Nazis in that way . . ." Crane says, his brow furrowing.

"You get my point, though. I came across a reference to it in a book on writing, in a section about how not to write passive characters. And I am *not* the passive character in my own story."

"Indiana Jones is not a passive character!" Crane says, and he's surprisingly animated. "And I am not Indiana Jones in this scenario! Wait—you think of me like Indiana Jones?"

Outwardly I pretend to brush that off, but I take a mental picture of the flush that hits his cheeks just then. "You're getting distracted. My point is, you're not in charge of my safety. You're reducing me to some kind of walking target when I'm actually contributing a lot here."

He's quiet for a moment, and just when I think he's going to silently dump me off at my mum's house, he turns toward the gallery. "All right. But if there's even a *hint* of danger, you run. Meaning if I tell you to get out, you do it, no questions asked."

"Agreed," I say. "I'm glad you at least have the confidence that I can outrun a couple of seventy-five-year-old museum volunteers."

"The snark can take a back seat, though," he says, putting the car in park.

"I'll leave it safely buckled in for the drive home," I reply.

He shakes his head, but we get out of the car together, walk up the marble stairs, and enter through the front door.

The main desk is empty, but Crane rings the little bell there. "Hello?" he calls, and starts doing the casual pacing he does—the kind that's anything but casual and is actually him scanning the place for anything of interest or any potential threat.

"In here," calls a voice.

I point to the sculpture gallery, and we head down the long corridor that leads to it.

"Marie Cavanaugh?" Crane asks as we enter the room. I'm taken aback by the change in the exhibition—namely, that all of Felicity's work, which was on the various display pillars, has gone. The plaques describing each piece are now empty plastic holders, waiting for new descriptions to be slotted into them.

"Yes?" Marie turns to us.

"My name is Detective Crane, and this is Annie, she's . . . assisting me with some fact-checking in an investigation I'm working on."

I don't take issue with his "fact-checking assistant" because I want Marie to talk to us. I'm not about to wave my arms at Crane and say, "Remember what we talked about? How important I am?" But it suddenly occurs to me that when I met Marie previously, I'd lied and said I was writing an article about the museum. I'm not stupid enough to lie again and say, "Oh, that was just my cover. I'm actually with the police." I just have to hope Marie either doesn't remember me or doesn't really care about the lie.

"How can I help you?" Marie says. Her eyes narrow at me for a moment, but she turns away. She has a cloth and is running it over the empty displays, though they seem immaculate to me.

"We'd like to ask you some questions about a cold case we're reopening. A woman named Vera Huntington was murdered in 1968, and a surgeon you worked with at the time was convicted of her murder. Dr. Alasdair Huntington?" Crane says.

Marie pauses at the mention of Vera's name, and I see her eyes widen in surprise. But she controls her features quickly and dutifully resumes dusting. "Why do you want to know about all that?" she asks, sounding irritated. "It was decades ago."

"If you could indulge us and answer the question," Crane says evenly, "we'd appreciate it."

"Yes, I remember the incident," she says, and lets the cloth fall to her side. Her brow furrows, like she's trying to recall details of something far more mundane than murder. Like a shopping list, or what was on TV the night before. It's an odd reaction, and I feel instinctively that she's hiding something. "I don't see why you want to reopen that case. It seemed clear that Alasdair was guilty."

"What makes you say that?" I ask. "We have a reliable witness who says that you not only worked closely with the doctor, but that you might have had knowledge of some unethical medical choices he made."

Marie purses her lips and looks at the floor. "It was a long time ago, and I left the hospital not long after Dr. Huntington was arrested. I stopped nursing altogether and moved to Canada. I couldn't take the pressure of bad memories. I only came back to London in the nineties." Marie looks up at me, then at Crane. "There's really nothing more to say. I don't know why you'd need to talk to me about Vera. I didn't even know her."

"But you knew Dr. Huntington," Crane says. "And our source tells us you knew what he was up to. He was using the homeless population of London to perform experimental surgical techniques. Techniques that had an extremely high mortality rate and hadn't been approved by any medical boards. Whenever someone came into his operating theater and he knew they had no home and no family, he used them as human lab rats. Is that right?"

"I don't know what you're talking about," Marie says. "Now, if you'll excuse me . . ." She turns and fidgets with the empty plastic label holders that had recently held information about Felicity's work. She's clearly not going to tell us anything she knows about Dr. Huntington, and why would she? How would that help? Even if he was guilty of all those deaths, he died decades ago.

Crane looks at the ceiling, clearly following the same line of thought. But my eyes catch the sculptures around the edges of the room, things that must be part of the permanent collection, and I realize there's far more to Marie than her past as a nurse. Because why on earth is she here? Volunteering with Max?

Max, Marie, and this gallery are the link between Vera and Felicity. Two women who died in the same way, decades apart. And they both had work on display in this gallery.

"I wonder, then, if you can tell me about the sculptures that used to be here." I gesture to the empty plinths in front of us. "I visited only the other day and saw an entire series of wire sculptures by a woman named Felicity Rowe."

Marie doesn't look at me; she just keeps fidgeting with the plastic labels, so I press on. "You see, Felicity was apprentice to my mum, Laura Adams."

At that, Marie starts and looks at me wide-eyed. She shifts her expression quickly to neutrality, but I saw the moment of alarm when I revealed who I was.

"You're aware of the connection between Laura Adams and this gallery?" Crane asks, stepping closer to Marie.

"She was a great benefactor for us," Marie says, but I see a twitch in her jaw. "Years ago she made a very sizable donation."

"Do you know much about her art?" I ask. I'm wondering just how much Marie knows about the blackmail, and about Vera's body of work. "How long have you been working here?"

Marie sighs, finally understanding that being forthcoming will make us leave her alone faster. "I started here in 1992, a couple of years before Laura Adams became a household name. I don't know about her art, just that she kept the gallery open with her donation." Marie looks at me briefly, then away. "What a generous family you come from."

That last is said almost like a threat, or as if it's layered with a double meaning that I'm failing to grasp. If she was genuinely happy Mum had donated to keep the gallery running, and believed she'd done so out of the goodness of her heart, she'd have been more cheerful when she heard who I was.

"Marie?" A new voice echoes from the corridor, another volunteer—a young man.

Marie doesn't acknowledge him, just stares at me in an increasingly worrying way. Like a snake about to strike. Even Crane can sense it—he squares his shoulders and takes a step closer to me.

Finally, she surfaces, as if coming back from somewhere far away, and turns to the young man. "I'm sorry. I forgot who I was for a moment there."

"There's a call for you on line six," the young man says.

"I'll take it in the office." She turns from us without saying good-bye.

We watch her walk away, with the same hunch I noticed

earlier, like she's making herself small rather than curved with age.

I take Crane to see the painting of Max, and we stare at it in silence for a while before exiting the gallery. It's dark, and past time for me to check on Mum. Before I descend the steps toward Crane's car, the smell of cigarette smoke to my left catches my attention. I see Marie for only a moment, before she tucks herself into the shadows. But before she disappears, I take in the cloud of her cigarette, her milk-curdling glare, and the flash of the flame from her lighter before it clicks shut.

CHAPTER 33

"WE NEED TO FIND MAX TORRENCE," I SAID TO FORD AS I emerged from the police station. "Now."

"Are you . . . okay?" Ford asked, placing his arm around my shoulders. "They didn't threaten you, or upset you?"

I gave him a cynical smile. "Of course I'm okay. What did you think would happen? That I'd come out shaking and need smelling salts?"

He laughed, looking genuinely relieved. "I'm sorry. I forgot who I was dealing with."

I reached over and cupped a hand under his chin. "Mind you don't do it again," I said, and grinned at him. "Because the correct question to ask would have been, 'Frances, what clever inside information did you glean from the police while they thought they had the upper hand?'"

"Ah yes. That was the second item on my list of things to ask you," he said.

"Well, this brings us back to Max Torrence. Apparently, Vera's husband, celebrated surgeon and—I'm certain—a certifiably psychopathic individual, never saw her body. It was formally identified by Max Torrence. And I want to know what he's not saying to the police about it."

"Well then," Ford said, opening the car door for me, "where might Max be now?"

I smiled with rather twisted satisfaction when I realized that Professor Dane had scheduled an extra lecture today, to take the place of the usual seminar. "If you don't mind dropping me at the university, I'm just in time for my favorite lecture."

"HELLO, MAX," I said as I settled into the seat next to him. It was his usual spot, and I imagined him getting there and feeling smug satisfaction to see my empty chair. He'd have been picturing me in the police interrogation room, confident that he'd gotten away with murder.

His shirt was rumpled, making me suspect he was in yesterday's clothes. I hated to have anything in common with him, but his outfit was a reminder that I was in the same boat after my night with Ford. I smoothed a hand down my trousers but stopped halfway. There were bigger problems in the world.

Even though Max looked a little the worse for wear, he was as relaxed as ever. He leaned back in his seat and regarded me with all the attention you'd give a prized horse, sizing me up for speed, longevity, breeding power. It made me inwardly recoil, but I kept my composure.

"Is Elaine not joining us today?" I asked him.

Elaine had not been in the chair at the police station when I left. She was either being questioned or had fled straight home.

Max's eyes darted around the classroom, but his expression remained fixed. If he was worried not to see Elaine, he didn't show it. Though something told me he wouldn't be worried for her specifically, but worried about what she might have said to the police.

Professor Dane entered the lecture theater, and his familiar energy, well-kept tweed, and cheerful greetings made me feel anchored. Max Torrence needed to be exposed for what he was, and I was determined to see to it.

"Hello, everyone," Professor Dane said. "Today I've got a rather invigorating lecture for you on fratricide—a tale as old as Cain and Abel. Let's discuss the reasons why murder might run in families, in particular, with siblings."

If I hadn't already believed in fate, I would have started right then.

The lecture was fascinating. The professor talked about the toxicity of family dynamics, how favoritism from parents toward one child could warp the minds of siblings, about power and abuse, and the role human nature plays in the competition for resources even within the family unit.

"So often the reason someone kills comes down to the unwavering belief that another person is going to take what they have. Or someone has already taken it from them, whether that's the love of a parent, or material things they think they deserve, or the integrity of their reputation."

Whispers broke out in the lecture theater at that last comment, and I looked around to see if I'd missed something. The whispers turned to murmurs; the murmurs turned to voices. Max's complexion reddened as he saw someone pass a newspaper along the aisle. He reached out and snatched it, unfolding it to see the front page fully.

Professor Dane had noticed the commotion but was continuing to talk over it. I leaned toward Max, though I hated to close any distance between us, and began to read. And I knew then that I didn't need to fight to take down Max Torrence. His own corrupt family had fallen, and taken him down with them.

CHAPTER 34

THE NEXT DAY, I PAD DOWNSTAIRS TO START SOME coffee on the stove when there's a loud knocking at the door. It's not particularly early—I get out my phone and see that it's nearly 10 A.M.—but I know it won't be Crane because he'd call first. I peer through the peephole in the door and see an elderly woman with shoulder-length dyed-brown hair. She reaches out to the large brass door knocker and pounds it several more times.

She seems harmless, and she isn't Max or Sam, or even Marie. She's probably just here to remind us to fill in our voting registration cards or is collecting for charity, but the urgency with which she's knocking suggests otherwise.

"Can I help you?" I feel a blast of icy morning air as I open the door, reminding me I'm in a vest top and flannel pajama bottoms that have seen better days.

She looks at me with a rather direct gaze—the kind that reveals she knows exactly who I am. She's here on an agenda, and it's not the innocent kind.

"Annabelle Adams?" she asks.

"That's me," I say, though we both know she didn't need to check.

"Yes, you look just like your Instagram," she says. It's almost funny, seeing this curt older woman on my doorstep admitting at the get-go that she's been social media stalking, but it's served to make me extra curious. She starts to peer past me into the house. I give her a cynical glare and angle the door closer to my body so she can't see inside.

"My name is Elaine Torrence," she says. "Can I please come in? There's something I need to talk to you about."

Elaine is a rather elusive subject in Aunt Frances's diary. Frances could never quite draw her out, and I'm keen to pencil in the rest of her. I open the door to her out of curiosity more than anything. That, and I'm getting cold. I do know that old ladies are not always as harmless as they seem, but Mum is upstairs somewhere and I've got Crane on speed dial.

"You're Max's ex-wife," I say, gesturing for her to come inside.

"That's right," Elaine says as she enters. "One of a long list of bad choices I've made, but heigh-ho." She has a breeziness about her that feels a little kooky, like one of those ladies who, as they get further into their later years, start doing more and more random adventurous things just because they can. I take in her fuzzy purple wool hat and matching plastic purple costume jewelry and decide I could easily see this woman bungee jumping in Australia just to prove she's still got it.

In Aunt Frances's account of her brief friendship with Elaine, the woman was conniving, if a bit clumsy and predictable. But she wasn't particularly clever, and tended to attempt elaborate schemes to undermine people, only to have them easily foiled. She was a curiosity, this woman.

"Would you like some coffee? Or tea?" I ask, as she follows me to the kitchen.

"Do you have an espresso machine?" she asks cheerfully. "I just learned what a cortado is. I went to Spain and they were all the rage."

Yes, I decide. Bungee jumping in Australia is definitely an accurate assumption for how Elaine is spending her later years.

I smile. "We don't have one, but that's not a bad idea. I might do some online shopping later." And I'm surprised to find that I mean it. I keep forgetting that I have a bank account that won't scream every time I buy something. I've yet to make even one truly extravagant purchase since I inherited Aunt Frances's wealth. Perhaps it's past time for that. I could order an espresso machine from Italy that's the price of a used car.

"Then coffee is fine," Elaine says, taking a seat.

"Milk? Sugar?"

"Oh, I take my coffee black," she says. "Like my heart." She says the last phrase so deadpan that I freeze, thinking of the animal hearts on the doorstep. I wonder how long it will be before I stop seeing death whenever anyone says *heart*.

Elaine laughs, her serious expression vanishing. "Don't look so rattled, dear. It's an old joke. A friend of mine used to say it."

I nod, a little distracted now. I light the ancient gas hob with a long match and place the heavy kettle on it. It's already warm, and half-full, so I imagine Mum isn't still sleeping upstairs, as I originally thought. She's likely down in her studio, contemplating the empty space that's there now, since her canvases have all gone to the gallery where her show will open in a few days.

I realize with a start that the small canvas of Vera's I brought from Castle Knoll is in the kitchen, lying flat and unassuming on the worktop, face down. I brought it downstairs this morning with a view to locking it in the old safe that sits in the study. If it's the last of Vera's work and is clearly something most people would recognize as an original Laura Adams, I want it out of sight again where no one can lay eyes on it. I'd burn it, but that feels like a crime. I'd never burn a book, and art fits into that sort of category for me.

My eyes fall on the pencil marks on the back of the canvas, and I notice the title *Bleeding Heart* written there, with Vera's signature underneath it, also in pencil, not easy to spot. It's embarrassing that I never looked close enough to notice the pencil on the back before, but I never felt a need to look at the other side of the painting. Until all this happened, I barely even looked at the front of it. I just thought, oh yes, one of Mum's, and tucked it away.

"What brings you here?" I ask, sitting across from her.

Elaine glances at the face-down canvas. No spark of recognition shows on her face, and I relax a bit. Not only would it be unlikely for her to recognize Vera's work from the blank reverse side, bearing only her penciled name, but she probably never saw the abstract series Vera produced that Mum made famous as her own. She'd have said something by now, told the press she recognized those paintings when Mum was everywhere in the nineties.

The kettle whistles and I pour water into the waiting cafetière, though something tells me Elaine will turn up her nose at Mum's budget coffee from Aldi, after enthusiastically discovering cortados. But when I set a cup in front of her, she takes it gratefully.

"Laura and I have a lot in common, you know," Elaine says, surprising me yet again. "We're both banned from the gallery where Max works, for a start."

"You know Mum?" I ask.

Elaine ignores my question and continues as if I've not said anything. "I've known something was off about that gallery for decades, but I was barred from entering it after we had a rather messy divorce in 1990. It was Max's playground in the eighties, for drug-fueled parties and infidelities, and I think he wanted to make doubly sure I couldn't turn up there and give him an earful," she says. She blows across her coffee and takes a sip. "Max's sister was murdered, you know," she says. "In the same way as Laura's friend Felicity."

"I know," I say. "Is that what brought you here? Did you see the news about Felicity, and want to talk about Vera?"

"She was magnetic, Vera was. Her death never sat right with me—I mean, it was horrible, so of course it wouldn't, but there were a lot of rich and powerful men trying to mess with the facts."

I give her an assessing stare. "My great aunt Frances kept rather detailed diaries of that time."

"I know," Elaine replies. "I used to sneak into her flat and read them. She hid them in a very predictable place—under the mattress. I do wish sometimes things had been different, and we'd been able to truly be friends, but . . ."

"But you threw her under the bus by planting evidence and getting her arrested," I say.

Elaine sighs. "I was threatened into doing that," she replies. "And I regret so much how easily I was bullied in my youth. One of the many bad choices I mentioned earlier. They've all rather piled up one by one, and they weigh me down, like a heavy string of pearls."

"You were threatened by whom? Those steaks with the stitches in them, do you know who did that?" I ask.

She looks at me for a long moment. "You think it was Max who killed her, don't you?" A bitter laugh escapes her, and she takes a long sip from her mug. "I often do too. Sometimes I think it really was Alasdair Huntington, but . . ."

"Actually, lately I've been wondering if it was you," I say, just to see her reaction. The Elaine in Frances's diary wouldn't have been smart enough to pull off this kind of frame-up, unless she was double bluffing, playing the rather dim slapdash meddler to cover up the fact that she was really capable all along.

Elaine laughs. "I'd hoped you'd inherited your great aunt's intellect," she says.

"Then who stitched up those steaks? Who was practicing to imitate the doctor's work?"

"Those steaks came from the doctor's own refrigerator," Elaine says. "And the police even asked his local butcher if they'd been bought by someone in his household, and it was confirmed that Vera had bought them. I think she always did the shopping. They had a housekeeper, but Vera was particular about her meat. That was one of the things that helped put the doctor away for her murder."

"It doesn't make sense, though," I say. "Why would the doctor need to practice on steaks? Even beginners in medical school use other things to practice stitching on. I read somewhere they use pig's feet most often, closer to human skin." I shudder just thinking about it, but people have to learn somehow.

"That was Dr. Huntington's defense as well, but the prosecution used it as evidence of his unstable personality. Alongside testimony about his egotistical rants at dinner parties, and the sadistic way he used to cut up meat. He'd bring out bones and crack them to show how to break into a human rib cage . . ." Elaine looks into her cup. "He might not have killed Vera, but he was unquestionably a psychopath."

"Vera had information that confirmed that," I say. "In the red handbag that Frances gave to you to pass along to her."

"I know," Elaine says. "Anyway, it was the doctor's people who threatened me. They didn't want to get rid of the steaks; they wanted them somewhere that could bring suspicion away from Dr. Huntington. Max would have been the best person to plant them on, but I was explicitly instructed to find someone who probably couldn't afford a lawyer. I planted them in Frances's place really sloppily to make easy work for whoever would help exonerate her."

"So you didn't really want to hurt Frances," I say slowly.

"No, I didn't. I just didn't know how to say no to the doctor's people—he had this crooked lawyer who really gave me the creeps. So I did the best I could, by making a bad job of it." Elaine pauses and looks down at her hands. "I've come here to try to help," she says finally. "I remembered something, and I think it's related to the new girl who died. I wanted to come here first, before the police, because in the past the police have only made things worse."

I sit up straighter. "Anything you think might help would be really welcome," I say. "We're all at a bit of a loss when it comes to who would have killed Felicity. I keep feeling like the murders are connected, but I'm running out of facts to prove it."

"Well, maybe this detail will help. It was something Max

said, back when we were married. I'd been trying to get to the bottom of what happened to Vera for years, and Max's behavior about it always made me feel uneasy. He blocked me at every turn and rarely even spoke about Vera. For a while I thought it was grief, but it was almost like he didn't trust himself when speaking about her—perhaps he was worried he might let something slip."

"You think he knew more about what really happened than he let on? Or that he might have actually killed her?" I ask.

"Like I said, I'm too deep in the weeds to be sure. But once, a few years after Vera died, we had too much to drink and he started talking about Vera's art. She was always unpredictable, chasing new styles and approaches to capture the chaos of her mind." Elaine's face turns extra serious as she meets my eyes. "And I know Frances's account of me in that diary is probably erratic, but please believe me when I say that Vera *was* mentally unwell. Frances wanted badly to believe that the men in Vera's life were trying to discredit her by assigning mental problems, but two things can be true at once. One, that Vera had information that was dangerous to her, and two, that she was unstable and needed help.

"Anyway, Max was tipsy and spoke about Vera's obsession with hearts. Apparently, it was something that followed her from childhood, when she once stumbled upon a mouse her cat had killed. Max said that Vera had one foolproof way of terrifying him from then on. Any time her cat killed something—a bird, a rat, a mouse—Vera would remove its heart and put it somewhere for Max to find."

I blink, trying to make sense of what she's saying. "Someone left an animal heart on our doorstep the day before Felicity was killed," I say. "And recently too."

"Then I think whoever killed Felicity knew Vera very, very well," Elaine says.

The doorbell rings, and I start. "Excuse me for a moment," I say, and get up to answer it.

I look through the peephole and see Crane looming on the steps, his brow furrowed as he looks directly back at me. "Annie," Crane says as I open the door. "There's been a rush with the exhumation order for Vera's body, given the information Kabir provided on the autopsy. A judge approved it straightaway, and an exhumation company is bringing up her body as we speak."

"That's good news," I say, leading him into the foyer. "Elaine is here," I add. "She actually sort of just . . . turned up. She's in here."

But when we get to the kitchen, Elaine is gone. She's clearly gone out the back door, through the garden and out the back gate—the one that leads to the alley where the skip is. I can see out the window that it's slightly ajar.

There are two photographs on the table, next to her half-empty cup of coffee. I pick up the top one and examine it carefully. It's a man in his forties, wearing a white lab coat and a smug grin. He's got his arm around the waist of a woman in a nurse's uniform, and she's giving the camera a demure close-lipped smile. They're standing in a garden, squinting slightly in the sun. I flip it over and see pencil scrawling on the back. *Alasdair and Marie, 1967.*

The second one is of two women, with the same backdrop, the same sun squints. It looks like it was taken only moments later than the other photograph, or maybe moments before. The woman in the nurse's uniform—who must be Marie Cavanaugh—has both arms around another woman. She's taller, but only by a fraction, and they're both blond. Marie isn't looking at the camera this time, but at the other woman, her grin full and unfettered. I turn it over to look at the back, and the same penciled handwriting greets me. *Vera and Marie, 1967.*

Crane is watching me silently, as my mind is swirling with new theories. Marie killing Vera because she was having an affair with Alasdair, framing him out of anger when Alasdair refused to leave his wife. Or Marie killing Vera because she and Vera were lovers, and Vera refused to leave her husband. Either way, Marie could have had reason to hurt them both, because if these pictures told any story, it was that the three of them were close.

Elaine's words about the animal heart echo in my mind. *I think whoever killed Felicity knew Vera very, very well.*

I look away from the photos to Crane, but my eyes catch on the scene just behind him. The normally cluttered kitchen worktop is a bit too clean.

Vera's last painting, the only remaining one with Mum's signature on the front and Vera's on the back, is gone.

CHAPTER 35

"BEWARE THE HEART KEPT IN DARKNESS." I RECITE PEony Lane's words out loud, still looking at the empty place on the worktop where Vera's last painting lay only moments ago. "*It will be death's catalyst if brought into the light without its proper name.*"

"You'll have to catch me up, Annie," Crane says, looking at me quizzically. "Why was Elaine here? And what does your fortune have to do with her running off?"

I pace over to the kitchen sink, where I can stare out the window in the direction of the skip where I found Felicity. My mind is racing through the backstreets of Chelsea, wondering where Elaine could have gone with the painting, and what her plans are with it. I'm itching to try to find her, but I've no idea where to start. "It's less about Elaine," I reply, "and more about the fact that she took the painting I pulled out of Frances's files. The one that was in my room. Its title is *Bleeding Heart*, and it was the only painting left that wasn't publicly displayed and sold as Mum's, or isn't in police Evidence currently. It has to be *the heart kept in darkness* from my fortune. That was the last painting, and now Elaine has it."

"What do you think she plans to do with it?" Crane asks.

"I have no idea. I can only hope she'll just keep it or destroy it. But she said she'd been trying to find out what really happened to Vera for years and that she felt something has always been off about the gallery," I say. "I don't know, she seemed rather harmless. But the fact that she took it and left while I was distracted . . . She wouldn't have known we had any of Vera's work here unless Max told her years ago. Maybe it was just a crime of opportunity. She saw something connected to Vera, so she took it before it could be hidden away again."

Crane comes to join me at the kitchen sink and follows my gaze out the window. "Start from the beginning, and tell me everything she said, if you can."

So I relate everything I can recall—the insistence that Vera was mentally unwell, regardless of Frances's feelings about it; how Elaine was forced to plant evidence and where that evidence initially came from. Once I finish telling him about Vera's way of taunting Max with animal hearts, he's clearly concerned.

"So," he says, "Elaine came to say that the thing she remembered, the thing she wanted to tell you, was that Vera used to torment Max by leaving animal hearts where he could find them?"

I nod and meet his eyes but don't say anything.

"Annie, Elaine wouldn't have known that you'd had the same threat—the appearance of an animal heart on your front steps the day before Fliss was found. It wasn't reported on the news. It's in the police file, but that's it. Unless Laura was talking about it with anyone else?"

"The only person I could think she'd share that with is my dad," I say. "And you met Sam—he likely has fingers in a lot of pies, but I can't think how he'd ever cross paths with Elaine, let alone have that come up in conversation. I think maybe she just wanted to share some things she knew."

"Or she wanted access to this house," Crane says.

"She couldn't have known about the painting," I remind him again. I hear the din of music from the stairs to the basement. "Actually . . . Mum needs to know the painting is gone," I say. "But I think there's more we need to ask her."

Crane's phone buzzes with an incoming call, and he pauses to check the number. "You go," he says. "I've got some things I can follow up on. We'll reconvene later."

I nod and give him a small wave as he walks toward the door, phone to his ear. I make my way down the stairs, where the whitewashed walls of Mum's studio look almost clinical without the large colorful canvases up against them. The chaos of splattered paint and art supplies still litters the space, but you can see the outlines of where the canvases were resting while she painted. It's like someone has come and pulled the teeth out of the place, and we're staring at the open wounds.

Mum is sitting in the center of the floor, cross-legged and wearing faded denim dungarees. She's staring at the space in a meditative way, but the overall effect of her pose and her expression is of a child who can see ghosts.

"Mum?" I say, and sit next to her on the floor.

We are silent for a while, and I think of so many things I could ask her. Things that aren't related to Vera or Felicity, but are about how she feels to have her name associated with things she never created, or how Sam Arlington could worm his way back into her heart, or whether or not Felicity ever got the guidance she was searching for when she came to Mum asking for an apprenticeship.

Each thought crowds on top of the others until I feel suffocated by them. But one thing floats to the surface, and it's an image from her new collection. It was something I saw when I came down here days ago to look at the paintings that are no longer here. Each one had echoes of the small canvas from Frances's files, of Vera's work—but those echoes were like a ghostly image behind Mum's bolder centerpieces. I now realize they were replicas of Vera's hearts, but rendered in black. I thought they were shadows when I looked at them at first, but it was as if she was bringing out pieces of Vera, killing them off, and then letting the bold images of her own evolved style thrive in their place.

"Mum, can I ask you about the new series? I saw it briefly, but knowing what I know now, about Vera's work and Dad's duplicity in forcing a public plagiarism of her work on you . . ."

Mum nods and rubs the back of her neck. "I call it the *Black Heart* series," she says. "I've felt so powerless for so long. I could have come forward and confessed that those paintings weren't mine back when they first made their splash. But the person behind the threats—the person speaking through that Folkestone man—didn't want the name Vera Huntington in the papers ever again. That was what they said over the phone in that horrible, modulated voice. So I was damned if I did, damned if I didn't. They'd hurt us both if I admitted to the theft of her work, and they'd hurt us if I kept the money from the paintings."

"Did the person making the threats ever say anything else about Vera?" I ask.

"Just that her name didn't deserve to be remembered," Mum says. "I didn't like the way they said that, because even after all the pain and stress Vera's paintings have caused me in my life, I still greatly admire her as an artist. She must have been something, when she was alive. So this series is the only kind of reply I can make to the voice on the other end of the phone. A reminder to them that I remember Vera, and that my art would never have been the same without her. She's always there, standing just behind everything I ever paint." Mum's voice is sad, but it's a resigned sort of sadness. The kind that signals she's working through her own memories, and the various ghosts that have haunted her over the years, and using her art as her voice.

She breathes deeply and says, "Can you ever forgive me, Annie? I've lied. I've lied *so many times* to you."

She's crying softly, so I put my arm around her shoulders, and it feels strange enough there that I pull it back. We don't really hug, Mum and I—and I don't like false displays of affection. They've always felt to me like steps in a social dance that neither Mum nor I have ever bothered with. It's funny—the lack of hugs between us actually feels like one of our comfort zones. We both know the other feels odd about them, and so we're released from those kinds of obligations when it's just us.

Our affection is in other things—I hug her every time I call the council about cutting the hedges that overhang her garden, or when I pay the water bill she's forgotten about. Her affection for me has, for years, been tied up in trying to protect me from dangers I didn't know about, and from my inconsistent father, and from Aunt Frances's isolated life that always threatened to loom large if Mum didn't put up boundaries. The shadow of Vera was haunting Mum all this time, but I think it became less about Laura Adams not being the real artist, and more about Vera Huntington being the name that signaled danger to her family.

Without its beating heart, your family will fall one by one. Peony Lane's words had seemed so clear to me when I sped up to Chelsea from Castle Knoll, but now . . . now I don't know who my family's beating heart could be. Part of me wonders if it was Frances, and after she died we've been falling one by one in slow succession. Mum is the first domino, toppling as the specter of Vera Huntington threatens the life she's worked hard to build.

But what if the beating heart of the family isn't a person at all? It could be *this*—this right here, the sideways fractured relationship between me and Mum, the feeble bridge between the two people who make up our tiny family. *One by one* gives the illusion of many people waiting to fall, but all you need for that to work is a pair of people ready to let a bridge burn.

"I forgave you almost immediately," I say. "I mean, I do wish you hadn't shut me out, and that you'd told me about everything when I was old enough to handle it, but . . ."

"I know, I'm so sorry. Sam probably wouldn't have had any hold on me if I'd had you to confide in, but I just didn't want to put all this on you," she says.

"Speaking of Sam, where is he? He hasn't been calling you, or coming by at all?" I ask.

Mum looks around the room, as if my dad will be just sitting to one side, but the worry lines in her face tell me there's more going through her mind than that.

But I don't have a chance to ask her more, because my phone buzzes with several texts from Crane.

Sorry to run, incident at the graveside of Vera Huntington. Max and Elaine both arrested for trying to stop the exhumation.

Then, a minute later: *That held us up, but going ahead now. Forest Hills cemetery, Marylebone.*

Two minutes go by, and one further message comes through: *xx*

CHAPTER 36

Number Ten Hopeful Forrest Linneman Goes Down in Scandal—Anonymous Source Sends Evidence of His Involvement in Torrence-Funded Pornography Business

The headline couldn't have been more sensational, but as I read the details over Max's shoulder, the story became even more salacious.

The well-respected dean of the Department of Psychology at University College London, Andrew Torrence, has been exposed as the primary funder of a prominent distributor of pornography. While the material produced by the company is strictly legal, a politician's ties to it have soiled his reputation beyond repair, as his campaign leans heavily on the "bring back morality" of conservative politics. Forrest Linneman has come out against the "loose moral values of the London youth," citing the sex shops in Soho, and the swinging and drug use of their clientele, as one of the main problems he hopes to eradicate in his borough.

But documents have been sent directly to the *Post* detailing not only the hypocrisy of Mr. Linneman—who has tried (and failed) to cover his financial tracks in funding the production of pornographic magazines—but also the extent of Mr. Torrence's pornography empire.

Andrew Torrence has long been a member of London's wealthy elite, and his family was also recently in the papers due to the murder of his daughter, socialite Vera Huntington. The *Post* has been in contact with University College London, who have informed us that Mr. Torrence is stepping down from his role immediately. We have also learned that several other prominent aristocrats associated with the Torrence family are distancing themselves from them, implying that the family name now carries seedy connections not suitable for upstanding individuals.

Andrew Torrence has a son, Max, who is currently studying in the department his father has just left. No word yet on whether Max will stand by his father and take up the more scandalous branch of the family business or if his hands are clean.

I watched Max carefully, as did much of the class. Professor Dane continued to talk about cases in which a sibling had killed another, and asked the class for analysis in each one. There was a case in which one twin killed the other to cleanse his own reputation and assume that of his brother after he had run up debts. Money was a common theme—people either wanted it or had lost it and blamed their sibling. Jealousy was at the core of most of the problematic sibling relationships. Jealousy and competition.

"You're wondering who could have leaked this information, aren't you?" I whispered to Max.

I admit that I was poking the bear a bit, but I was in a room full of people and Ford was waiting for me outside. Max might have been angry, but he wasn't stupid. He looked at me as if he could reduce me to ash with only his eyes. I refused to flinch, and I sensed that this bothered him.

Suddenly his expression changed—he'd had an idea. He gave me a predatory smile that made my skin crawl. "You know, my father's slimy side business may be news to me, but I have to admit it's got potential. I bet he knows a model who looks remarkably like you. In fact, I bet if I ask nicely, he'll pay her extra to pose in some extremely compromising ways and cook up the most entertaining interview to accompany it."

"You wouldn't dare. That's slander," I spat back at him. "Or libel, or something. I don't know, but Ford's got an excellent lawyer who will make sure your father's business is burned to the ground simply for the threat *of you doing that."*

"I can see the article taking shape, meet the model: Frances Adams tells us all the ways she loves to bake, and all the angles she loves to take it from while her bread rises." Max's words cut off as the slap I dealt him echoed throughout the lecture hall. I'd really wound my hand back before delivering it as well, so that the force of it against his face left a red mark in the shape of my handprint.

Max stood, gave me a look that said war had been declared, and marched out of the room.

"Well," Professor Dane said, "I think we'll just assume he deserved that, and move on."

CHAPTER 37

THE PICTURES ELAINE LEFT ARE TUCKED INTO FRANces's diary, which sits in the passenger seat of Mum's beaten-up Renault Mégane as I drive. I left her in her studio, still contemplating her life's work, sifting through emotions in the internal way that she does. There are probably endless conversations Mum and I should have, in order to develop a healthy mother-daughter relationship, but there's only so much emotional shoveling I can take in the middle of a murder investigation.

And then there's Crane, with his afterthought of digital kisses in a text message, that little *xx* rattling around my brain like loose change. The more I think about my fortune from Peony Lane, the more I realize it could be about my emotional life rather than my safety.

But it will be your own heart, if left unguarded, that's ripe for the knife.

If I were Aunt Frances, I'd see Felicity's murder as a template for someone who was coming for me. A literal translation of my fate, that like Felicity and Vera, I was destined to die by having my heart cut out.

But as I think about Crane, how careful he is around me, always some measure of his guard up, I feel like he's guarding my heart for me. And coming off this sticky conversation with Mum, knowing that arm's length is our comfort zone and our communication is always cloaked behind something else—her art, my help with organizing—it occurs to me that I don't know how to function in any other way.

Maybe I should change. Maybe I should give Peony Lane's fortune the metaphorical middle finger and crash through the romantic barriers between me and Crane, no longer dancing around the tension between us. I can leave my goddamn heart unguarded if I want to, Peony Lane.

Is that who I want to be? A new Annie who actually communicates how she feels, even when it's scary?

I forgot who I was for a moment there.

The words from Frances's diary come unbidden to my mind. I'm almost at the cemetery where Vera's exhumation is happening, but I see a good spot to pull over, so I do. I flip through the pages of Frances's diary, searching.

There it is—Vera said it to Frances, twice. Once, after they'd been dancing at Hatchetts, she said, *Let's go dancing again soon. That was the most fun I've had in ages. I almost forgot who I was for a moment there.* And then, again, when she found Frances in Ronnie Scott's on the night she was murdered. She'd come to Frances for help, and Frances said something that clearly set off a plan in Vera's mind.

I flip the pages and reread the entire passage, my heart starting to hammer as the pieces of this mystery come together.

I turned to Vera and watched her expression change when she saw the determination in my face. "What if you got to him first?" I asked.

The music filled the club, and Vera stared at the stage, transfixed. "I could . . . You're right. What if I got to him first?"

I sensed that her mind was racing—she was miles away. I had the sudden worry that I'd set off a spark that had struck a powder keg within her. "Vera?" I prodded her gently. She started nodding as if I'd just said something significant, still watching the stage.

"I think . . . yes. Thank you, Frances. I forgot who I was for a moment there," she said. It was the second time I'd heard her say that, and something about it unsettled me. But we were quiet for the rest of the set, me watching Vera from the corner of my eye, and Vera transfixed by the musicians but clearly not seeing them at all.

I shut the diary and start the car again, racing toward Crane and the cemetery. I see several vans parked just inside the gates, and police tape cordoning off a space where a digger has pulled up the earth that's been covering the grave of Vera Huntington for the past fifty-four years. A team of two men in white forensic jumpsuits have set up a pulley system. They've raised the coffin out of its resting place and are sliding it across the earth toward a ramp leading to the back of one of the vans.

Crane stands a little apart, his hands in his pockets, wearing a tan mac I've never seen him in before. It must have been in the back of his car, or borrowed from someone, but he very much looks like a man from another era. He's watching the scene solemnly, his dark beard striking against the neatly pressed lines of the coat. There's a gray mist in the air, the kind that can shift to rain without you noticing until you're wet through.

I park and rush out toward Crane. When he sees me he slides a hand across his jaw, a worried gesture of his that I can identify from a distance. He could be in a crowd of people at Glastonbury, me on an opposite hillside, and I'd still feel the pull of that stature like a magnetic force. All the lights and sounds would melt away and I'd spot him, an impossible task for anyone else.

"Annie, hey. You shouldn't be here; there was trouble earlier—this whole exhumation has been rather volatile," he says.

"Then why did you tell me where it was happening?" I ask. He opens his mouth to speak, but I barrel onward. "That doesn't matter," I say. "I've just discovered two very important things. Have they opened the coffin yet?"

"Only briefly, to confirm that there's a body inside," he says.

"And there was?"

Crane gives me a strange sideways look. "Yes. Why?"

We turn to watch the coffin being loaded into the back of the van, destined for Kabir's lab. The cherrywood has been wiped free of the wet soil that would have been clinging to it when they brought it back into the world of the living. There's a veneer of old lacquer and water damage visible on one side, and then the coffin slides into place and the van doors close.

"Because I think I know what Kabir is going to find when he examines the body," I say.

Crane turns back to me, and we stand in the gathering mist, only a foot or so between us.

"And what's that?" he asks.

"That the body in there isn't Vera Huntington's," I say. "It's Marie Cavanaugh's."

Crane's eyes widen a fraction, and the deep brown of them looks almost black in the flat January light. The mist has left droplets clinging to his hair, and I hastily run a hand through my own blond curls, feeling them starting to react to the moisture.

"How on earth did you work that out?" he asks, but one corner of his mouth is traveling upward, amused. He wants me to be right. He suspects that I might be. And I am, about this. I just hope I'm right about my second important discovery.

"I'll explain on the way, but I think we need to follow that body to the lab," I say.

He brushes back the damp hair from his forehead and watches the van as it drives through the gates of the cemetery and out onto the main road.

"All right, let's go," he says finally. "But what was the other important thing you discovered? You said there were two things. I'm assuming the wrong body in the coffin is the first one."

"It was. The second is, well . . . it's unrelated." I look at him and take another small step forward, so that I've closed the gap between us. Before I can hesitate, or change my mind, or pretend I was just leaning in to brush something off his shoulder, I slide both my hands up either side of his neck. Then I lean in and kiss him.

CHAPTER 38

"DO YOU REALLY THINK HE CAN DO THAT?" I SAID TO Ford as he drove us back to Chelsea. I told him what had happened with Max at the university, and while Ford's eyes remained fixed on the road, I could tell he was furious. His knuckles were white as they gripped the steering wheel, and he took the turns a little too fast. "Do you think Max can have someone who looks like me pose naked in a magazine and print a false interview as if it really is me?"

"It would be defamation," Ford said. "He could do it, but we would sue the life out of him, and we'd win. It depends on how much of his business and reputation he wants to stake on causing you harm. He might be the type to risk it all, simply because he'd know you'd suffer distress in the process."

"I wish there was a way for us to strike first," I said. "I think he killed Vera, and I want to prove it. That would stop him."

Ford looked worried and gave me several glances while driving, as if checking I was still there. "Try not to let him get to you," he said. "It's what he wants—to rattle you. To make you feel powerless. And you aren't powerless, Frances. Far from it."

My hand still stung from the slap I'd dealt Max, even though at least fifteen minutes had passed. I took a deep breath and nodded. Something about being near Ford made me feel stronger, more powerful. If Max wanted a war, I'd give him one. Ford and I would give him one.

Ford slowed the car when we turned down Tregunter Road, because it became clear someone was waiting on the steps for us. He was leaning back across several steps in a sort of sprawl, and as we drew nearer I straightened in my seat.

"That's Brian Folkestone," I said warily.

When Ford pulled up across the road from the house—parked illegally, but he was the type to park where he liked and pay the fine like it was nothing—Brian's face was thrown into sharp relief, and he looked utterly distraught. Straightaway my fear melted, because I could see the red of his eyes, the hunch of his shoulders. He was miserable. There was a half-empty bottle of vodka near his side, and he was swaying slightly.

I reached for the car door handle, but Ford put his hand on my arm. "Frances, I don't care how hopeless the man looks, you're to stay here. Let me deal with this."

I gave Ford a stern look. "You're welcome to come with me, but I'm going to talk to him. I need to. There are things I have to know." I opened the car door and got out. Ford was by my side in seconds, his arm around my waist.

"There are times where I admire how headstrong you are, Frances, but this isn't one of them. You might have missed my enthusiasm for you as a person, but I'll reiterate now that I am deeply in love with you and that means your safety is of paramount importance to me."

My grin was so broad I could barely contain it, but I simply said, "Thank you. I hope you'll balance that concern for my safety alongside your faith in my judgment. And I'll add that I love you too."

He nodded wearily, but his lips held a slight smile. "Thank you for the addendum. And I relent. Let's talk to him together."

By then we were at the bottom of the steps, and Brian had been watching us coming. He hadn't moved, except to lift his head from the steps to sit up a bit better, so that he could take a swig from the vodka bottle.

"Hello, Brian," I said. "I'd ask you what you're doing here, but I have a feeling it has something to do with Vera. Is that right?"

Brian looked up at me blearily. "I just came to tell you, so that your boyfriend doesn't set his dogs on me"—Brian eyed Ford with what little drunken menace he could muster—"that I keep getting instructions to scare you, intimidate you to stop you sniffing around." He nodded at me. "But I wanted to tell you I ain't gonna do it, on account of Vera."

"What do you mean, on account of Vera?" I asked.

"Just what I said," Brian slurred. "She liked you, she told me. You were a good 'un, she told me. I'm not to hurt you." His eyes watered, and his expression crumpled.

I gently stepped out of the circle of Ford's arm, and he let me. I moved to the step where Brian sat, and crouched down near him. "I'm sorry she's gone," I said. "I miss her too. And I'm grateful you shared that with us. It'll help keep me safe. Can you tell me who was instructing you to silence me?"

Brian shook his head forcefully, which must have set off a wave of drunken dizziness, and he took a moment to stop swaying. I was worried he might be sick, but he swallowed hard and said, "Can't, sorry. I'll go now, won't darken your step." He struggled to his feet, and Ford helped steady him when he swayed. "But just know, I love Vera. Loved. Loved her. There's nothing I wouldn't do for her."

CHAPTER 39

I SENSE CRANE'S SHARP INTAKE OF BREATH AS I KISS him—I've surprised him, but he hasn't moved away. His hands take a worrying amount of time to find my waist, and I think for a moment he's frozen out of some objection. But then we sink into the kiss, and as I start enjoying how soft his lips are and the slight brush of his beard against my chin, I feel his hands at the small of my back.

They move to my waist and pull me in for a moment, but then he makes a small noise at the back of his throat and gently nudges me away. I imagine that his mouth leaves mine reluctantly, and days later I'll replay this moment, thinking I hear the slight sound of lips parting that signals two people who have ended a kiss with the energy of having wanted it. Not one person silently backing away, which is the shadow the memory creates when I question my own reading of it.

He looks at me for what seems like a lifetime, and I think he might be considering pulling me toward him again and resuming what I started, but he puts one hand into his coat pocket for his keys.

"I—" he starts, and I flush with embarrassment as it occurs to me that I've overstepped.

"Sorry," I say instinctively, "I shouldn't have, I mean . . ." I'm still watching him for subtle hints that this wasn't just me, that there's some spark on his side that's right here with me. His cheeks flush a little, but I can't tell if it's the cold creeping around us as the mist has turned to rain.

"No, don't be sorry," he says, and stares at the ground while he rummages in his pockets. I'm certain he found his keys in there ages ago, but he keeps rattling them and dropping them back into the depths of his pocket in order to have somewhere for his hands to be that isn't near me. Or that's the small insult I'm choosing to see, as the seconds stretch out between us and he doesn't step back to me to close the distance again.

"No, this was terrible timing," I say, and I wince as I realize how true that is. "We're graveside at an exhumation, in the middle of a murder investigation. I don't know what I was thinking, and—"

His eyes meet mine and I stop babbling. "It's, um . . . yeah, the timing was pretty interesting," he adds slowly, "but I don't want you to think I don't . . ." He stops, and his hand leaves his pocket to make a frustrated pass through his damp hair. He bites his lip. I don't know if I've ever seen him do that before. It's unnerving how much electricity there is in that one small gesture. "There are things I need to explain . . . Maybe not now, though. Another time?"

I feel my chest squeeze in on itself, like the rejection blow is physical. Because that's a rejection, isn't it?

I nod and swallow hard. "Another time," I manage to choke out.

"I'll meet you at the pathology lab, then," he says, and he

doesn't wait for my answer before turning and walking to his car.

I make some kind of noise of agreement. And then I'm back behind the wheel of Mum's car, and while I fight the traffic to University College Hospital, I begin the agonizing spiral of analyzing every moment of closeness I've ever had with Rowan Crane.

Perhaps I had it wrong all this time. His arm around my waist only ever happened when I was upset; he only ever reached for my hand if I needed comfort. He's the steadfast type, calm and sincere, and wouldn't let someone sit near him in tears without offering consolation.

I slam my hands against the steering wheel, letting the emotions flow out of me while I'm alone in traffic and not on display in a pathology lab trying to solve a murder. I want to get all these feelings out so that I can pack them all away again, neatly, under a boulder of embarrassment and worry that I've irrevocably changed the one friendship that I'd really come to depend on.

I breathe in deeply through my nose, trying to stop the tears that have already erupted down my face. Showing up puffy eyed and snotty from crying would be setting fire to the last feeble strand of my dignity, and I will *not* have that.

"Pull yourself together, Annie," I say as I search for a space in the hospital car park. "You took a risk. So what if it was weird? That's on him. You were the one who was brave, and sometimes bold moves mean bitter consequences." I flip down the sun visor and check in the tiny mirror on the back that my mascara hasn't run. Mercifully, I look okay. My hair is starting to expand to new dimensions from the moisture outside, but my face looks relatively normal.

I open the glove compartment to see if Mum has any hair

ties in there and only find one of her many boho scarves. I roll it into a thin band, pile my curls on top of my head, and tie the scarf around it several times so that the fabric doesn't hang down. I look like a teenager with a prom updo, but it's better than the eighties frizz I was sporting. And messing with my hair gives me something to focus on that isn't Crane. Jesus, I can't even call him by his first name in my own head. What was I thinking, kissing him?

I swallow the shame that threatens to make me lock all the car doors and never set foot outside again. The temptation to sit in this car forever and just slowly waste away is strong. If I recline the seat and lie down in it, weeks could go by before anyone decides to look any closer.

"Stop your melodrama, Annie," I say to myself. "And get your arse out of the car. Also, no more talking to yourself."

I'm still giving myself an internal pep talk as I walk to the car park lifts, but as I walk I scan the rows of cars for signs of Rowan's silver VW. There, I did it—Rowan. His name is Rowan. If I was ever admitting to having feelings for him, I'd need to be on a first-name basis with the man. Even if it's only mentally.

I wish for the lift to be dreadfully slow, stopping at every floor, but it whooshes to the pathology lab in what feels like an unfairly small amount of time. To calm myself down, I do what I always do—I run through the facts of the case in my head. There are puzzles to be solved, crimes to be unpacked. Murderers to be caught.

I knock lightly on the door to Kabir's office and hear him call, "Come in!"

I push the door slightly open but stand on the other side of it so I'm not looking in. "Um, it's Annie Adams, and I have to warn you, I'm not the type of person who can see a dead body and remain conscious. So, if you don't mind giving me a heads-up of what you've got on display in there, I'd appreciate it?"

A moment later Kabir's face peers around the door and he gives me a sympathetic smile. "No worries, I completely understand. Pathology isn't for everyone. You'd best stay out here, then."

"Um, is Detective Crane in there? He was on his way here. I'm just not sure if I beat him through traffic," I say.

"I haven't seen him," Kabir says. "I'm just starting the preliminary examination of the body, but is there something I can help you with in the meantime?"

I think quickly, wondering if I should share my theories with Kabir instead. It feels weirdly like a betrayal of my partnership with Crane, but then, I don't know if time is on our side with this case. The exhumation of this body will have set off alarm bells to everyone who was involved in Vera's original case.

I feel my phone buzz in my pocket, and motion for Kabir to step into the hall with me. He does, and I glance briefly to see a text from Crane: *Sorry, problem with Elaine and Max. There was nothing to hold them for other than disturbing the peace while trying to disrupt our exhumation, so they were cut loose an hour ago. Heading to the gallery to follow up your lead.*

I wait a beat, but there's no *xx* that follows. He's probably thinking that every friendly gesture he's ever given me was misunderstood as affection, because I'm emotionally stunted and don't know how to properly connect with someone. *Stop it, Annie, focus.*

"If I could run something by you?" I say to Kabir, who is patiently standing there watching me as I contain an internal crisis of self. "I think I've discovered something, and it might help your autopsy if I flag a few things for you to check."

"Of course," he says. "What do you have?"

I'm holding Frances's diary. I flip through it and take out the photos of Alasdair and Marie, and Marie and Vera. I hold them out to him.

"This woman here is Marie Cavanaugh. She was a nurse who worked with Alasdair Huntington and was a witness to his crimes. The doctor was playing God—he was performing unethical experimental surgeries on patients who'd been living on the streets."

Kabir lets out a long whistle. "That's quite a discovery," he says.

"Well, there's more, but I need you to bear with me through this one—it's an extremely twisted set of events. But you remember how, when you first looked at the old autopsy of Vera for us, you flagged that something wasn't right with the dental records?"

"The autopsy report said there were signs of blue in her gums, which signifies heavy metal poisoning," Kabir says. "But the dental records didn't reflect that."

"I think the dental records included in that file are Vera's, but the body isn't. I think the body is actually Marie Cavanaugh's," I say. "I think Vera Huntington found out what her husband was doing, worried he was going to have her killed, and plotted to stop him for good by framing him for her own murder. Conveniently, there was another person Vera saw as Alasdair's accomplice, someone she also felt should suffer for his crimes—Marie Cavanaugh. Vera and Marie bore a passing resemblance to each other, and I think Vera killed Marie in order to punish both Marie and her husband. Alasdair would go to prison for Vera's murder, and Marie would no longer be making a bad system worse. And Vera could disappear as Marie."

"Marie didn't keep working at the hospital after Vera died, I assume?" Kabir asks.

"She conveniently quit her job by phone, saying the Huntington case was too traumatic for her and she was going to start a new life with her sister in Canada. Which I think Vera probably did do, minus the sister. I suspect she only came back to the UK once everyone who could identify her was gone."

"Wow," Kabir says. "I mean . . ." He trails off, lost for words, then laughs nervously.

"You think I've lost it, don't you?" I say. The embarrassment from earlier is still sitting in my stomach like a coiled snake, and the way Kabir's features shift when he looks at me is threatening to wake it back up again. His expression is patient but clearly skeptical. At least he doesn't look condescending, and for that he's still in my good books.

"I'll admit, it's . . . a lot. But I'll see about Marie Cavanaugh's dental records, which will tell us for sure. But slowly poisoning someone with heavy metals isn't a reliable way to kill them, if Vera was feeling threatened and wanted to disappear quickly."

"That wasn't the cause of death, though," I add. "You said the blue lines in her gums threw doubt on the cause of death, which meant we could exhume her body."

Kabir looks thoughtful, then says, "Yes, I'd say the heavy metals, while at toxic levels, weren't what killed her. And that could have been incidental—it was the 1960s, after all, and lead paint was still common in houses and on furniture back then. There were even old houses where lead pipes hadn't been changed, so it could have got into her system that way. I'll double-check everything, but I think you're onto something."

I feel my jaw unclench, but just a little. "Thanks, Kabir," I say. "Even if you're just humoring me, I appreciate it."

"It's no problem. And I'm not humoring you; it's like you said. Something doesn't add up about those dental records, and you've given me a leg up in the job of finding out what it is."

I smile at him, relieved.

"Can I have your number?" he asks. His cheeks color slightly, and he adds, "To call you with what I find."

"Oh, um, sure," I say. He pulls his phone out of his pocket and enters my number as I rattle it off for him. "Call me as soon as you find anything." I turn to walk back to the lifts.

"Um, Annie?" Kabir calls after me.

"Yeah?"

"Can I also maybe just . . . call you? For a coffee or a drink or something sometime?"

My own phone is still in my hand and hasn't buzzed since that last message from Crane. I look down at it once more, at Crane's words on the screen, all perfunctory and straightforward and just about the case. No warmth, just business.

Kabir's face is open and easygoing, and it's clear that he's asking me out because he's interested in me. It feels, I don't know . . . nice to be noticed in that way.

"Yeah," I say. "I'd like that."

CHAPTER 40

"ANNIE ADAMS, THIS IS BRIAN FOLKESTONE," A VOICE says as I pick up a call from an unknown number. Mum's old Renault doesn't have Bluetooth, so I have to mildly break the law by picking up the call manually while the light is red, then putting the phone on speaker and jamming it into the cup holder. I'm driving back from the hospital, trying not to think of Rowan Crane and how even my slight encouragement of Kabir feels like cheating. But what else was I supposed to do? Kabir seems nice. He's extremely attractive. He's an actual doctor, which is an upgrade from the string of irresponsible musicians I dated before moving to Castle Knoll.

But not only does my brain keep replaying that kiss with Crane, it keeps finding all the small things about it that might signal hope. The tiny beat when he pulled me closer. The way he bit his lip when he was watching me try to backpedal and apologize, and the fact that he told me not to be sorry. And that small half sentence, when he started to say,

But I don't want you to think I don't, that he never finished. Was he about to say he didn't want me to think he wasn't interested?

Crane is headed to the Knightsbridge gallery to confront Marie, who is actually Vera. A confrontation with Max Torrence is probably looming as well, as I'm almost certain he has helped cover for Vera all these years and could even have helped her kill Marie. I'm still unsure which one of them killed Felicity, but that could have been a team effort as well.

Brian Folkestone, on the other hand, was probably one step behind the pair of them and almost always in danger of finding them out. Much like Elaine, he was someone Vera used, and his affection for her would have blinded him. From what I read in Frances's diary, he sank deeply into his grief for Vera, and his life became a shadow of what it once was.

"Mr. Folkestone, how can I help you?" I ask as I drive.

"I . . . I have information for you, because I really don't want any more people to get hurt," he says.

"If someone is in danger, you need to call the police," I say, but not unkindly.

"I did," Folkestone says. "I tried Detective Crane, but he said he was tied up with something else. Then I called the normal police, but my whole explanation for why someone's in danger sounded so mad to them that they brushed me off."

"Okay, back up a minute and maybe tell me the details," I say. "Who exactly is in danger?"

"Your mum. Something's been set in motion, and I had to call to try to stop it," he says. His voice sounds breathy, like he's walking somewhere quickly.

I feel my pulse spike, cursing myself for thinking Mum would be out of the firing line as long as she stays in the house with the doors locked. I imagined Crane and I would confront Max and Vera and defuse the threat without Mum ever having to know that things got tense.

"What's been set in motion? I'm in the car, so I can get to wherever I need to be. What's happening?"

"I live at the Barbican, right? In one of the towers. And Laura's exhibition is opening here tonight. It must have been some twist of fate, but when I was eating outside at the café, I saw Max's ex-wife Elaine crossing the courtyard with a canvas. A small one, but unmistakably one of Vera's that Laura had signed."

My thoughts race. I think of Felicity and those canvases in black bin bags. The threats Mum got on her life and mine, if any more of Vera's art was put out into the world with Mum's name on it. I don't know what Elaine's game is, but if Vera killed Marie, she could have killed Felicity too. It would have been her fight from the shadows to keep her remaining work out of the limelight in the hope that her name would never come up again. She wouldn't want people to start looking too closely at her life and her "death."

"The police are at the gallery in Knightsbridge. They're going to make an arrest for Vera's murder," I say. "I think Mum will be safe. Those threats won't hold once the culprit is behind bars." I don't mention that Vera's been alive all this time. It's too much to explain and I'm mostly just wanting to hear what Brian has to say.

I'm driving south down Gower Street, and I know the way to the Barbican by heart, because Mum and I go there all the time. It's an art hub—concerts, talks, exhibitions—a brutalist concrete jungle that feels like a second home to me. I calm my jumpy nerves by thinking about the Barbican's various towers, looking like beehives with plants on overstuffed balconies. When I was in my teens I always wanted to live in a flat there. I had dreams of moving out of Mum's house and renting one, where I'd spend all day writing novels and turning one of the spare bedrooms into a photo-developing suite. It was an independence that never materialized, and I realize I feel a bit of a loss for that.

"I really think you should come here. Whatever Elaine is planning to do to your mum's exhibition—you're the best person to stop it," Brian says. "If there's security, they'll let you in. You can interfere on behalf of Laura."

I nod, even though I know he can't see me. "Okay, I'm on my way. I know where the exhibition's being set up, and you've given me enough time to go and get that painting before it gets added to the collection, or before Elaine does something drastic to expose Mum's duplicity. I'm sure Mum would like to come clean for Vera sometime, but I want her to have a chance to do it on her own terms." I pause, focusing on a tight turn, and then add, "Thanks, Brian."

"It's the least I could do," Brian says. "Like I said, I don't want anyone else to get hurt."

I find a car park and try calling Mum, but she's not picking up. She's likely still in the studio, and she often leaves her phone somewhere upstairs while she's down there. It's not cause for huge concern, but Folkestone saying that Mum might be in danger has me on high alert. I think, most likely, it's her reputation that's really at stake here. Crane will arrest Max and Vera, and even if that canvas was added to the show, no one will know it wasn't Mum's.

Unless that's what Elaine is actually planning—and I suspect it is. After all these years, Elaine has finally worked out that Mum has been using Vera's art as her own, and Elaine is ready to set the record straight. Elaine is probably feeling rather noble, bringing back the memory of her dead friend.

Because if Elaine has been barred from the gallery since Vera's return as Marie, I'm betting she wasn't in on Max and Vera's frame-up job in the first place. She likely still believes Vera's dead.

I call Crane, and to my surprise, he picks up on the third ring. I'd thought he'd have his hands full, with Max and Vera.

"Annie, everything okay?" he asks.

I push down the swirl of feelings that come up when I hear his voice and try to stay focused on the matter at hand. After all, that's what Crane would do.

"Yeah, relatively okay," I say, as I make my way to the Sculpture Court and through the doors toward the Art Gallery. It's on the third floor, and I take the stairs two at a time. "I'm at Mum's venue at the Barbican Centre. I think Elaine is planning to use that remaining canvas for some kind of public revenge against Mum. I think she knows Mum got famous using Vera's art, but it wasn't clear to Elaine until she recognized Vera's handwriting and message on the back of that canvas at the house. I don't think Elaine ever saw any of Vera's more abstract work back in the sixties. Frances hid that at Ford's soon after Vera left it with her."

"So what are you going to do? Annie? Don't confront Elaine. I'll make my way there. That space should be locked anyway, right? The art is extremely valuable."

I reach the doors to the gallery, and a man is slumped against them. "Oh . . . *shit*," I say.

"What? Annie? What is it?"

"It's Mum's broker, Bobby. He's . . . he's not bleeding, but can you call the Barbican, get their security up here, and have them send an ambulance? I really hope he's just unconscious." I feel his neck for a pulse, then realize I'm only doing that because it's what people do on TV and I actually don't know the proper spot to take a pulse. With a flood of relief, I notice he's breathing. I shake him gently, and he slumps further, until he's lying on the floor.

I feel my palms start to sweat as the worry hits me. Mum isn't answering her phone. What if it's because she's already here? What if she's inside the gallery, lured out of the house somehow by Max and Vera? Elaine may want to ruin Mum's reputation by exposing her fraud, but Max and Vera have reason to silence her permanently.

"Rowan," I say, my voice wavering. I've used his first name, which should be enough to signal how afraid I am. If I barge through those doors and have to confront the murder of my mother . . . It's a loss I can't bear to think about.

Without its beating heart, your family will fall one by one.

"It's okay, Annie, I'm coming. Just get somewhere safe, I'm on my way," he says, his voice steady but barely hiding an edge of concern.

"Folkestone said he called you," I say quickly, as I check the handle to the gallery door and find it unlocked. Elaine must have used the broker's keys, though I have no idea how she incapacitated him. "But he said you told him you were in the middle of something. He saw Elaine come this way. Can you get her description out there?"

I step into the dark space, and I'm greeted by the shadows of Mum's paintings all around me—the colors are sapped of all their vibrancy in this light. I scan the room for Mum, and exhale when I see it's clear. Then I look at the walls for any kind of sabotage, or for the last canvas hanging among the originals. I wouldn't put it past Elaine to splash them all with paint, covering them like an animal-rights protester.

But there's nothing.

"Did you get them? Max and Vera?" I ask quietly. "Crane?"

There's a small silence, then the sound of a car door unlocking in the background.

"Annie," Crane says, his voice suddenly colored with angry concern, "Folkestone never called me."

And that's when I feel it—the cold metal of the knife against my throat.

CHAPTER 41

MY PHONE CLATTERS TO THE FLOOR AS FOLKESTONE knocks it out of my hand, pressing the knife a little deeper against my skin. It's sharp. I can feel the sting of a thin line where the blade is, and the hot prickle of blood. I swallow hard, trying to push down the fear and lightheadedness that press at me in tandem, then regret the movement of my throat as it just meets the blade more completely.

My brain is a mixture of fragments of my fortune, and words from Frances's diary.

A drunken Brian on the Chelsea steps, saying to Frances, *I love Vera. Loved. Loved her. There's nothing I wouldn't do for her.* He slipped then. He said *love* first, because he knew she was still alive. Because he'd killed for her.

But it will be your own heart, if left unguarded, that's ripe for the knife.

I consider shoving an elbow backward into Folkestone's ribs, but he's significantly larger than I am, and I imagine the force of it simply giving the hand holding the knife more chance to bite into my neck.

Instead I take a shaky breath and raise my hands higher into the air. "What do you want from me, Brian?" I ask.

"That one's simple," he says. "I was going to kill Laura, but she's been hard to get to, never leaving her house, never alone. So you'll do nicely—I'll be able to take something from Laura, something she values. Just like she took something valuable from Vera."

"You know my mum wasn't the person who forged her name on Vera's work, right? My dad was behind that," I say, forcing calm into my voice.

"She's just as guilty. She's lived all these years using Vera's work as her own!" he growls.

"You know that Vera's been alive all this time," I say, "because you helped her fake her own death. What does Vera think about the paintings? Surely you've talked to her. It was quiet after Mum gave away all that money. She never would have used any more of Vera's work if Elaine hadn't taken that last canvas."

"Vera won't see me," he says, and he pushes me farther into the darkened gallery space.

"But you were the middleman who extorted Mum," I say, confused. I try to slow my breathing, thinking. If Folkestone's only aim is to kill me to hurt Mum, he's not going to want to take his time about it. I'm not sure how to negotiate with someone whose only goal is endgame. Brian will know by now that it's all unraveling—if we've found Vera, it's just a matter of time before he loses everything.

"Vera just wanted out, to keep her name out of the papers. She said she didn't care about Laura using her work. But she didn't see the injustice of it all! After everything she went through to be free, free of Alasdair, who wouldn't let her paint, free of her father, who told her she was mad . . ."

"So, was it only ever you who pressured Mum for that money?"

"The money was the easiest way to get to Laura, until now. I just didn't realize how much I was willing to sacrifice for Vera. My Vera, a true visionary, someone so special they only come around once in a generation. The only person who wanted to get justice for my sister, who wanted to stop her horrible husband killing more people." His breath beats against the back of my neck, and I recoil. He smells of stale beer and cigarettes. For some reason I think of whisky, and his comment at the pub about why he never drinks it—it's too easy to hide the taste of poison.

"That's how you got to Marie, isn't it? You put something in her drink. Whisky, was it? The pathologist said it looked like lead poisoning."

"Mercury, from a thermometer," he says. "A lethal dose, though it took her a full day to die," he adds, and for a moment he sounds almost wistful, as if he wishes he could be back there. It's then that I realize I'm dealing with someone with zero moral compass and that negotiating is going to be pointless. I feel a horrible stretch of helplessness and start looking around the room for something—anything—I can use as a weapon.

For a moment I think I see the shadow of movement, and hope flutters for a second that Crane might have made it here. Or possibly Elaine? Though I think Folkestone's story about Elaine and that canvas was a ruse.

I don't want to provoke him further, but Vera seems to be something of a fixation for him, and the only idea I've got left is to keep him talking about her until Crane gets here. As long as I can keep him off the topic of what he plans to do with me, I might survive a bit longer.

"Vera must have had the idea though, to kill Marie?" I try. "You aren't guilty completely, if you both planned it together." Which is not true at all, but I'm fishing for any kind of out I can find. "If you loved her, she manipulated you to help her, she used you," I say. "And Frances even gave her the idea," I add. "In her diary, she told Vera, *What if you got to him first?* As in, what if you took down your husband before he could kill you?"

"Vera isn't guilty of anything. This was all me!" he says, getting agitated again. "She may have liked the idea of framing her husband—she even practiced his stitching and would go over different plans for how we'd find a body so we could imitate his work on it. But she never wanted to kill anyone. She wanted me to get a body out of the morgue at the hospital, a Jane Doe. But the doctor couldn't go to prison and have his accomplice just walk free. Marie had to die, and she'd solve a problem for us in the process. That means Vera's clean."

It doesn't actually mean that, but I'm not about to argue with him. The shadow moves again, and I feel my pulse in my mouth. There's definitely someone in here, but whether it's someone who's going to help me or someone like Elaine—who might not care if I die—I can't say. But by their shape and the way they move, I know it isn't Crane.

"So, Felicity was your work too?" I say, eyeing the shadow. I consider lunging to my left, because Folkestone is right-handed and my priority right now is avoiding his knife. He's considerably taller than I am and may not expect me to move downward. I consider how I might shift my weight away from him in a direction he won't expect. "I suppose Felicity's chest cavity wasn't closed up neatly, like Marie's. You wanted to imitate the doctor's work but couldn't. Because it was Vera who helped you sew up Marie's chest. But why kill Felicity, who was just trying to keep more of Vera's work out of circulation?"

"That wasn't what she was doing," the shadow says, and it's a man's voice. He steps closer to us, and I recognize the cheap suit and bad haircut of my dad, Sam Arlington.

CHAPTER 42

"OH, YOU'VE GOT TO BE JOKING," I SAY, MY VOICE GOing breathy. The last bits of hope I had drain from me, and I feel like my legs might give way. There's no way Sam is here to offer any help, and this is looking like a terrible partnership I could never have predicted.

But Brian's arm slackens just a bit, and whether it's out of surprise or confusion, I'm not sure. But I'm not going to wait for a second chance. I let all my weight shift left, and lunge that way while falling to the floor.

It doesn't entirely work. While I'm momentarily away from his knife, it just gives him a chance to tackle me and pin me down. He braces his knee against both of my legs, and in seconds I'm in a worse position than I was before. The knife isn't at my throat now. Instead, it's hovering over my heart.

Right where Peony Lane said it would be.

Sam is circling behind Folkestone, his expression impossible to read. Shadows are still hiding most of him, but I think about how he's never made any effort to find me, talk to me, even send me a birthday card or make a phone call. The man doesn't know me at all, and in that sense, he probably doesn't care if I die. Realizing that, I feel a stab in my chest that's unrelated to the knife pressing there.

Why didn't he want to know me all these years? What did I ever do that meant I was inconsequential, someone to ignore until I could be maneuvered like just another game piece in a long con? For decades I told myself he was some loser who didn't want a daughter. But lying here, watching him hover on the sidelines while a madman prepares to cut my heart out, I realize it isn't that he doesn't want a daughter. It's that he doesn't want *me.*

And now if I die, it means all the things I know die, too—no one else would know he was ever here. Which . . . Why is he here?

Folkestone's knife bites into the cotton top I'm wearing, and he's got it right under my left breast, to the side of my sternum. The knife tip doesn't move but I see his shoulders rise slightly as his arms tense, preparing the force he'll need to break through my ribs and hit straight at my heart. I squirm—it's the only thing I can do, try to shift the alignment of the knife at my heart so that he would miss and I might stand a chance if he stabs me, but it's a feeble move.

Folkestone's eyes are glassy but intense, like he's in the moment but also somewhere far away. Like a smoker taking their first drag of a cigarette in a long time. This man is a killer, and Vera was likely only an excuse for him to unleash that.

He inhales, ready to strike—and then a hand grasps his throat from behind, unsteadying him. The knife breaks my skin as he pushes forward to shake Sam off. I feel the hot bloom of blood and the searing pain as he nicks my rib. I scream, but Sam's other hand comes around Folkestone's back and pulls at the arm holding the knife. Sam isn't as tall or as strong as Folkestone, but it's enough to allow me to get my knees up between us, and I kick at his chest, hard.

Sam is still behind him, squeezing his neck, and Brian stumbles backward, pinning Sam underneath him. I reach into the hole in my top and feel the tacky flow of blood. It'll be a fight for me to stay conscious, given how badly I handle blood. But as the world starts to swim, the realization that Sam is trying to help sends a spark of adrenaline through me, and I lunge at Brian before he can turn on Sam.

Together, Sam and I wrench the knife out of his hand, but since I'm the one he's facing, he's able to take his other fist and hit me in the face. I reel backward, but I hold on to the knife. Sam throws a punch at Brian's face and misses, and Brian flies at me.

I hold the knife outward, so that if he tries to use the force of his body to pin me again, he'll meet the blade. I never thought I'd be the kind of person to kill someone, and I truly don't want to invite that memory into my life, but I realize then that if I have to, I'll kill Brian Folkestone. And I won't even be conflicted about it. I'll feel awful, having taken a life, but I won't wish I'd done something differently.

But Brian knows how to fight far better than I do, and he comes at me slightly sideways, grabbing my arm and twisting it outward, forcing my fingers to release the knife or my wrist will snap. I scream again as the knife clatters to the floor. It's slippery now, and the realization that it's my blood sends me to my knees. Stars spot my vision, and I feel for the cut on my chest again. It's minor. I let loose an almost-maniacal laugh when I understand that most of the blood is from my nose, from when Brian hit me. My injuries are superficial, but my wooziness with blood is what actually knocks me out.

The last thing I see is Brian's face—determined, angry, and then contorted with pain. His mouth opens and shuts above me like a sinister fish, and as my hearing fades and black swallows my vision, I'm almost certain that Sam has stabbed him in the back.

CHAPTER 43

MY CONSCIOUSNESS COMES BACK SLOWLY—IT'S NOT like in the movies, where people faint and then suddenly open their eyes later and say, "What happened?" When I pass out from some kind of panic, I usually lie on the ground for a minute or so, dimly hearing the world around me as the volume slowly returns to normal and I open my eyes. But it takes another couple of minutes for me to be able to sit up and not feel as if I might vomit.

When I'm able to face the scene of Brian with the knife in his back, he's face down and thankfully Sam has moved me farther away from his body, so I'm not staring at him. Instead, I focus on breathing and look at the ceiling, which is the speckled Styrofoam of office buildings and schools the world over, with flat plastic panes covering tubes of fluorescent light. Mercifully, they're still off.

"Annie?" Sam hovers over me, out of breath and looking terrible. "Are you okay?" He's feeling for my pulse, which is laughably pointless, seeing how I'm blinking at him and clearly alive. But I get it; it's a gesture that says, *I'm not sure what else to do, but I don't want to do nothing.*

"Yeah," I say, and my voice still sounds a bit far away. I swallow, and my mouth feels like sand. "How . . . Why are you here? What did you . . ." I trail off and try to swallow again. "Please tell me you didn't kill Felicity."

"I didn't," he says. "But I threatened her. I discovered she'd found out about the art fraud your mum and I were behind, and that she had the rest of Vera's canvases. She was planning to go public, and I couldn't have that. Not again, after how hard your mum had worked to move on from all this and reinvent herself. Fliss agreed to hand over the paintings to me if I paid her for her silence. We were going to meet to do the handover, but what I didn't know was that she'd contacted Brian Folkestone as well. She wanted a bidding war over those canvases, to get the most money she could."

"How did she know about Brian?" I ask.

"She confronted Laura about the fraud when she pieced together some details from the things left in the attic. It was Vera's remaining paintings up there that were the smoking gun, really. I told Laura we should have gotten rid of them years ago, but Laura didn't have the heart to." He winces at the phrasing, but continues. "And so Laura pleaded with Fliss and told her about Brian and the threats. But of course Fliss then thought Brian represented the gallery, which had money to throw at securing Vera's works," Sam says. "I only found this out recently. I've been trying to piece it all together myself."

"So Felicity smuggled the remaining paintings out in black bin bags and went to meet Brian to try to arrange a handover," I say slowly. "Presumably he was her highest offer."

Sam nods.

"So you didn't set her up as Mum's apprentice and tell her about the art fraud as a way to force Mum to take her in?" I ask.

"No," Sam says, and his smile is rueful, like he's not at all surprised I'd have multiple theories in which he was the villain. "I know it's out of character for your mum to take on an apprentice, but, Annie, I genuinely think that when you decided to stay in Castle Knoll . . . Laura was lonely. Fliss's email was one of a stack sent to Laura's agent asking to meet, and Laura decided that, since Fliss also came from Castle Knoll, she'd be a good person to open up to and take in." He pauses, then adds, "I think even after your mum found out Fliss wanted to go public about the art, she still wanted things to work out. She really did like her. She saw a lot of potential in Fliss and her art."

There's an awkward silence as I blink at him, trying to understand his role in the events that have just taken place. "How did you know I was here?"

"I just . . . I've been following you." He has the good sense to look sheepish at the horrified look I give him. "Laura asked me to." He puts his hands into the air between us, the universal gesture for *hear me out.* "Your mum was worried about what might happen to you if you weren't with that detective fellow, and I'm pretty good at surveillance. I'm glad she persuaded me to do that. Maybe you are too?" He raises one eyebrow, and I let out a conciliatory sigh.

"Yeah, I suppose I should say thank you," I say. "For saving my life."

He waves one hand, like it was a throwaway thing. "I mean, I owe you one. Or a few."

There's another awkward silence, because . . . he sort of does. Owe me.

"Why—" I start, then clamp my jaws shut, trying to figure out how to phrase this. "Where were you my whole life? I never heard from you. No calls, no cards. I'm not hard to find. And don't say you sent things and Mum never gave them to me to protect me or some garbage. There are ways around that even if it's true. Which I know it isn't."

He has the grace to look ashamed. He glances around the room, back at the still form of Brian, face down in the corner. Then he looks back to me. "I suppose it's long overdue that I explain." He draws a long breath. "I was in prison. For a very long time. I killed someone, and it's a long story you don't need right now. I know I could have called or contacted you even from prison, but I just . . . my life isn't a safe space. It never really has been, but . . ." He pauses as the sound of voices echoes up from the courtyard outside.

He stands abruptly and takes off his jacket, which is smeared with blood. He turns it inside out and puts it back on. He drops his voice and starts to talk faster. "Laura knows I was in prison, but I only told her recently. But Frances knew from the start." When I give him a confused look, he says, "Surely you saw clippings about my arrest in Frances's files."

When I shake my head, he rushes on. "Well, that's interesting. Maybe Frances was trying to protect you—you and Laura—once I was out of the picture. She must have kept those secrets buried, since I was arrested under an alias. Enough googling might have uncovered my other name, but—"

"I never googled you," I say, "and neither did Mum." He looks almost hurt for a moment, but the voices from the courtyard start to sound from the foyer, and his eyes dart to the door.

I look from him to the body and back to him again. "This

was self-defense. You'll be fine," I plead. I don't want him to go. "If you've served your time, I'll just explain and it'll be okay."

"No, Annie, they don't give the benefit of the doubt to guys like me," he says. "It's better if I make myself scarce."

"I have loads of money," I say. "I can get a great lawyer for you, if there's any trouble!" I blink, my eyes stinging. I don't trust Sam Arlington, but he did just save my life. He was following me, trying to keep me safe. And in doing that, he made it so that I didn't have to stab Brian and live with the horror of having killed someone. But that act would put him back under the microscope. "You've . . . you've done something else, haven't you? Some other crime I don't know about, but you're afraid if the police interview you about Brian, they'll connect you to something else."

Sam's lips are pursed in a thin line, but even in the dim light I can see tears welling, and he nods. "It's for the best," he says, and his voice is hoarse. "And, Annie, for what it's worth? I'm really sorry."

And then he's out the door, and I'm alone again.

CHAPTER 44

I FEEL LIKE BOTH MY BODY AND MY EMOTIONS HAVE been run through a mincer, so the last person I want to see is Rowan Crane. But also the first person I want to see is Rowan Crane. I hate this feeling of being torn in two—the confusion of that kiss is sitting alongside the fact that right now, when I'm feeling raw and horrible, he's the person I want to sink into and cry about it with.

So when he comes rushing through the door to the gallery, I just lean against the wall and shut my eyes to block everything out. He's not alone—several other police officers are there, and I hear them gathering and talking at the other side of the room, where Brian's body is. There's the flicker of the overhead lights, and I become even more committed to keeping my eyes shut, because I don't want to see the reality of the scene in full color.

I've taken off my cardigan and am holding it under my nose, tipping my head back.

But I can't shut out the familiarity of Crane's voice, and the gentle nudge of his hands on either side of my face, coaxing my head down so he can look me over, check that I'm not seriously hurt. He's still the picture of professionalism, prodding at my nose a little and shining a light into my eyes to check for head trauma. As he fusses over me, he's asking questions that I'm not ready to answer about what happened. I murmur that I'm okay, that I just need a minute.

And then this woman comes gliding in—and she's Marie Cavanaugh but not. The Marie I met in the gallery, who hunched to make herself smaller, mumbled a bit, and looked as bland as possible, is gone. And even though the white pixie cut and curves are the same, this woman is standing with a poise you only see in old films.

Instantly she's Vera, and she looks both proud and relieved to be able to walk around in that skin. She takes several long strides into the center of the room, her eyes scanning the canvases on the walls. Her eyes show interest when they catch the art, but dim at the sight of Brian on the floor.

I give Crane a confused look, and I don't even have to voice my question about how Vera got here before he says gently, "One of the officers tracked her down at the gallery, just before we got the call about a disturbance here. Technically Vera is coming in for questioning voluntarily, but"—his eyes dart to her and back to me—"she's a bit of a spitfire. She lied to one of the other officers and said she'd drive herself to the station. Clearly she'd overheard what was going on here and decided on a detour."

Another officer approaches Crane, keeping his voice low. "My fault. She pulled a sweet-old-lady routine on PC Johnson over there." He angles his chin toward a young woman who is arguing with a superior in the corner.

"So that's done, then," Vera says. She sounds almost bored,

with an edge of relief—like Brian was a long-running inconvenience that had finally burned itself out. I remember then who this woman is. She may not have killed Marie, but she helped use her to frame Alasdair Huntington. Never mind that Alasdair deserved to be put away for other crimes, Vera set the wheels in motion that led to Marie's murder, and then sewed her chest shut, imitating her husband's surgeries.

"Vera," I say, and stand shakily. Crane tries to help steady me by taking my arm, but I shrug him off. I press my cardigan to the cut on my rib, choosing not to look at the bloodstains. If I don't look at the blood, I can effectively pretend it isn't there and try to regain some composure. It stings, and it'll probably need stitches, but it's nothing serious.

Vera nods but doesn't really see me. She's looking at the paintings. "These are Laura's?"

"Yes," I say. "She was trying to . . ." I struggle, attempting to remember the words Mum used to explain her reconciliation with the fraud she committed with her first series.

"I can see what she was trying to do," Vera says, cutting me off. "You don't explain art to the viewer; you let it speak for itself."

So I'm quiet, and watch her regarding the paintings. She gives nothing away, but walks from one to the next, giving each its own consideration. It's interesting to watch—it's as if she's greeting guests arriving at a party. Sizing them up, deciding who is properly dressed for the occasion, who has the wittiest jokes or the most interesting stories.

Finally, I break the silence, because I need to know if Vera is going to hurt Mum. Whether that's by dragging her name through the mud or physically harming her, I want some indication of what we're in for. After all, this was the woman who, as a child, had taunted her brother with animal hearts. Had she been angry with Mum all along, about the art?

"Was that you, putting the bloody heart on our steps?" I ask.

She blinks, coming out of whatever reverie the canvas in front of her has sent her into. "Heart? No, that wasn't me." She sighs and walks back to me. Crane is standing next to me, quiet, but watching. I try not to focus on the fact that he doesn't seem to be watching Vera as much as he's watching me.

"Max knew from the beginning, didn't he?" I ask. "He identified your body. He helped cover up that you were still alive."

"He did," she says. "It was Brian who made sure Marie didn't look like Marie," she adds. I see a flinch, but it's barely there. This woman gives off the impression of being a carved block of ice. "But Max knew what I was planning. He may have been morally ambiguous, in the way he treated Elaine and in his business dealings, but he cares about me."

"So, the hearts left on our steps?" I push.

"That must have been Brian," she says, with a cursory glance to the corner. "One of the reasons I refused to see him when I came back from Canada was that he'd been reliving the murder of Marie for decades. He was fixating on the things I used to talk to him about—I'd become an obsession, my own dark personality from back then melded with his murderous tendencies, and he just became a specter that haunted me. I'm sorry he started haunting you too." There's a moment when her expression softens, but it's only for a heartbeat, and her mask snaps back into place.

"I have to ask . . ." I hesitate, wondering how to phrase

this. "Your art that my mum used, that she made famous under her name. You knew straightaway, I presume?"

Vera nods. "I was the one who called Laura, using a device to distort my voice. I admit my threats were horrible at first, but I was angry, so I threatened to hurt her whole family if she ever used any of that art again. But she sounded so young and scared. She didn't know who I was, just thought I was someone representing Vera's estate, but she explained that she was under the thumb of a conniving husband. Inwardly, I knew just what that felt like. I didn't know I was opening the door for Laura to be extorted by Brian, and Max decided to ban her from the gallery anyway, on principle. He wouldn't go after Laura, but he's been angry about the situation for years. It only added fuel that this was a relative of Frances Adams. He never got over the way she bested him."

"I think, knowing Mum, she was probably happy to see that money go. She's been happy in Chelsea, living life on a shoestring. We always got by just fine," I say.

One of the uniformed police officers who had been examining Brian's body comes toward us, and it's clear she's looking for her moment to ask me some questions. Crane steps forward, almost like he wants to be the go-between. Now that I'm feeling more alert, I can practically see the wheels of his mind turning. He looks at the six-foot-two athletic form of Brian Folkestone on the floor, with the knife in his back at an angle that's clearly higher than the five-foot-four Annie Adams would naturally plunge it in at. Even though Brian was around seventy-five, realistically I was no match for him alone.

The police officer steps up to us. "Miss Adams, if you don't mind, we're going to need a statement from you. I don't know if you want to do this here or come down to the station or—"

"She won't need to go to the station," Crane interjects.

"Sir, begging your pardon, but we've got a body on the floor, and we need to get to the bottom of who killed the man," she says.

I think it through quickly, in the span of heartbeats. Sam, on the run because his slate isn't clean. He knew he'd be under fire for the murder of Folkestone, but he still did it. And he did it for me.

"I can solve that for you," I say. "I did."

Crane gives me a quizzical look, then narrows his eyes. And I know he knows I'm lying. They'll find my prints on that knife, and they'll find Sam's too. But even I know that just because Sam was here, it doesn't mean he killed Brian.

"Brian Folkestone lured me here and attacked me. I fought and managed to get the knife in his back when he slipped and was on the floor," I say.

"And no one else was here?" Crane asks, his voice low.

"No one else was here," I say.

CHAPTER 45

April 2, 1969

MAX TORRENCE DIDN'T RETURN TO THE UNIVERSITY the next week or the week after. Ford asked around discreetly and found out that Max had abandoned his degree after his father left the department, probably because he no longer felt quite so untouchable without him.

It didn't seem right that Max could disappear, just sink into the ether and cause new problems for somebody else—and he would; I knew he would. I just had to hope it wouldn't be me. Imagine if Max just bides his time in the shadows, and waits until I become complacent and happy with my life, only to strike then. Max could be my eventual murderer, if my fortune proves true.

But winter took hold further, and the fires in the house in Chelsea crackled as Ford and I settled into a true partnership that made me feel like my life was just starting—finally. He relaxed around me; the careful guard he'd kept up so closely since I'd met him had evaporated in the alliance we'd formed around Vera, Max, Elaine, and their secrets and lies. We fitted together, Ford and I, and it took our investigations for us to really see that. There had been hints of it before, but I was so relieved when we finally fell into step together. It was easy, him and me. And Chelsea was home.

He asked me to marry him at the end of November, and I had no hesitation in saying yes. I'll continue my psychology course, and Ford and I will live here in Chelsea for as long as we like. Or go back to Castle Knoll and live in Gravesdown Hall, if I can face the place.

Just after he proposed, I asked him about Vera's things, the dresses, paintings, and the tiara. He said he'd packed them in one of the unused wardrobes in a guest room. Something tugged at me then. I can't explain why, but I wanted to see her things again. Wonder what she would have been, if Max hadn't ended her life.

I wondered about my own guilt, about what I'd said that last night we were out. What if you got to him first? *I'd said. Had I been instrumental in her death that night? Had my words convinced her to confront Max, or her father, or her husband?*

I swallowed the feeling and opened the wardrobe. I pulled out the canvases, one by one—there were so many. It was as if they'd doubled in number since I'd come back to my flat that day to find all her things.

I ran my hand over a beaded Chanel dress that hung in the wardrobe, and a mink coat that looked ghostly in the shadows there. Finally, I reached for the box that held the tiara and opened it carefully. My palms broke into a sweat as my brain played a terrible image behind my eyes before I lifted the lid. I imagined opening it to find a rat's heart, another threat—a sign that someone not only wanted me silenced but knew where I lived and how to get inside.

Instead, the tiara winked up at me like a mischievous child, and I breathed a little easier. Then I saw the note—yet another thing I could swear wasn't there when I first got the tiara months before. My name was on the envelope.

My hands shaking, I opened it and slid out the card from inside.

Frances, my dear—

I want you to have these things. No matter what happens to me, don't think of them as bad luck. I've always been given precisely what I wanted, and I want to pass a bit of that along to you. Wear this tiara on your wedding day. Your Ford is a good man. He'll keep you safe, I'm sure of it.

This world is a terrible and uncertain place, but you've a good heart and a keen mind. Use both of those, always.

V

I must have missed the note the first time. The box was silk-lined and had folds of tissue to cover the tiara. It had probably slipped down initially, and when Ford put these things away he'd looked in the box and moved the note to its proper place. But then, why not tell me about it?

I asked him later, and he said he hadn't opened the box. It must have been the housekeeper, who had tidied the things away at his request.

"I can't decide whether it's ominous or serendipitous, us getting engaged, and then me finding this note from Vera telling me I should wear her tiara at our wedding. I don't know if I can. It feels wrong to wear something from a murdered friend on such a happy day," I said. "But not honoring the wishes of someone who has died also feels unlucky. I just . . ." I rubbed my arms, which had broken out in gooseflesh.

Ford gave me an understanding smile and moved toward me.

He wrapped his arms around me from behind, like a shield from anything that might creep up on me unexpectedly. "I think that the heart of Vera's note comes from a place of good wishes and appreciation for your friendship. No choice you make regarding it will be unlucky."

I smiled, and the swirl of worry and fixation on what might be lucky or unlucky quietened in my mind. Ford was like that, and I knew that it would always be the greatest gift he ever gave me—that sense of safety, not just from the world but from the darkness of my own mind.

And the appreciation he has for the way that mind doesn't need to be fully shielded from the darkness, but must plunge into it periodically in an effort to figure it out. In an effort to fight it.

I wore the tiara proudly, and was grateful for Vera's generosity, and for the life she lived.

We honeymooned in Afghanistan when the university term ended for Christmas, and I finally got to feel the wideness of the world and taste new things and see history from an angle I'd never looked from before. I loved every moment of it, and Ford and I are planning so many more adventures abroad together.

Now that we're back, and I'm Ford's wife and this is my home—our home—all I feel is joy when I think of the future. My studies have taught me so much more than I expected, because the notes I've kept and squirreled away out of worry for my fate—I look at them now as just the beginning of a person who was, in reality, a scholar of psychology.

I may have started out as a collector of secrets, but I've evolved into a student of the human mind. And that's not only the healthier way to be, it's far more powerful.

CHAPTER 46

I WEARILY THROW MY KEYS AND MY PHONE ONTO the coffee table in the sitting room, where the chill of a dead fireplace threatens to bring me to tears. Crane is at my heels, and for some reason, all I can think about is that part of Aunt Frances's diary where she wrote about herself and Ford in this very same room. An evening when the fire was crackling and he was finding paper and pen to help her get the facts straight about the various problems and lies she was trying to investigate and untangle. His unwavering support of her, and her realizing she loved him.

I look at the cold ashes in the fireplace, then at Crane, hovering back a few feet from me, as if worried I might lose control and try to kiss him again. I feel tired, shaky, and rather traumatized at having almost been killed, then lying to the police to protect my dad. There are stitches in my chest, just over my heart, and they feel tight with every step I take.

Needing something to do with my hands, I cross over to the fireplace and pull some logs from the basket next to it.

There's a bit of kindling left at the bottom, and I busy myself stacking it all in the grate. I take the long lighter from the mantelpiece and coax the kindling to life, blowing on it, willing it to crackle and give me some kind of warmth in this room.

When I can't bear to feel Crane's eyes on my back any longer, I turn and walk back to stand in front of the sofa. He's still near the wall, thinking.

Finally he meets my eyes. "I need to talk to you," he says. "About earlier. About the cemetery."

I tear my eyes from his and focus on a point where the wallpaper is peeling, just over his shoulder. Maybe if I keep that in my sights, I can hold it together through this. But he takes a step toward me, followed by another, and soon he's hovering within my reach and looking at me like I might be the one breaking *his* heart.

I take a deep breath and try not to look at him. I fail, and meet his eyes, and his cheeks color.

"I've been agonizing over everything," I say, my words tumbling out. "Replaying all the times you put your arm around me, or reached for my hand. If that was just you being comforting, and trying to make me feel better in the middle of some hard moments of an investigation, I need to know. Because to me it wasn't nothing."

He reaches for my hand then, his fingers rough as they entwine with my own, but his touch carrying that characteristic Rowan gentleness. "It's not nothing to me either," he says quietly. "But trust me when I say"—he pauses and moves his other hand to cup my chin—"I'll do anything to keep you safe. Even if that means breaking your heart."

I blink as the heat of tears floods my vision. "Hey." I put my hand over his, where it still rests under my chin, like I could hold it there and freeze this moment. "If I need to stand here and give you a speech about why I'm getting a lot harder to kill, I can do that," I say, and offer a small smile.

He closes his eyes for a beat and looks slightly pained. "The events of today sort of go against that point, Annie," he says. And he takes a step back, removing his hands as he does. I feel the absence of them like a cold spot in a warm lake, the kind of feeling that makes you shiver because it feels wrong in a way that hints at depths you're swimming over without realizing.

I haven't even taken my coat off, and instinctively I reach into my pockets and try to find something to grab on to. A tissue I can crumple, or a ChapStick to cap and uncap. My left hand finds the fortunes I've been carrying around with me all winter. Mine, and a stack of about six more. Something about always having them there feels like I've got a pocket reference to the beyond. I've still not opened any but my own, but I take them all out and fidget with them. I shuffle the front envelope to the back, and the back to the front, not really seeing them. Names flash back and forth, a host of Castle Knoll residents whose fates are still unknown until I decide to unleash them.

Finally mine floats to the top, and it's without its envelope and dog-eared. I let my thumb find the edges of the paper, and it unfolds in my hand. My eyes skim past all of it, until the last line.

But it will be your own heart, if left unguarded, that's ripe for the knife.

I never knew if she meant literally or figuratively, but I now know it was both. The tears that are welling up start to betray me and spill over, and I breathe in deeply, the smell of the smoke from the fire filling my nostrils and reminding me of the big fireplaces in Castle Knoll.

Maybe if I convince him enough, he'll give us a try. My safety feels like such an abstract reason for him not to be with me. Perhaps I just need to show him that life isn't always going to be dangerous, that sometimes it could be beautiful. Maybe Peony will be wrong, if I can just show him that we could be really good together. I feel my throat constrict, as a tiny voice at the back of my mind tells me that if he really wanted me, he'd need no convincing.

There it is again, that twist of the knife.

"What are you not telling me?" I ask. I hold up the fortunes. "Don't let her be *right*, Rowan!"

His eyes find the fortunes, and he shakes his head. He's biting his lip again—hard.

"Why have you been carrying those around?" he asks, his voice carrying a low heat that's more worrying than if he were shouting. I don't want him angry with me, but I feel like he's looking for reasons to keep me at arm's length. Picking them out of the air. "Frances hid away and lost all credibility with her friends and relatives and became obsessed with her own future. Her own murder. I can't watch you do the same."

I let my hurt shift to a flash of rage and give him a withering look as I march over to the window, the fortunes still in my hands. Wordlessly, I show him the stack, lift the sash, and then feed them to the wind. The papers flutter away immediately, floating up and out of my sight in seconds.

"I don't think that was why she did that," I say, more quietly now. "I think . . ." My throat constricts as I think of Frances and her deep connection with Ford. ". . . I think that descent only really happened when she lost her husband." I blink, and more tears hit my cheeks. Crane is quiet, studying me. "If you don't have feelings for me, just say it." I look at him, searching.

And in his face, I see something—I can't be imagining it. He's unguarded, afraid, and there's something else. Longing. Then he shuts down his expression, his jaw tight.

"What aren't you telling me?" I ask again. "There's something else, isn't there?"

He swallows hard. "People I care about get killed, Annie," he says eventually.

"Felicity wasn't your fault," I say. "We've gotten to the bottom of that whole thing; that *wasn't you*."

"No, no, you don't—" He stops and stares at the fire, where the air is shifting with the invisible waves of heat the flames are giving off. Tiny gray fragments of ash float upward here and there, like severed moth wings. "You don't understand. I'm not talking about Fliss, I'm talking about *me*. There's something—it's followed me for years."

He starts pacing, his hand periodically reaching up to absently rub his jaw. "Annie, I know I've alluded to an old case that haunts me. What I didn't tell you was that the killer keeps contacting me. Taunting me."

I open my mouth to reply, but it hangs there a moment, surprised. Of all the things I expected him to say, that wasn't it.

His jaw tightens and he nods. "I know Fliss was just a coincidence, and we've caught who did that. But her death really hammered home the fact that whoever has been sending me notes all these years—and it's been *years*, Annie—they mean what they're threatening." The look he gives me is absolute agony.

"You get close to me, and you'll be just another name on

his list. You'll jump right to the top of it. Whoever he is, he already knows about you. And I can't have you involved. I just . . . I just can't," he says, and that last almost comes out like a cry.

And then he's gone.

CHAPTER 47

MY CASE FOR SELF-DEFENSE IS MURKY, SO CRANE presses me to hire a lawyer—by perfunctory text of course, devoid of any *xx*—and I do. Sam's fingerprints aren't on the knife—no one's are. He wiped it down while it was still in Folkestone's back, knowing it could come back to him. I think he assumed I'd flee the scene, too, and the mystery of who killed Brian Folkestone would just be left to rot in the file in a police station somewhere, in time becoming just another cold case. Or perhaps I'm being naive—my blood was all over the scene too.

But even though Brian had been stabbed in the back, I do some of the best writing of my life and come up with a relatively plausible story. Brian and I were grappling on the floor and in a panic I stabbed outward, not looking where he was. I was very afraid, I was stabbing at the air and happened to get him in the back. Given the amount of evidence they found, the fact that Brian had been watching our house and putting dead animal parts on our doorstep, not to mention the fact that he had lured me to the gallery so he could ambush me—all after having killed Fliss—I was let off the hook pretty easily.

Vera faced a few criminal charges in relation to her role in posing as Marie Cavanaugh—desecrating a corpse, identity theft, fraud. And, of course, concealing the facts of a murder, because she knew all along what Brian had done to Marie. Vera and her lawyer are still working their way through a fair amount of legal tangles, but she seems confident there are enough loopholes that fines can be paid and life can go on. And all those criminal charges just make her even more of a source of intrigue. She's a pop-culture fascination now, and as far as I've seen, she's come back out of her shell and embraced it. A socialite from a bygone era, back from the dead.

But she and Mum did have to have some professional mediation in place to hammer out the legal issues with the art in perpetuity. Vera wasn't going to come for Mum—but lines were drawn and both parties have moved forward.

The real story is that when Vera came to the crime scene and saw the paintings Mum had created hanging there, she felt a deep connection to the way Mum paints. Or so she said. Mum offered to come clean about using Vera's work, but Vera didn't want that. Those paintings were a purge of a violence and a person Vera no longer was, she explained. Laura putting them into the world was actually the best way for them to be seen, and Vera felt that Laura was far better placed to be the face of that series than she was.

That was the benevolent spin Vera put on it, but underneath it all, there's still tension between Mum and Vera, a sense that Mum owes her. It's a dynamic I don't like but have very little power over.

Elaine has been keeping her distance, though I think she

genuinely wanted to find out what happened to Vera, and she took that painting from our kitchen because it felt like a clue in her own journey to find answers about a rather fraught time in her life. She just didn't know how to confront me about it and decided to abscond with it. She brought it to the Barbican on a hunch, to compare with Mum's new series, because things she saw in the house had her making connections. Brian saw her at the Barbican, so he had extra ammo to lure me there when he phoned—but when Elaine saw Mum's unconscious broker by the door, she ran. Once the events of the rest of that day came to light, she got in touch, returned the painting, and apologized.

I get postcards from my dad now and then, though they never say anything of significance. One came from New Mexico: *I saw this cactus and thought it was cool.* And another came from Big Sur: *Finally reading Kerouac, thought you'd approve.* Perhaps the significance is simply in their arrival. It's the first gesture he's ever made that says, *I'm here, and I'm thinking of you.*

I feel strongly that I have to help put Felicity and Marie Cavanaugh to rest. Brian Folkestone's crimes need to be exposed, along with a host of other secrets. After Vera's identity theft was brought to light, as well as her role in framing her husband, the list of people Alasdair Huntington killed on his operating table grows. An inquest is launched, and the history of his medical negligence continues to be analyzed and uncovered. But a lot of people who had been forgotten because they were living on the streets and, as Alasdair put it in a statement in the sixties, "circling the drain of society," become remembered through the unearthing of a long-covered-up injustice. Even some of the nameless—people who were signed into the hospital as John and Jane Doe only to meet the knife of Alasdair Huntington—are identified through old records and good research.

I start a project looking into their pasts and telling their stories. What were their lives like before they lost their homes? Some were victims of domestic violence; some fell into addiction; some had mental health problems that were never treated.

Along with the police researchers, I start making files—with the assistance of many of the families, once the victims are identified. I feel like Great Aunt Frances, but these aren't individual secrets people want to hide. These are the things society should have seen when looking at someone without a home, even if that person was a husk of their former self by the time they were on the streets.

I start with Susan Folkestone. I find a cousin of hers, who tells me a story about how, as a child, she had a teddy named Sandwiches. She had heard that bears liked picnics and named him Sandwiches because that way he'd never be far from food—"It's there in the name," she reportedly said. Her best friend from secondary school told me a story about how she collected stamps and had pen pals all around the world. I gather photos, objects, images, and stories and put them up in visual arrangements. Like murder boards, but for lifetimes. Not *Who killed this person?* but *How did this person live?*

And with each victim I find heartbreak after heartbreak—the things life threw at each of them to knock them back, the times they tried to resurface into life only to have their hand slapped away or slip from someone's grasp.

I stay in London with Mum, thinking I'll take just another week. A month goes by, then two. Mum and I drink whisky, sneak into cinemas like we used to, then make large donations to charities supporting young filmmakers from marginalized backgrounds, or film schools struggling with supplies. She paints; I research and piece together the stories of the victims of Alasdair Huntington. Crane calls sometimes, and sometimes I call him, but we still only talk of victims or cases. It's become a reminiscing, almost—going through all the facts of past things we've worked on together, to try to remember that feeling of clicking together so well.

Each time I hang up the phone wondering if we'll ever get that partnership back.

Mum's broker puts me in touch with someone at the Wellcome Trust, and I put together my first exhibit. It's called *Family Humanity: The Lives and Deaths of London's Forgotten in the 1960s.* The night of the opening, Mum arrives with a flurry of flashbulbs following her.

I'm in the foyer of the brightly lit museum space, greeting people and drinking champagne, with Jenny acting as emotional support for my nerves. She's back from her contract with Macy's in New York, where she took her talents designing window displays to new heights. I give her a nervous smile, then wave at Kabir over her shoulder as he enters the gallery. He smiles back, both of us brushing off the fact that I keep pushing back our date. I've genuinely been really busy, between the fallout from the murder solving, and the project on Dr. Huntington's victims, so half my excuses haven't been complete lies. But some of them have been . . . not entirely the truth. Really, I need more time. It feels wrong to go out with Kabir right now, when I feel so romantically torn.

My eyes scan the guests as they take in my exhibition. I've got very mixed feelings about putting my writing aspirations on hold to tell different kinds of stories, but sometimes you just have to follow the narrative that wants telling.

Someone from *The Guardian* is asking me questions about the visual nature of storytelling, and whether or not I'm the newest campaigner for homeless charities. But then he sees Mum, says, "Do you mind?," and rushes over to talk to her.

She spends five minutes answering questions but finally pushes the reporter toward the bar, where there's still free champagne on offer.

"I'm sorry, Annie," Mum says apologetically as she kisses my cheek.

"It's okay," I say. "I'm used to having a famous artist for a mother. And let's face it, you're interesting."

Mum glances upward, where the exhibit I've made fills the second floor, and the lives Alasdair claimed are being given a bit more voice. When she looks back at me, she gives me a broad smile and links her arm with mine. "I think it's past time that my projects aren't center stage. I realize I can use up all the air in a room, you know. And you've spent your life not breathing as deeply as you could, just to make space for me to be me."

I blink back tears, because this is the closest Mum has ever come to admitting that it's rather hard being the least colorful person in a house with someone as bright as Laura Adams. But of course I can't go out and say that; I can already feel my emotional discomfort bubbling up, so I just say, "What a very Laura Adams metaphor. Ten out of ten. I've got zero editorial notes for you on that one."

I'm jostled by people angling to get through the crowded space, and I'm grateful for it—it breaks up the awkwardness of Mum and me having to be sentimental for another second.

The evening goes by in a flurry of people shaking my

hand, smiling at me, and asking me questions that I can tell are phrased to be as philosophical or deep as possible, because the exhibit I've created is Important™.

At the end of the evening, just as the last of the visitors filter out and the catering team is clearing up stray champagne glasses, I notice a small envelope on the table next to where I've left my bag.

My heart jumps into my mouth, because the small square nature of it is unmistakable—as is the handwriting on the front. It's one of the envelopes from Peony Lane. One of the fortunes I *know* I threw out the window.

I take several shaky steps toward it and pick it up. It's not impossible that it's here, but it's got a feeling of the uncanny about it. I'm certain I saw the wind whip it away—but its existence sends a clear message. It's a warning. I think of the person in the shadows sending threats to Rowan for years. Watching him. Because this fortune being here, while impossible, bears the only name from that whole pile of fortunes that really matters to me.

And it's then that I know what my future holds—I'm going back to Castle Knoll.

Because as much as I want to avoid making any hard choices, this is a name that I won't deny can always call me home.

Rowan Crane.

ACKNOWLEDGMENTS

First and definitely foremost, I would like to thank all the readers, booksellers, and bookstores championing my series—thank you so much for sticking with Annie and Frances for yet another adventure; your enthusiasm and support for my work is the reason these adventures can keep happening. So please consider this a big hug from me through the page. I appreciate you all so very much.

As always, a massive thank-you to the TBA crew—Zoë Plant, Jenny Bent, Victoria Cappello, Martha Perotto-Wills, Aminah Amjad, and Emma Lagarde—you all take such fantastic care of me and my ideas; I couldn't have asked for a better team to represent me.

I was lucky enough to have three talented editors working with me for this book: Florence Hare and Vanessa Phan at Quercus, and Cassidy Sachs at Dutton. I can't describe how excited (and relieved) I was when you all expressed your delight at Annie's and Frances's adventures in London, and your excitement at the risks I took with the story this time around. No matter how many books deep we get, that feeling of being in such safe hands never goes away, and I am beyond grateful for that.

To the wider team at Quercus—Stefanie Bierwerth, Katie Blott, Charlotte Gill, Ayo Okojie, Ella Patel, Emily Patience—I am so lucky to have you all. Thank you to the US team at Dutton—Emily Canders, Isabel DaSilva, Ella Kurki, John Parsley, LeeAnn Pemberton, Dora Mak, Ashley Tucker, Hannah Poole, Erika Semprun, Clare Shearer, Melissa Solis, Stephanie Cooper, and Amanda Walker—you are all amazing.

Also, thank you to the all the copy editors, proofreaders, designers, and team members behind the scenes at both publishers who have worked so hard to make the finished copy you hold in your hands possible. To the jacket designers who have worked absolute magic with this series—Amanda Hudson for the US edition, and Andrew Smith and Nathan Burton for the UK edition—I won the book jacket lottery with you all, and you continuously knock it out of the park with every new cover. Also, a heartfelt thank-you goes to the translators and individual publishers in countries all over the world making it possible for this book to be read in so many languages.

My beautiful Harrogate group (or, the Harry Writers)—you have grown in number and I wish I could list you all, but you know who you are! Thank you all for the amazing community you've built, and for being a soft space for me to land with any of my random questions or general publishing spirals. Every writer needs a group like you lot, and I'm so lucky to be among your ranks.

Particular thanks go to Hannah Brennan, Jessica Bull, Grace Curtis, Rose Diell, Amy Dillmann, Maz Evans, Henry Fry, Alex Hay, Hannah Matthewson, Kelly Mullen, Ande Pliego, Holly Race, Tania Tay, and Teri Terry for their friendship and writerly support. And a big thank-you to DF for your insights on police procedure in the UK, and for always being up for answering the most random questions about what a detective would do in various scenarios! Any mistakes I've made in that regard are mine and mine alone. A special shout-out goes to Cara Miller, fellow writer and wonderful friend, who has taught me how to incorporate writing events with adventures abroad—thank you for being my travel buddy and helping me expand my horizons again; I hadn't realized just how small I'd let my world get while behind my keyboard. I'm so grateful to have been brought out into the sun a bit more.

To my critique partners, who have stuck with me and weathered the ups and downs of many books now—Ashley Chalmers, Mary Osteen, Kate Poels, Tyffany Neiheiser, and Hannah Roberts—your insights and patience with brainstorms, feedback, and general cheerleading have been a huge part of what has gotten me through this series, and I cannot thank you enough.

And finally, to my friends and family, thank you all for listening to my endless chatter about all things writing and publishing related. I'd like to say I'll learn to dial it back and talk about more standard subjects, but we all know that's not true. Thank you for tolerating me anyway. And because I know my children will delight in seeing their names in print yet again, Eloise and Quentin, you are both the most hilarious, clever, curious, and delightful human beings I've ever met, and I'm lucky to be your mom. And to my husband, Tom (who, in true English style, doesn't like a fuss), I'll just say thank you. Because after twenty years, you know just what I mean, even when I only use a few words.

ABOUT THE AUTHOR

Kristen Perrin is originally from Seattle, Washington, where she spent several years working as a bookseller before immigrating to the UK to do a master's and PhD. Her debut, *How to Solve Your Own Murder*, is the first Castle Knoll Murder Mystery and has been translated into more than twenty languages. The book was also a *Good Morning America* Buzz Pick, was featured on *The Tonight Show Starring Jimmy Fallon*, and has been a *New York Times*, IndieBound, *USA Today*, and *Der Spiegel* bestseller. She lives with her family in Surrey, England, where she is hard at work on more books in the series.